# SCIENCE FICTION

## REDISCOVERED PLANETS

(Book 1)

# SCIENCE FICTION REDISCOVERED PLANETS:

***THE MAD PLANET***

Murray Leinster

***PLANET OF THE DAMNED***

Harry Harrison

**Edited by**

# H. L. Osterman

(Book 1)

ABSOLUTELY AMAZING eBOOKS

**ABSOLUTELY AMAZING eBOOKS**

Published by Whiz Bang LLC, 926 Truman Avenue, Key West, Florida 33040, USA.



For information contact:
Publisher@AbsolutelyAmazingEbooks.com

ISBN-13: 978-1949504125 (Absolutely Amazing Ebooks)
ISBN-10: 1949504123

# INTRODUCTION TO
# TWOFERS

We all have opinions on what constitutes a "Golden Age" – whether in literature, cinema, science, you name it.

A Golden Age is defined as "an idyllic, often imaginary past time of peace, prosperity, and happiness." The term comes from Greek and Roman mythology, referring to when mankind lived in a better time and was pure,

But for our purpose it refers to the period when a specified art, skill, or activity is at its peak.

Science fiction is divided into various ages. From early precursors ("One Thousand and One Arabian Nights") to the 19th Century (Jules Verne and H.G. Wells) to the 20th Century (birth of the pulps), to the 1940s and '50s (The Golden Age) to the 1960s and '70s (The New Wave) to the '80s (Cyberpunk) to beyond (Contemporary) we have a continuum of imaginative thought.

But each of these so-called ages have peaks, Golden Age notwithstanding.

Science Fiction is a genre of speculative fiction based on imagined future scientific or technological advances and major social or environmental changes. It often deals with such concepts as scientific innovation, spaceflight, time travel, and extraterrestrial life.

Sci-fi master Isaac Asimov observed: "Science fiction can be defined as that branch of literature which deals with the reaction of human beings to changes in science and technology."

~ ~ ~

Nonetheless, fans of science fiction have favorite stories from a variety of so-called ages – all "golden" to him or her.

So I make no apologies that this new series of two-for-one sci-fi volumes are my personal pairings of novels that sparked my imagination – and I enjoyed enough to want to share them with you.

This Twofer series is Absolutely Amazing eBooks' way of

*Twofer Science Fiction: Rediscovered Planets*

offering all-but-forgotten novels at an economy price – ebooks for less than a buck each!

You'd spend a lot more to get a neutralizer or sonic screwdriver.

- H. L. Osterman

# THE MAD PLANET

Murray Leinster

# 1

In All His lifetime of perhaps twenty years, it had never occurred to Burl to wonder what his grandfather had thought about his surroundings. The grandfather had come to an untimely end in a rather unpleasant fashion which Burl remembered vaguely as a succession of screams coming more and more faintly to his ears while he was being carried away at the top speed of which his mother was capable.

Burl had rarely or never thought of the old gentleman since. Surely he had never wondered in the abstract of what his great grandfather thought, and most surely of all, there never entered his head such a purely hypothetical question as the one of what his many-times-great-grandfather – say of the year 1920 – would have thought of the scene in which Burl found himself.

He was treading cautiously over a brownish carpet of fungus growth, creeping furtively toward the stream which he knew by the generic title of "water." It was the only water he knew. Towering far above his head, three man-heights high, great toadstools hid the grayish sky from his sight. Clinging to the foot-thick stalks of the toadstools were still other fungi, parasites upon the growth that had once been parasites themselves.

Burl himself was a slender young man wearing a single garment twisted about his waist, made from the wing-fabric of a great moth the members of his tribe had slain as it emerged from its cocoon. His skin was fair, without a trace of sunburn. In all his lifetime he had never seen the sun, though the sky was rarely hidden from view save by the giant fungi which, with monster cabbages, were the only growing things he knew. Clouds usually spread overhead, and when they did not, the perpetual haze made the sun but an indefinitely brighter part of the sky, never a sharply edged ball of fire. Fantastic mosses, misshapen fungus growths, colossal molds and yeasts, were the essential parts of the landscape through which he moved.

Once as he had dodged through the forest of huge toadstools, his shoulder touched a cream-colored stalk, giving the whole fungus a tiny shock. Instantly, from the umbrella-like mass of pulp overhead, a fine and impalpable powder fell upon him like snow. It was the season when the toadstools sent out their spores, or seeds, and they had been dropped upon him at the first sign of disturbance.

Furtive as he was, he paused to brush them from his head and hair. They were deadly poison, as he knew well.

Burl would have been a curious sight to a man of the twentieth century. His skin was pink, like that of a child, and there was but little hair upon his body. Even that on top of his head was soft and downy. His chest was larger than his forefathers' had been, and his ears seemed almost capable of independent movement, to catch threatening sounds from any direction. His eyes, large and blue, possessed pupils which could dilate to extreme size, allowing him to see in almost complete darkness.

He was the result of the thirty thousand years' attempt of the human race to adapt itself to the change that had begun in the latter half of the twentieth century.

At about that time, civilization had been high, and apparently secure. Mankind had reached a permanent agreement among itself, and all men had equal opportunities to education and leisure. Machinery did most of the labor of the world, and men were only required to supervise its operation. All men were well-fed, all men were well-educated, and it seemed that until the end of time the earth would be the abode of a community of comfortable human beings, pursuing their studies and diversions, their illusions and their truths. Peace, quietness, privacy, freedom were universal.

Then, just when men were congratulating themselves that the Golden Age had come again, it was observed that the planet seemed ill at ease. Fissures opened slowly in the crust, and carbonic acid gas – the carbon dioxide of chemists – began to pour out into the atmosphere. That gas had long been known to be present in the air, and was considered necessary to plant life. Most of the plants of the world took the gas and absorbed its carbon into themselves, releasing the oxygen for use again.

Scientists had calculated that a great deal of the earth's increased fertility was due to the larger quantities of carbon dioxide released by the activities of man in burning his coal and petroleum. Because of those views, for some years no great alarm was caused by the continuous exhalation from the world's interior.

Constantly, however, the volume increased. New fissures constantly opened, each one adding a new source of carbon dioxide, and each one pouring into the already laden atmosphere more of the gas – beneficent in small quantities, but as the world learned, deadly in large ones.

The percentage of the heavy, vapor-like gas increased. The whole body of the air became heavier through its admixture. It absorbed more moisture and became more humid. Rainfall increased. Climates grew warmer. Vegetation became more luxuriant – but the air gradually became less exhilarating.

Soon the health of mankind began to be affected. Accustomed through long ages to breathe air rich in oxygen and poor in carbon dioxide, men suffered. Only those who lived on high plateaus or on tall mountaintops remained unaffected. The plants of the earth, though nourished and increasing in size beyond those ever seen before, were unable to dispose of the continually increasing flood of carbon dioxide.

# 2

**By** the middle of the twenty-first century it was generally recognized that a new carboniferous period was about to take place, when the earth's atmosphere would be thick and humid, unbreathable by man, when giant grasses and ferns would form the only vegetation.

When the twenty-first century drew to a close the whole human race began to revert to conditions closely approximating savagery. The low-lands were unbearable. Thick jungles of rank growth covered the ground. The air was depressing and enervating. Men could live there, but it was a sickly, fever-ridden existence. The whole population of the earth desired the high lands and as the low country became more unbearable, men forgot their two centuries of peace.

They fought destructively, each for a bit of land where he might live and breathe. Then men began to die, men who had persisted in remaining near sea-level. They could not live in the poisonous air. The danger zone crept up as the earth-fissures tirelessly poured out their steady streams of foul gas. Soon men could not live within five hundred feet of sea level. The low-lands went uncultivated, and became jungles of a thickness comparable only to those of the first carboniferous period.

Then men died of sheer inanition at a thousand feet. The plateaus and mountaintops were crowded with folk struggling for a foothold and food beyond the invisible menace that crept up, and up –

These things did not take place in one year, or in ten. Not in one generation, but in several. Between the time when the chemists of the International Geophysical Institute announced that the proportion of carbon dioxide in the air had increased from .04 per cent to .1 per cent and the time when at sea-level six per cent of the atmosphere was the deadly gas, more than two hundred years intervened.

Coming gradually, as it did, the poisonous effects of the deadly stuff increased with insidious slowness. First the lassitude, then the heaviness of brain, then the weakness of body. Mankind ceased to grow in numbers. After a long period, the race had fallen to a fraction of its former size. There was room in plenty on the mountaintops – but the danger-level continued to creep up.

There was but one solution. The human body would have to inure itself to the poison, or it was doomed to extinction. It finally developed a toleration for the gas that had wiped out race after race and nation after nation, but at a terrible cost. Lungs increased in size to secure the oxygen on which life depended, but the poison, inhaled at every breath, left the few survivors sickly and filled with a perpetual weariness. Their minds lacked the energy to cope with new problems or transmit the knowledge which in one degree or another, they possessed.

And after thirty thousand years, Burl, a direct descendant of the first president of the Universal Republic, crept through a forest of toadstools and fungus growths. He was ignorant of fire, or metals, of the uses of stone and wood. A single garment covered him. His language was a scanty group of a few hundred labial sounds, conveying no abstractions and few concrete things.

He was ignorant of the uses of wood. There was no wood in the scanty territory furtively inhabited by his tribe. With the increase in heat and humidity the trees had begun to die out. Those of northern climes went first, the oaks, the cedars, the maples. Then the pines – the beeches went early – the cypresses, and finally even the forests of the jungles vanished. Only grasses and reeds, bamboos and their kin, were able to flourish in the new, steaming atmosphere. The thick jungles gave place to dense thickets of grasses and ferns, now become tree ferns again.

And then the fungi took their place. Flourishing as never before, flourishing on a planet of torrid heat and perpetual miasma, on whose surface the sun never shone directly because of an ever-thickening bank of clouds that hung sullenly overhead, the fungi sprang up. About the dank pools that festered over the surface of the earth, fungus growths began to cluster. Of every imaginable shade and color, of all monstrous forms and malignant purposes, of huge size and flabby volume, they spread over the land.

The grasses and ferns gave place to them. Squat footstools, flaking molds, evil-smelling yeasts, vast mounds of fungi inextricably mingled as to species, but growing, forever growing and exhaling an odor of dark places.

The strange growths now grouped themselves in forests, horrible travesties on the vegetation they had succeeded. They grew and grew with feverish intensity beneath a clouded or a haze-obscured sky, while above them fluttered gigantic butterflies and huge moths, sipping daintily of their corruption.

The insects alone of all the animal world above water, were able to endure the change. They multiplied exceedingly, and enlarged themselves in the thickened air. The solitary vegetation – as distinct from fungus growths – that had survived, was now a degenerate form of the cabbages that had once fed peasants. On those rank, colossal masses of foliage, the stolid grubs and caterpillars ate themselves to maturity, then swung below in strong cocoons to sleep the sleep of metamorphosis from which they emerged to spread their wings and fly.

The tiniest butterflies of former days had increased their span until their gaily colored wings should be described in terms of feet, while the larger emperor moths extended their purple sails to a breadth of yards upon yards. Burl himself would have been dwarfed beneath the overshadowing fabric of their wings.

It was fortunate that they, the largest flying creatures, were harmless or nearly so. Burl's fellow tribesmen sometimes came upon a cocoon just about to open, and waited patiently beside it until the beautiful creature within broke through its matted shell and came out into the sunlight.

Then, before it had gathered energy from the air, and before its wings had swelled to strength and firmness, the tribesmen fell upon it, tearing the filmy, delicate wings from its body and the limbs from its carcass. Then, when it lay helpless before them, they carried away the juicy, meat-filled limbs to be eaten, leaving the still living body to stare helplessly at this strange world through its many faceted eyes, and become a prey to the voracious ants who would soon clamber upon it and carry it away in tiny fragments to their underground city.

# 3

Not all the insect world was so helpless or so unthreatening. Burl knew of wasps almost the length of his own body who possessed stings that were instantly fatal. To every species of wasp, however, some other insect is predestined prey, and the furtive members of Burl's tribe feared them but little as they sought only the prey to which their instinct led them.

Bees were similarly aloof. They were hard put to it for existence, those bees. Few flowers bloomed, and they were reduced to expedients once considered signs of degeneracy in their race. Bubbling yeasts and fouler things, occasionally the nectarless blooms of the rank, giant cabbages. Burl knew the bees. They droned overhead, nearly as large as he was himself, their bulging eyes gazing at him with abstracted preoccupation. And crickets, and beetles, and spiders –

Burl knew spiders! His grandfather had been the prey of one of the hunting tarantulas, which had leaped with incredible ferocity from his excavated tunnel in the earth. A vertical pit in the ground, two feet in diameter, went down for twenty feet. At the bottom of that lair the black-bellied monster waited for the tiny sounds that would warn him of prey approaching his hiding-place (*Lycosa fasciata*).

Burl's grandfather had been careless, and the terrible shrieks he uttered as the horrible monster darted from the pit and seized him had lingered vaguely in Burl's mind ever since. Burl had seen, too, the monster webs of another species of spider, and watched from a safe distance as the misshapen body of the huge creature sucked the juices from a three-foot cricket that had become entangled in its trap.

Burl had remembered the strange stripes of yellow and black and silver that crossed upon its abdomen (*Epiera fasciata*). He had been fascinated by the struggles of the imprisoned insect, coiled in a hopeless tangle of sticky, gummy ropes the thickness of Burl's finger, cast about its body before the spider made any attempt to approach.

Burl knew these dangers. They were a part of his life. It was his accustomedness to them, and that of his ancestors, that made his existence possible. He was able to evade them; so he survived. A moment of carelessness, an instant's relaxation of his habitual caution, and he would be one with his forebears, forgotten meals of long-dead, inhuman monsters.

Three days before, Burl had crouched behind a bulky, shapeless fungus growth while he watched a furious duel between two huge horned beetles. Their jaws, gaping wide, clicked and clashed upon each other's impenetrable armor. Their legs crashed like so many cymbals as their polished surfaces ground and struck against each other. They were fighting over some particularly attractive bit of carrion.

Burl had watched with all his eyes until a gaping orifice appeared in the armor of the smaller of the two. It uttered a shrill cry, or seemed to cry out. The noise was, actually, the tearing of the horny stuff beneath the victorious jaws of the adversary.

The wounded beetle struggled more and more feebly. At last it collapsed, and the conqueror placidly began to eat the conquered before life was extinct.

Burl waited until the meal was finished, and then approached the scene with caution. An ant – the forerunner of many – was already inspecting the carcass.

Burl usually ignored the ants. They were stupid, short-sighted insects, and not hunters. Save when attacked, they offered no injury. They were scavengers, on the lookout for the dead and dying, but they would fight viciously if their prey were questioned, and they were dangerous opponents. They were from three inches, for the tiny black ants, to a foot for the large termites.

Burl was hasty when he heard the tiny clickings of their limbs as they approached. He seized the sharp-pointed snout of the victim, detached from the body, and fled from the scene.

Later, he inspected his find with curiosity. The smaller victim had been a minotaur beetle, with a sharp-pointed horn like that of a rhinoceros to reinforce his offensive armament, already dangerous because of his wide jaws. The jaws of a beetle work from side to side, instead of up and down, and this had made the protection complete in no less than three directions.

Burl inspected the sharp, dagger-like instrument in his hand. He felt its point, and it pricked his finger. He flung it aside as he crept to the hiding-place of his tribe. There were only twenty of them, four or five men, six or seven women, and the rest girls and children.

Burl had been wondering at the strange feelings that came over him when he looked at one of the girls. She was younger than Burl – perhaps eighteen – and fleeter of foot than he. They talked together, sometimes, and once or twice Burl shared with her an especially succulent find of foodstuffs.

# 4

The next morning he found the horn where he had thrown it, sticking in the flabby side of a toadstool. He pulled it out, and gradually, far back in his mind, an idea began to take shape. He sat for some time with the thing in his hand, considering it with a far-away look in his eyes. From time to time he stabbed at a toadstool, awkwardly, but with gathering skill. His imagination began to work fitfully. He visualized himself stabbing food with it as the larger beetle had stabbed the former owner of the weapon he had in his hand.

Burl could not imagine himself coping with one of the fighting insects. He could only picture himself, dimly, stabbing something that was food with this death-dealing thing. It was no longer than his arm and though clumsy to the hand, an effective and terribly sharp implement.

He thought: Where was there food, food that lived, that would not fight back? Presently he rose and began to make his way toward the tiny river. Yellow-bellied newts swam in its waters. The swimming larvae of a thousand insects floated about its surface or crawled upon its bottom.

There were deadly things there, too. Giant crayfish snapped their horny claws at the unwary. Mosquitoes of four-inch wing-spread sometimes made their humming way above the river. The last survivors of their race, they were dying out for lack of the plant-juices on which the male of the species lived, but even so they were formidable. Burl had learned to crush them with fragments of fungus.

He crept slowly through the forest of toadstools. Brownish fungus was underfoot. Strange orange, red, and purple molds clustered about the bases of the creamy toadstool stalks. Once Burl paused to run his sharp-pointed weapon through a fleshy stalk and reassure himself that what he planned was practicable.

He made his way furtively through the forest of misshapen growths. Once he heard a tiny clicking, and froze into stillness. It was a troop of four or five ants, each some eight inches long, returning along their habitual pathway to their city. They moved sturdily, heavily laden, along the route marked with the black and odorous formic acid exuded from the bodies of their comrades. Burl waited until they had passed, then went on.

He came to the bank of the river. Green scum covered a great deal of its surface, scum occasionally broken by a slowly enlarging bubble of some gas released from decomposing matter on the bottom. In the center of the placid stream the current ran a little more swiftly, and the water itself was visible.

Over the shining current, water-spiders ran swiftly. They had not shared in the general increase of size that had taken place in the insect world. Depending upon the capillary qualities of the water to support them, an increase in size and weight would have deprived them of the means of locomotion.

From the spot where Burl first peered at the water the green scum spread out for many yards into the stream. He could not see what swam and wriggled and crawled beneath the evil-smelling covering. He peered up and down the banks.

Perhaps a hundred and fifty yards below, the current came near the shore. An outcropping of rock there made a steep descent to the river, from which yellow shelf-fungi stretched out. Dark red and orange above, they were light yellow below, and they formed a series of platforms above the smoothly flowing stream. Burl made his way cautiously toward them.

On his way he saw one of the edible mushrooms that formed so large a part of his diet, and paused to break from the flabby flesh an amount that would feed him for many days. It was too often the custom of his people to find a store of food, carry it to their hiding place, and then gorge themselves for days, eating, sleeping, and waking only to eat again until the food was gone.

Absorbed as he was in his plan of trying his new weapon, Burl was tempted to return with his booty. He would give Saya of this food, and they would eat together. Saya was the maiden who roused unusual emotions in Burl. He felt strange impulses stirring within him when she was near, a desire to touch her, to caress her. He did not understand.

He went on, after hesitating. If he brought her food, Saya would be pleased, but if he brought her of the things that swam in the stream, she would be still more pleased. Degraded as his tribe had become, Burl was yet a little more intelligent than they. He was an atavism, a throwback to ancestors who had cultivated the earth and subjugated its animals. He had a vague idea of pride, unformed but potent.

No man within memory had hunted or slain for food. They knew of meat, yes, but it had been the fragments left by an insect hunter, seized and carried away by the men before the perpetually alert ant colonies had sent their foragers to the scene.

If Burl did what no man before him had done, if he brought a whole carcass to his tribe, they would envy him. They were preoccupied solely with their stomachs, and after that with the preservation of their lives. The perpetuation of the race came third in their consideration.

They were herded together in a leaderless group, coming to the same hiding place that they might share in the finds of the lucky and gather comfort from their numbers. Of weapons, they had none. They sometimes used stones to crack open the limbs of the huge insects they found partly devoured, cracking them open for the sweet meat to be found inside, but they sought safety from their enemies solely in flight and hiding.

Their enemies were not as numerous as might have been imagined. Most of the meat-eating insects have their allotted prey. The sphex – a hunting wasp – feeds solely upon grasshoppers. Others wasps eat flies only. The pirate-bee eats bumblebees only. Spiders were the principal enemies of man, as they devour with a terrifying impartiality all that falls into their clutches.

Burl reached the spot from which he might gaze down into the water. He lay prostrate, staring into the shallow depths. Once a huge crayfish, as long as Burl's body, moved leisurely across his vision. Small fishes and even the huge newts fled before the voracious creature.

After a long time the tide of underwater life resumed its activity. The wriggling grubs of the dragonflies reappeared. Little flecks of silver swam into view – a school of tiny fish. A larger fish appeared, moving slowly through the water.

Burl's eyes glistened and his mouth watered. He reached down with his long weapon. It barely touched the water. Disappointment filled him, yet the nearness and the apparent practicability of his scheme spurred him on.

He considered the situation. There were the shelf-fungi below him. He rose and moved to a point just above them, then thrust his spear down. They resisted its point. Burl felt them tentatively with his foot, then dared to thrust his weight to them. They held him firmly. He clambered down and lay flat upon them, peering over the edge as before.

The large fish, as long as Burl's arm, swam slowly to and fro below him. Burl had seen the former owner of his spear strive to thrust it into his opponents, and knew that a thrust was necessary. He had tried his weapon upon toadstools – had practiced with it. When the fish swam below him, he thrust sharply downward. The spear seemed to bend when it entered the water, and missed its mark by inches, to Burl's astonishment. He tried again and again.

He grew angry with the fish below him for eluding his efforts to kill it. Repeated strokes had left it untouched, and it was unwary, and did not even try to run away.

Burl became furious. The big fish came to rest directly beneath his hand. Burl thrust downward with all his strength. This time the spear, entering vertically, did not seem to bend. It went straight down. Its point penetrated the scales of the swimmer below, transfixing that lazy fish completely.

An uproar began. The fish, struggling to escape, and Burl, trying to draw it up to his perch, made a huge commotion. In his excitement Burl did not observe a tiny ripple some distance away. The monster crayfish was attracted by the disturbance, and was approaching.

The unequal combat continued. Burl hung on desperately to the end of his spear. Then there was a tremor in Burl's support, it gave way, and fell into the stream with a mighty splash. Burl went under, his eyes open, facing death. And as he sank, his wide-open eyes saw waved before him the gaping claws of the huge crayfish, large enough to sever a limb with a single stroke of their jagged jaws.

# 5

**He** opened his mouth to scream – a replica of the terrible screams of his grandfather, seized by a black-bellied tarantula years before – but no sound came forth. Only bubbles floated to the surface of the water. He beat the unresisting fluid with his hands – he did not know how to swim. The colossal creature approached leisurely, while Burl struggled helplessly.

His arms struck a solid object, and grasped it convulsively. A second later he had swung it between himself and the huge crustacean. He felt a shock as the mighty jaws closed upon the corklike fungus, then felt himself drawn upward as the crayfish released his hold and the shelf-fungus floated to the surface. Having given way beneath him, it had been carried below him in his fall, only to rise within his reach just when most needed.

Burl's head popped above water and he saw a larger bit of the fungus floating nearby. Less securely anchored to the rocks of the river bank than the shelf to which Burl had trusted himself, it had been dislodged when the first shelf gave way. It was larger than the fragment to which Burl clung, and floated higher in the water.

Burl was cool with a terrible self-possession. He seized it and struggled to draw himself on top of it. It tilted as his weight came upon it, and nearly overturned, but he paid no heed. With desperate haste, he clawed with hands and feet until he could draw himself clear of the water, of which he would forever retain a slight fear.

As he pulled himself upon the furry, orange-brown upper surface, a sharp blow struck his foot. The crayfish, disgusted at finding only what was to it a tasteless morsel in the shelf-fungus, had made a languid stroke at Burl's wriggling foot in the water. Failing to grasp the fleshy member, the crayfish retreated, disgruntled and annoyed.

And Burl floated downstream, perched, weaponless and alone, frightened and in constant danger, upon a flimsy raft composed of a degenerate fungus floating soggily in the water. He floated slowly down the stream of a river in whose waters death lurked unseen, upon whose banks was peril, and above whose reaches danger fluttered on golden wings.

It was a long time before he recovered his self-possession, and when he did he looked first for his spear. It was floating in the water, still transfixing the fish whose capture had endangered Burl's life. The fish now floated with its belly upward, all life gone.

So insistent was Burl's instinct for food that his predicament was forgotten when he saw his prey just out of his reach. He gazed at it, and his mouth watered, while his cranky craft went downstream, spinning slowly in the current. He lay flat on the floating fungoid, and strove to reach out and grasp the end of the spear.

The raft tilted and nearly flung him overboard again. A little later he discovered that it sank more readily on one side than on the other. That was due, of course, to the greater thickness – and consequently greater buoyancy – of the part which had grown next the rocks of the river bank.

Burl found that if he lay with his head stretching above that side, it did not sink into the water. He wriggled into this new position, then, and waited until the slow revolution of his vessel brought the spear-shaft near him. He stretched his fingers and his arm, and touched, then grasped it.

A moment later he was tearing strips of flesh from the side of the fish and cramming the oily mess into his mouth with great enjoyment. He had lost his edible mushroom. That danced upon the waves several yards away, but Burl ate contentedly of what he possessed. He did not worry about what was before him. That lay in the future, but suddenly he realized that he was being carried farther and farther from Saya, the maiden of his tribe who caused strange bliss to steal over him when he contemplated her.

The thought came to him when he visualized the delight with which she would receive a gift of part of the fish he had caught. He was suddenly stricken with dumb sorrow. He lifted his head and looked longingly at the river banks.

A long, monotonous row of strangely colored fungus growths. No healthy green, but pallid, cream-colored toadstools, some bright orange, lavender, and purple molds, vivid carmine "rusts" and mildews, spreading up the banks from the turgid slime. The sun was not a ball of fire, but merely shone as a bright golden patch in the haze-filled sky, a patch whose limits could not be defined or marked.

In the faintly pinkish light that filtered down through the air, a multitude of flying objects could be seen. Now and then a cricket or a grasshopper made its bullet-like flight from one spot to another. Huge butterflies fluttered gayly above the silent, seemingly lifeless world. Bees lumbered anxiously about, seeking the cross-shaped flowers of the monster cabbages. Now and then a slender-waisted, yellow-stomached wasp flew alertly through the air.

Burl watched them with a strange indifference. The wasps were as long as he himself. The bees, on end, could match his height. The butterflies ranged from tiny creatures barely capable of shading his face to colossal things in the folds of whose wings he could have been lost. And above him fluttered dragonflies, whose long, spindle-like bodies were three times the length of his own.

Burl ignored them all. Sitting there, an incongruous creature of pink skin and soft brown hair upon an orange fungus floating in midstream, he was filled with despondency because the current carried him forever farther and farther from a certain slender-limbed maiden of his tiny tribe, whose glances caused an odd commotion in his breast.

~ ~ ~

The day went on. Once, Burl saw upon the blue-green mold that spread upward from the river, a band of large, red Amazon ants, marching in orderly array, to raid the city of a colony of black ants, and carry away the eggs they would find there. The eggs would be hatched, and the small black creatures made the slaves of the brigands who had stolen them.

The Amazon ants can live only by the labor of their slaves, and for that reason are mighty warriors in their world. Later, etched against the steaming mist that overhung everything as far as the eye could reach, Burl saw strangely shaped, swollen branches rearing themselves from the ground. He knew what they were. A hard-rinded fungus that grew upon itself in peculiar mockery of the vegetation that had vanished from the earth.

And again he saw pear-shaped objects above some of which floated little clouds of smoke. They, too, were fungus growths, puffballs, which when touched emit what seems a puff of vapor. These would have towered above Burl's head, had he stood beside them.

And then, as the day drew to an end, he saw in the distance what seemed a range of purple hills. They were tall hills to Burl, some sixty or seventy feet high, and they seemed to be the agglomeration of a formless growth, multiplying its organisms and forms upon itself until the whole formed an irregular, cone-shaped mound. Burl watched them apathetically.

Presently, he ate again of the oily fish. The taste was pleasant to him, accustomed to feed mostly upon insipid mushrooms. He stuffed himself, though the size of his prey left by far the larger part uneaten.

He still held his spear firmly beside him.

It had brought him into trouble, but Burl possessed a fund of obstinacy. Unlike most of his tribe, he associated the spear with the food it had secured, rather than the difficulty into which it had led him. When he had eaten his fill he picked it up and examined it again. The sharpness of its point was unimpaired.

Burl handled it meditatively, debating whether or not to attempt to fish again. The shakiness of his little raft dissuaded him, and he abandoned the idea. Presently he stripped a sinew from the garment about his middle and hung the fish about his neck with it. That would leave him both hands free. Then he sat cross-legged upon the soggily floating fungus, like a pink-skinned Buddha, and watched the shores go by.

Time had passed, and it was drawing near sunset. Burl, never having seen the sun save as a bright spot in the overhanging haze, did not think of the coming of night as "sunset." To him it was the letting down of darkness from the sky.

Today happened to be an exceptionally bright day, and the haze was not as thick as usual. Far to the west, the thick mist turned to gold, while the thicker clouds above became blurred masses of dull red. Their shadows seemed like lavender, from the contrast of shades. Upon the still surface of the river, all the myriad tints and shadings were reflected with an incredible faithfulness, and the shining tops of the giant mushrooms by the river brim glowed faintly pink.

Dragonflies buzzed over his head in their swift and angular flight, the metallic luster of their bodies glistening in the rosy light. Great yellow butterflies flew lightly above the stream. Here, there, and everywhere upon the water appeared the shell-formed boats of a thousand caddis flies, floating upon the surface while they might.

Burl could have thrust his hand down into their cavities and seized the white worms that inhabited the strange craft. The huge bulk of a tardy bee droned heavily overhead. Burl glanced upward and saw the long proboscis and the hairy hinder legs with their scanty load of pollen. He saw the great, multiple-lensed eyes with their expression of stupid preoccupation, and even the sting that would mean death alike for him and for the giant insect, should it be used.

The crimson radiance grew dim at the edge of the world. The purple hills had long been left behind. Now the slender stalks of ten thousand round-domed mushrooms lined the river bank and beneath them spread fungi of all colors, from the rawest red to palest blue, but all now fading slowly to a monochromatic background in the growing dusk.

The buzzing, fluttering, and the flapping of the insects of the day died slowly down, while from a million hiding places there crept out into the deep night soft and furry bodies of great moths, who preened themselves and smoothed their feathery antennae before taking to the air. The strong-limbed crickets set up their thunderous noise – grown gravely bass with the increasing size of the organs by which the sound was made – and then there began to gather on the water those slender spirals of tenuous mist that would presently blanket the stream in a mantle of thin fog.

# 6

Night fell. The clouds above seemed to lower and grow dark. Gradually, now a drop and then a drop, now a drop and then a drop, the languid fall of large, warm raindrops that would drip from the moisture-laden skies all through the night began. The edge of the stream became a place where great disks of coolly glowing flame appeared.

The mushrooms that bordered on the river were faintly phosphorescent (*Pleurotus phosphoreus*) and shone coldly upon the "rusts" and flake-fungi beneath their feet. Here and there a ball of lambent flame appeared, drifting idly above the steaming, festering earth.

Thirty thousand years before, men had called them "will-o'-the-wisps," but Burl simply stared at them, accepting them as he accepted all that passed. Only a man attempting to advance in the scale of civilization tries to explain everything that he sees. The savage and the child is most often content to observe without comment, unless he repeats the legends told him by wise folk who are possessed by the itch of knowledge.

Burl watched for a long time. Great fireflies whose beacons lighted up their surroundings for many yards – fireflies Burl knew to be as long as his spear – shed their intermittent glows upon the stream. Softly fluttering wings, in great beats that poured torrents of air upon him, passed above Burl.

The air was full of winged creatures. The night was broken by their cries, by the sound of their invisible wings, by their cries of anguish and their mating calls. Above him and on all sides the persistent, intense life of the insect world went on ceaselessly, but Burl rocked back and forth upon his frail mushroom boat and wished to weep because he was being carried from his tribe, and from Saya – Saya of the swift feet and white teeth, of the shy smile.

Burl may have been homesick, but his principal thoughts were of Saya. He had dared greatly to bring a gift of fresh meat to her, meat captured as meat had never been known to be taken by a member of the tribe. And now he was being carried from her!

He lay, disconsolate, upon his floating atom on the water for a great part of the night. It was long after midnight when the mushroom raft struck gently and remained grounded upon a shallow in the stream.

When the light came in the morning, Burl gazed about him keenly. He was some twenty yards from the shore, and the greenish scum surrounded his now disintegrating vessel. The river had widened out until the other bank was barely to be seen through the haze above the surface of the river, but the nearer shore seemed firm and no more full of dangers than the territory his tribe inhabited. He felt the depth of the water with his spear, then was struck with the multiple usefulness of that weapon. The water would come to but slightly above his ankles.

Shivering a little with fear, Burl stepped down into the water, then made for the bank at the top of his speed. He felt a soft something clinging to one of his bare feet. With an access of terror, he ran faster, and stumbled upon the shore in a panic. He stared down at his foot. A shapeless, flesh-colored pad clung to his heel, and as Burl watched, it began to swell slowly, while the pink of its wrinkled folds deepened.

It was no more than a leech, sharing in the enlargement nearly all the lower world had undergone, but Burl did not know that. He thrust at it with the side of his spear, then scraped frantically at it, and it fell off, leaving a blotch of blood upon the skin where it came away. It lay, writhing and pulsating, upon the ground, and Burl fled from it.

He found himself in one of the toadstool forests with which he was familiar, and finally paused, disconsolately. He knew the nature of the fungus growths about him, and presently fell to eating. In Burl the sight of food always produced hunger – a wise provision of nature to make up for the instinct to store food, which he lacked.

Burl's heart was small within him. He was far from his tribe, and far from Saya. In the parlance of this day, it is probable that no more than forty miles separated them, but Burl did not think of distances. He had come down the river. He was in a land he had never known or seen. And he was alone.

All about him was food. All the mushrooms that surrounded him were edible, and formed a store of sustenance Burl's whole tribe could not have eaten in many days, but that very fact brought

Saya to his mind more forcibly. He squatted on the ground, wolfing down the insipid mushroom in great gulps, when an idea suddenly came to him with all the force of inspiration.

He would bring Saya here, where there was food, food in great quantities, and she would be pleased. Burl had forgotten the large and oily fish that still hung down his back from the sinew about his neck, but now he rose, and its flapping against him reminded him again.

He took it and fingered it all over, getting his hands and himself thoroughly greasy in the process, but he could eat no more. The thought of Saya's pleasure at the sight of that, too, reinforced his determination.

With all the immediacy of a child or a savage he set off at once. He had come along the bank of the stream. He would retrace his steps along the bank of the stream.

Through the awkward aisles of the mushroom forest he made his way, eyes and ears open for possibilities of danger. Several times he heard the omnipresent clicking of ants on their multifarious businesses in the wood, but he could afford to ignore them. They were short-sighted at best, and at worst they were foragers rather than hunters. He only feared one kind of ant, the army-ant, which sometimes travels in hordes of millions, eating all that it comes upon. In ages past, when they were tiny creatures not an inch long, even the largest animals fled from them. Now that they measured a foot in length, not even the gorged spiders whose distended bellies were a yard in thickness, dared offer them battle.

The mushroom forest came to an end. A cheerful grasshopper (*Ephigger*) munched delicately at some dainty it had found. Its hind legs were bunched beneath it in perpetual readiness for flight. A monster wasp appeared above – as long as Burl himself – poised an instant, dropped, and seized the luckless feaster.

There was a struggle, then the grasshopper became helpless, and the wasp's flexible abdomen curved delicately. Its sting entered the jointed armor of its prey, just beneath the head. The sting entered with all the deliberate precision of a surgeon's scalpel, and all struggle ceased.

The wasp grasped the paralyzed, not dead, insect and flew away. Burl grunted, and passed on. He had hidden when the wasp darted down from above.

The ground grew rough, and Burl's progress became painful. He clambered arduously up steep slopes and made his way cautiously down their farther sides. Once he had to climb through a tangled mass of mushrooms so closely placed, and so small, that he had to break them apart with blows of his spear before he could pass, when they shed upon him torrents of a fiery red liquid that rolled off his greasy breast and sank into the ground (*Lactarius deliciosus*).

A strange self-confidence now took possession of Burl. He walked less cautiously and more boldly. The mere fact that he had struck something and destroyed it provided him with a curious fictitious courage.

He had climbed slowly to the top of a red clay cliff, perhaps a hundred feet high, slowly eaten away by the river when it overflowed. Burl could see the river. At some past flood time it had lapped at the base of the cliff on whose edge he walked, though now it came no nearer than a quarter-mile.

The cliffside was almost covered with shelf-fungi, large and small, white, yellow, orange, and green, in indescribable confusion and luxuriance. From a point halfway up the cliff the inch-thick cable of a spider's web stretched down to an anchorage on the ground, and the strangely geometrical pattern of the web glistened evilly.

Somewhere among the fungi of the cliffside the huge creature waited until some unfortunate prey should struggle helplessly in its monster snare. The spider waited in a motionless, implacable patience, invincibly certain of prey, utterly merciless to its victims.

Burl strutted on the edge of the cliff, a silly little pink-skinned creature with an oily fish slung about his neck and a draggled fragment of a moth's wing about his middle. In his hand he bore the long spear of a minotaur beetle. He strutted, and looked scornfully down upon the whitely shining trap below him. He struck mushrooms, and they had fallen before him. He feared nothing. He strode fearlessly along. He would go to Saya and bring her to this land where food grew in abundance.

Sixty paces before him, a shaft sank vertically in the sandy, clayey soil. It was a carefully rounded shaft, and lined with silk. It went down for perhaps thirty feet or more, and there enlarged itself into a chamber where the owner and digger of the shaft might rest. The top of the hole was closed by a trap door, stained with mud and earth to imitate with precision the surrounding soil. A keen eye would have been needed to perceive the opening. But a keen eye now peered out from a tiny crack, the eye of the engineer of the underground dwelling.

Eight hairy legs surrounded the body of the creature that hung motionless at the top of the silk-lined shaft. A huge misshapen globe formed its body, colored a dirty brown. Two pairs of ferocious mandibles stretched before its fierce mouth-parts. Two eyes glittered evilly in the darkness of the burrow. And over the whole body spread a rough, mangy fur.

It was a thing of implacable malignance, of incredible ferocity. It was the brown hunting-spider, the American tarantula (*Mygale Hentzii*). Its body was two feet and more in diameter, and its legs, outstretched, would cover a circle three yards across. It watched Burl, its eyes glistening. Slaver welled up and dropped from its jaws.

And Burl strutted forward on the edge of the cliff, puffed up with a sense of his own importance. The white snare of the spinning spider below him impressed him as amusing. He knew the spider would not leave its web to attack him. He reached down and broke off a bit of fungus growing at his feet. Where he broke it, it was oozing a soupy liquid and was full of tiny maggots in a delirium of feasting. Burl flung it down into the web, and then laughed as the black bulk of the hidden spider swung down from its hiding place to investigate.

~ ~ ~

# 7

The tarantula, peering from its burrow, quivered with impatience. Burl drew near, and nearer. He was using his spear as a lever, now, and prying off bits of fungus to fall down the cliffside into the colossal web. The spider, below, went leisurely from one place to another, investigating each new missile with its palpi, then leaving them, as they appeared lifeless and undesirable prey. Burl laughed again as a particularly large lump of shelf-fungus narrowly missed the black-and-silver figure below. Then –

The trap door fell into place with a faint click, and Burl whirled about. His laughter turned to a scream. Moving toward him with incredible rapidity, the monster tarantula opened its dripping jaws. Its mandibles gaped wide. The poison fangs were unsheathed. The creature was thirty paces away, twenty paces – ten. It leaped into the air, eyes glittering, all its eight legs extended to seize, fangs bared–

Burl screamed again, and thrust out his arms to ward off the impact of the leap. In his terror, his grasp upon his spear had become agonized. The spear point shot out, and the tarantula fell upon it. Nearly a quarter of the spear entered the body of the ferocious thing.

It struck upon the spear, writhing horribly, still struggling to reach Burl, who was transfixed with horror. The mandibles clashed, strange sounds came from the beast. Then one of the attenuated, hairy legs rasped across Burl's forearm. He gasped in ultimate fear and stepped backward – and the edge of the cliff gave way beneath him.

He hurtled downward, still clutching the spear which led the writhing creature from him. Down through space, eyes glassy with panic, the two creatures – the man and the giant tarantula – fell together. There was a strangely elastic crash and crackling. They had fallen into the web beneath them.

Burl had reached the end of terror. He could be no more fear-struck. Struggling madly in the gummy coils of an immense web, which ever bound him more tightly, with a wounded creature shuddering in agony not a yard from him – yet a wounded creature that still strove to reach him with its poison fangs – Burl had reached the limit of panic.

He fought like a madman to break the coils about him. His arms and breast were greasy from the oily fish, and the sticky web did not adhere to them, but his legs and body were inextricably fastened by the elastic threads spread for just such prey as he.

He paused a moment, in exhaustion. Then he saw, five yards away, the silvery and black monster waiting patiently for him to weary himself. It judged the moment propitious. The tarantula and the man were one in its eyes, one struggling thing that had fallen opportunely into its snare. They were moving but feebly now. The spider advanced delicately, swinging its huge bulk nimbly along the web, paying out a cable after it came inexorably toward him.

Burl's arms were free, because of the greasy coating they had received. He waved them wildly, shrieking at the pitiless monster that approached. The spider paused. Those moving arms suggested mandibles that might wound or slap.

Spiders take few hazards. This spider was no exception to the rule. It drew cautiously near, then stopped. Its spinnerets became busy, and with one of its six legs, used like an arm, it flung a sheet of gummy silk impartially over both the tarantula and the man.

Burl fought against the descending shroud. He strove to thrust it away, but in vain. In a matter of minutes he was completely covered in a silken cloth that hid even the light from his eyes. He and his enemy, the giant tarantula, were beneath the same covering, though the tarantula moved but weakly.

The shower ceased. The web-spider had decided that they were helpless. Then Burl felt the cables of the web give slightly, as the spider approached to sting and suck the sweet juices from its prey.

# 8

The web yielded gently as the added weight of the black-bellied spider approached. Burl froze into stillness under his enveloping covering. Beneath the same silken shroud the tarantula writhed in agony upon the point of Burl's spear. It clashed its jaws, shuddering upon the horny barb.

Burl was quiet in an ecstasy of terror. He waited for the poison-fangs to be thrust into him. He knew the process. He had seen the leisurely fashion in which the giant spiders delicately stung their prey, then withdrew to wait without impatience for the poison to do its work.

When their victim had ceased to struggle, they drew near again, and sucked the sweet juices from the body, first from one point and then another, until what had so recently been a creature vibrant with life became a shrunken, withered husk – to be flung from the web at nightfall. Most spiders are tidy housekeepers, destroying their snares daily to spin anew.

The bloated, evil creature moved meditatively about the shining sheet of silk it had cast over the man and the giant tarantula when they fell from the cliff above. Now only the tarantula moved feebly. Its body was outlined by a bulge in the concealing shroud, throbbing faintly as it still struggled with the spear in its vitals. The irregularly rounded protuberance offered a point of attack for the web spider. It moved quickly forward, and stung.

Galvanized into fresh torment by this new agony, the tarantula writhed in a very hell of pain. Its legs, clustered about the spear still fastened into its body, struck out purposelessly, in horrible gestures of delirious suffering. Burl screamed as one of them touched him, and struggled himself.

His arms and head were free beneath the silken sheet because of the grease and oil that coated them. He clutched at the threads about him and strove to draw himself away from his deadly neighbor. The threads did not break, but they parted one from another, and a tiny opening appeared. One of the tarantula's attenuated limbs touched him again. With the strength of utter panic he hauled himself away, and the opening enlarged. Another struggle, and Burl's head emerged into the open air, and he stared down for twenty feet upon an open space almost carpeted with the chitinous remains of his present captor's former victims.

Burl's head was free, and his breast and arms. The fish slung over his shoulder had shed its oil upon him impartially. But the lower part of his body was held firm by the gummy snare of the web-spider, a snare far more tenacious than any bird-lime ever manufactured by man.

He hung in his tiny window for a moment, despairing. Then he saw, at a little distance, the bulk of the monster spider, waiting patiently for its poison to take effect and the struggling of its prey to be stilled. The tarantula was no more than shuddering now. Soon it would be still, and the black-bellied creature waiting on the web would approach for its meal.

Burl withdrew his head and thrust desperately at the sticky stuff about his loins and legs. The oil upon his hands kept it from clinging to them, and it gave a little. In a flash of inspiration, Burl understood. He reached over his shoulder and grasped the greasy fish; tore it in a dozen places and smeared himself with the now rancid exudation, pushing the sticky threads from his limbs and oiling the surface from which he had thrust it away.

He felt the web tremble. To the spider, its poison seemed to have failed of effect. Another sting seemed to be necessary. This time it would not insert its fangs into the quiescent tarantula, but would sting where the disturbance was manifest – would send its deadly venom into Burl.

He gasped, and drew himself toward his window. It was as if he would have pulled his legs from his body. His head emerged, his shoulders – half his body was out of the hole.

The colossal spider surveyed him, and made ready to cast more of its silken sheet upon him. The spinnerets became active, and the sticky stuff about Burl's feet gave way! He shot out of the opening and fell sprawling, awkwardly and heavily, upon the earth below, crashing upon the shrunken shell of a flying beetle which had fallen into the snare and had not escaped.

Burl rolled over and over, and then sat up. An angry, foot-long ant stood before him, its mandibles extended threateningly, while its antennae waved wildly in the air. A shrill stridulation filled the air.

In ages past, when ants were tiny creatures of lengths to be measured in fractions of an inch, learned scientists debated gravely if their tribe possessed a cry. They believed that certain grooves upon the body of the insects, after the fashion of those upon the great legs of the cricket, might offer the means of uttering an infinitely high-pitched sound too shrill for man's ears to catch.

Burl knew that the stridulation was caused by the doubtful insect before him, though he had never wondered how it was produced. The cry was used to summon others of its city, to help it in its difficulty or good fortune.

Clickings sounded fifty or sixty feet away. Comrades were coming to aid the pioneer. Harmless save when interfered with – all save the army ant, that is – the whole ant tribe was formidable when aroused. Utterly fearless, they could pull down a man and slay him as so many infuriated fox terriers might have done thirty thousand years before.

# 9

**B**url fled, without debate, and nearly collided with one of the anchoring cables of the web from which he had barely escaped a moment before. He heard the shrill sound behind him suddenly subside. The ant, short-sighted as all ants were, no longer felt itself threatened and went peacefully about the business Burl had interrupted, that of finding among the gruesome relics beneath the spider's web some edible carrion which might feed the inhabitants of its city.

Burl sped on for a few hundred yards, and stopped. It behooved him to move carefully. He was in strange territory, and as even the most familiar territory was full of sudden and implacable dangers, unknown lands were doubly or trebly perilous.

Burl, too found difficulty in moving. The glutinous stuff from the spider's shroud of silk still stuck to his feet and picked up small objects as he went along. Old ant-gnawed fragments of insect armor pricked him even through his toughened soles.

He looked about cautiously and removed them, took a dozen steps and had to stop again. Burl's brain had been uncommonly stimulated of late. It had gotten him into at least one predicament – due to his invention of a spear – but had no less readily led to his escape from another. But for the reasoning that had led him to use the grease from the fish upon his shoulder in oiling his body when he struggled out of the spider's snare, he would now be furnishing a meal for that monster.

Cautiously, Burl looked all about him. He seemed to be safe. Then, quite deliberately, he sat down to think. It was the first time in his life that he had done such a thing. The people of his tribe were not given to meditation. But an idea had struck Burl with all the force of inspiration – an abstract idea.

When he was in difficulties, something within him seemed to suggest a way out. Would it suggest an inspiration now? He puzzled over the problem. Childlike – and savage-like – the instant the thought came to him, he proceeded to test it out. He fixed his gaze upon his foot. The sharp edges of pebbles, of the remains of insect-armor, of a dozen things, hurt his feet when he walked. They had done so ever since he had been born, but never had his feet been sticky so that the irritation continued with him for more than a single step.

Now he gazed upon his foot, and waited for the thought within him to develop. Meanwhile, he slowly removed the sharp-pointed fragments, one by one. Partly coated as they were with the half-liquid gum from his feet, they clung to his fingers as they had to his feet, except upon those portions where the oil was thick as before.

Burl's reasoning, before, was simple and of the primary order. Where oil covered him, the web did not. Therefore he would coat the rest of himself with oil. Had he been placed in the same predicament again, he would have used the same means of escape. But to apply a bit of knowledge gained in one predicament to another difficulty was something he had not yet done.

A dog may be taught that by pulling on the latchstring of a door he may open it, but the same dog coming to a high and close-barred gate with a latchstring attached, will never think of pulling on this second latchstring. He associates a latchstring with the opening of the door. The opening of a gate is another matter entirely.

Burl had been stirred to one invention by imminent peril. That is not extraordinary. But to reason in cold blood, as he presently did, that oil on his feet would nullify the glue upon his feet and enable him again to walk in comfort – that was a triumph. The inventions of savages are essentially matters of life and death, of food and safety. Comfort and luxury are only produced by intelligence of a high order.

Burl, in safety, had added to his comfort. That was truly a more important thing in his development than almost any other thing he could have done. He oiled his feet.

It was an almost infinitesimal problem, but Burl's struggles with the mental process of reasoning were actual. Thirty thousand years before him, a wise man had pointed out that education is simply training in thought, in efficient and effective thinking. Burl's tribe had been too much preoccupied with food and mere existence to think, and now Burl, sitting at the base of a squat toadstool that all but concealed him, re-exemplified Rodin's "Thinker" for the first time in many generations.

For Burl to reason that oil upon the soles of his feet would guard him against sharp stones was as much a triumph of intellect as any masterpiece of art in the ages before him. Burl was learning how to think.

He stood up, walked, and crowed in sheer delight, then paused a moment in awe of his own intelligence. Thirty-five miles from his tribe, naked, unarmed, utterly ignorant of fire, of wood, of any weapons save a spear he had experimented with the day before, abysmally uninformed concerning the very existence of any art or science, Burl stopped to assure himself that he was very wonderful.

Pride came to him. He wished to display himself to Saya, these things upon his feet, and his spear. But his spear was gone.

# 10

With touching faith in the efficacy of this new pastime, Burl sat promptly down again and knitted his brows. Just as a superstitious person, once convinced that by appeal to a favorite talisman he will be guided aright, will inevitably apply to that talisman on all occasions, so Burl plumped himself down to think.

These questions were easily answered. Burl was naked. He would search out garments for himself. He was weaponless. He would find himself a spear. He was hungry – and would seek food, and he was far from his tribe, so he would go to them. Puerile reasoning, of course, but valuable, because it was consciously reasoning, consciously appealing to his mind for guidance in difficulty, deliberate progress from a mental desire to a mental resolution.

Even in the high civilization of ages before, few men had really used their brains. The great majority of people had depended upon machines and their leaders to think for them. Burl's tribefolk depended on their stomachs. Burl, however, was gradually developing the habit of thinking which makes for leadership and which would be invaluable to his little tribe.

He stood up again and faced upstream, moving slowly and cautiously, his eyes searching the ground before him keenly and his ears alert for the slightest sound of danger. Gigantic butterflies, riotous in coloring, fluttered overhead through the misty haze. Sometimes a grasshopper hurtled through the air like a projectile, its transparent wings beating the air frantically. Now and then a wasp sped by, intent upon its hunting, or a bee droned heavily along, anxious and worried, striving in a nearly flowerless world to gather the pollen that would feed the hive.

Here and there Burl saw flies of various sorts, some no larger than his thumb, but others the size of his whole hand. They fed upon the juices that dripped from the maggot-infested mushrooms, when filth more to their liking was not at hand.

Very far away a shrill roaring sounded faintly. It was like a multitude of clickings blended into a single sound, but was so far away that it did not impress itself upon Burl's attention. He had all the strictly localized vision of a child. What was near was important, and what was distant could be ignored. Only the imminent required attention, and Burl was preoccupied.

Had he listened, he would have realized that army ants were abroad in countless millions, spreading themselves out in a broad array and eating all they came upon far more destructively than so many locusts.

Locusts in past ages had eaten all green things. There were only giant cabbages and a few such tenacious rank growths in the world that Burl knew. The locusts had vanished with civilization and knowledge and the greater part of mankind, but the army ants remained as an invincible enemy to men and insects, and the most of the fungus growths that covered the earth.

Burl did not notice the sound, however. He moved forward, briskly though cautiously, searching with his eyes for garments, food, and weapons. He confidently expected to find all of them within a short distance.

Surely enough he found a thicket – if one might call it so – of edible fungi no more than half a mile beyond the spot where he had improvised his sandals to protect the soles of his feet.

Without especial elation, Burl tugged at the largest until he had broken off a food supply for several days. He went on, eating as he did so, past a broad plain a mile and more across, being broken into odd little hillocks by gradually ripening and suddenly developing mushrooms with which he was unfamiliar.

The earth seemed to be in process of being pushed aside by rounded protuberances of which only the tips showed. Blood-red hemispheres seemed to be forcing aside the earth so they might reach the outer air.

Burl looked at them curiously, and passed among them without touching them. They were strange, and to him most strange things meant danger. In any event, he was full of a new purpose now. He wished garments and weapons.

Above the plain a wasp hovered, a heavy object dangling beneath its black belly, ornamented by a single red band. It was a wasp – the hairy sand-wasp – and it was bringing a paralyzed gray caterpillar to its burrow.

Burl watched it drop down with the speed and sureness of an arrow, pull aside a heavy, flat stone, and descend into the ground.

It had a vertical shaft dug down for forty feet or more.

It descended, evidently inspected the interior, reappeared, and vanished into the hole again, dragging the gray worm after it. Burl, marching on over the broad plain that seemed stricken with some erupting disease from the number of red pimples making their appearance, did not know what passed below, but observed the wasp emerge again and busily scratch dirt and stones into the shaft until it was full.

The wasp had paralyzed a caterpillar, taken it to the already prepared burrow, laid an egg upon it, and rilled up the entrance. In course of time the egg would hatch into a grub barely as long as Burl's forefinger, which would then feed upon the torpid caterpillar until it had waxed large and fat. Then it would weave itself a chrysalis and sleep a long sleep, only to wake as a wasp and dig its way to the open air.

Burl reached the farther side of the plain and found himself threading the aisles of one of the fungus forests in which the growths were hideous, misshapen travesties upon the trees they had supplanted. Bloated, yellow limbs branched off from rounded, swollen trunks. Here and there a pear-shaped puff-ball, Burl's height and half as much again, waited craftily until a chance touch should cause it to shoot upward a curling puff of infinitely fine dust.

Burl went cautiously. There were dangers here, but he moved forward steadily, none the less. A great mass of edible mushroom was slung under one of his arms, and from time to time he broke off a fragment and ate of it, while his large eyes searched this way and that for threats of harm.

Behind him, a high, shrill roaring had grown slightly in volume and nearness, but was still too far away to impress Burl. The army ants were working havoc in the distance. By thousands and millions, myriads upon myriads, they were foraging the country, clambering upon every eminence, descending into every depression, their antennae waving restlessly and their mandibles forever threateningly extended. The ground was black with them, each was ten inches and more in length.

A single such creature would be formidable to an unarmed and naked man like Burl, whose wisest move would be flight, but in their thousands and millions they presented a menace from which no escape seemed possible. They were advancing steadily and rapidly, shrill stridulations and a multitude of clickings marking their movements.

The great helpless caterpillars upon the giant cabbages heard the sound of their coming, but were too stupid to flee. The black multitudes covered the rank vegetables, and tiny but voracious jaws began to tear at the flaccid masses of flesh.

Each creature had some futile means of struggling. The caterpillars strove to throw off their innumerable assailants by writhings and contortions, wholly ineffective. The bees fought their entrance to the gigantic hives with stings and wingbeats. The moths took to the air in helpless blindness when discovered by the relentless throngs of small black insects which reeked of formic acid and left the ground behind them denuded in every living thing.

Before the oncoming horde was a world of teeming life, where mushrooms and fungi fought with thinning numbers of giant cabbages for foothold. Behind the black multitude was – nothing. Mushrooms, cabbages, bees, wasps, crickets. Every creeping and crawling thing that did not get aloft before the black tide reached it was lost, torn to bits by tiny mandibles. Even the hunting spiders and tarantulas fell before the host of insects, having killed many in their final struggles, but overwhelmed by sheer numbers. And the wounded and dying army ants made food for their sound comrades.

There is no mercy among insects. Only the web-spiders sat unmoved and immovable in their colossal snares, secure in the knowledge that their gummy webs would discourage attempts at invasion along the slender supporting cables.

Surging onward, flowing like a monstrous, murky tide over the yellow, steaming earth, the army ants advanced. Their vanguard reached the river, and recoiled. Burl was perhaps five miles distant when they changed their course, communicating the altered line of march to those behind them in some mysterious fashion of transmitting intelligence.

Thirty thousand years before, scientists had debated gravely over the means of communication among ants. They had observed that a single ant finding a bit of booty too large for him to handle alone would return to the ant-city and return with others. From that one instance they deduced a language of gestures made with the antennae.

Burl had no wise theories. He merely knew facts, but he knew that the ants had some form of speech or transmission of ideas. Now, however, he was moving cautiously along toward the stamping grounds of his tribe, in complete ignorance of the black blanket of living creatures creeping over the ground toward him.

A million tragedies marked the progress of the insect army. There was a tiny colony of mining bees – Zebra bees – a single mother, some four feet long, had dug a huge gallery with some ten cells, in which she laid her eggs and fed her grubs with hard-gathered pollen. The grubs had waxed fat and large, became bees, and laid eggs in their turn, within the gallery their mother had dug out for them.

Ten such bulky insects now foraged busily for grubs within the ancestral home, while the founder of the colony had grown draggled and wingless with the passing of time. Unable to forage herself, the old bee became the guardian of the nest or hive, as is the custom among the mining bees. She closed the opening of the hive with her head, making a living barrier within the entrance, and withdrawing to give entrance and exit only to duly authenticated members of the extensive colony.

The ancient and draggled concierge of the underground dwelling was at her post when the wave of army ants swept over her. Tiny, evil-smelling feet trampled upon her. She emerged to fight with mandible and sting for the sanctity of the hive. In a moment she was a shaggy mass of biting ants, rending and tearing at her chitinous armor. The old bee fought madly, viciously, sounding a buzzing alarm to the colonists yet within the hive. They emerged, fighting as they came, for the gallery leading down was a dark flood of small insects.

# 11

For a few moments a battle such as would make an epic was in progress. Ten huge bees, each four to five feet long, fighting with legs and jaw, wing and mandible, with all the ferocity of as many tigers. The tiny, vicious ants covered them, snapping at their multiple eyes, biting at the tender joints in their armor – sometimes releasing the larger prey to leap upon an injured comrade wounded by the huge creature they battled in common.

The fight, however, could have but one ending. Struggle as the bees might, herculean as their efforts might be, they were powerless against the incredible numbers of their assailants, who tore them into tiny fragments and devoured them. Before the last shred of the hive's defenders had vanished, the hive itself was gutted alike of the grubs it had contained and the food brought to the grubs by such weary effort of the mature bees.

The army ants went on. Only an empty gallery remained, that and a few fragments of tough armor, unappetizing even to the omnivorous ants.

Burl was meditatively inspecting the scene of a recent tragedy, where rent and scraped fragments of a great beetle's shiny casing lay upon the ground. A greater beetle had come upon the first and slain him. Burl was looking upon the remains of the meal.

Three or four minims, little ants barely six inches long, foraged industriously among the bits. A new ant city was to be formed and the queen-ant lay hidden a half-mile away. These were the first hatchlings, who would feed the larger ants on whom would fall the great work of the ant-city. Burl ignored them, searching with his eyes for a spear or weapon.

Behind him the clicking roar, the high-pitched stridulations of the horde of army ants, rose in volume. Burl turned disgustedly away. The best he could find in the way of a weapon was a fiercely toothed hind leg. He picked it up, and an angry whine rose from the ground.

One of the black minims was working busily to detach a fragment of flesh from the joint of the leg, and Burl had snatched the morsel from him. The little creature was hardly half a foot in length, but it advanced upon Burl, shrilling angrily. He struck it with the leg and crushed it. Two of the other minims appeared, attracted by the noise the first had made. Discovering the crushed body of their fellow, they unceremoniously dismembered it and bore it away in triumph.

Burl went on, swinging the toothed limb in his hand. It made a fair club, and Burl was accustomed to use stones to crush the juicy legs of such giant crickets as his tribe sometimes came upon. He formed a half-defined idea of a club. The sharp teeth of the thing in his hand made him realize that a sidewise blow was better than a spear-like thrust.

The sound behind him had become a distant whispering, high-pitched, and growing nearer. The army ants swept over a mushroom forest, and the yellow, umbrella-like growths swarmed with black creatures devouring the substance on which they found a foothold.

A great bluebottle fly, shining with a metallic luster, reposed in an ecstasy of feasting, sipping through its long proboscis the dark-colored liquid that dripped slowly from a mushroom. Maggots filled the mushroom, and exuded a solvent pepsin that liquefied the white firm "meat."

They fed upon this soup, this gruel, and a surplus dripped to the ground below, where the bluebottle drank eagerly. Burl drew near, and struck. The fly collapsed into a writhing heap. Burl stood over it for an instant, pondering.

The army ants came nearer, down into a tiny valley, swarming into and through a little brook over which Burl had leaped. Ants can remain under water for a long time without drowning, so the small stream was but a minor obstacle, though the current of water swept many of them off their feet until they choked the brook-bed, and their comrades passed over their struggling bodies dry-shod. They were no more than temporarily annoyed, however, and presently crawled out to resume their march.

About a quarter of a mile to the left of Burl's line of march, and perhaps a mile behind the spot where he stood over the dead bluebottle fly, there was a stretch of an acre or more where the giant, rank cabbages had so far resisted the encroachments of the ever present mushrooms. The pale, cross-shaped flowers of the cabbages formed food for many bees, and the leaves fed numberless grubs and worms, and loud-voiced crickets which crouched about on the ground, munching busily at the succulent green stuff. The army ants swept into the green area, ceaselessly devouring all they came upon.

A terrific din arose. The crickets hurtled away in a rocketlike flight, in a dark cloud of wildly beating wings. They shot aimlessly in any direction, with the result that half, or more than half, fell in the midst of the black tide of devouring insects and were seized as they fell. They uttered terrible cries as they were being torn to bits. Horrible inhuman screams reached Burl's ears.

A single such cry of agony would not have attracted Burl's attention – he lived in the very atmosphere of tragedy – but the chorus of creatures in torment made him look up. This was no minor horror. Wholesale slaughter was going on. He peered anxiously in the direction of the sound.

A wild stretch of sickly yellow fungus, here and there interspersed with a squat toadstool or a splash of vivid color where one of the many "rusts" had found a foothold. To the left a group of awkward, misshapen fungoids clustered in silent mockery of a forest of trees. There a mass of faded green, where the giant cabbages stood.

With the true sun never shining upon them save through a blanket of thick haze or heavy clouds, they were pallid things, but they were the only green things Burl had seen. Their nodding white flowers with four petals in the form of a cross glowed against the yellowish green leaves. But as Burl gazed toward them, the green became slowly black.

From where he stood, Burl could see two or three great grubs in lazy contentment, eating ceaselessly on the cabbages on which they rested. Suddenly first one and then the other began to jerk spasmodically. Burl saw that about each of them a tiny rim of black had clustered. Tiny black motes milled over the green surfaces of the cabbages. The grubs became black, the cabbages became black. Horrible contortions of the writhing grubs told of the agonies they were enduring. Then a black wave appeared at the further edge of the stretch of the sickly yellow fungus, a glistening, living wave, that moved forward rapidly with the roar of clickings and a persistent overtone of shrill stridulations.

The hair rose upon Burl's head. He knew what this was! He knew all too well the meaning of that tide of shining bodies. With a gasp of terror, all his intellectual preoccupations forgotten, he turned and fled in ultimate panic. And the tide came slowly on after him.

# 12

**He** flung away the great mass of edible mushroom, but clung to his sharp-toothed club desperately, and darted through the tangled aisles of the little mushroom forest with a heedless disregard of the dangers that might await him there. Flies buzzed about him loudly, huge creatures, glittering with a metallic luster. Once he was struck upon the shoulder by the body of one of them, and his skin was torn by the swiftly vibrating wings of the insect, as long as Burl's hand.

Burl thrust it away and sped on. The oil with which he was partly covered had turned rancid, now, and the odor attracted them, connoisseurs of the fetid. They buzzed over his head, keeping pace even with his headlong flight.

A heavy weight settled upon his head, and in a moment was doubled. Two of the creatures had dropped upon his oily hair, to sip the rancid oil through their disgusting proboscises. Burl shook them off with his hand and ran madly on. His ears were keenly attuned to the sound of the army ants behind him, and it grew but little farther away.

The clicking roar continued, but began to be overshadowed by the buzzing of the flies. In Burl's time the flies had no great heaps of putrid matter in which to lay their eggs. The ants – busy scavengers – carted away the debris of the multitudinous tragedies of the insect world long before it could acquire the gamey flavor beloved by the fly maggots. Only in isolated spots were the flies really numerous, but there they clustered in clouds that darkened the sky.

Such a buzzing, whirling cloud surrounded the madly running figure of Burl. It seemed as though a miniature whirlwind kept pace with the little pink-skinned man, a whirlwind composed of winged bodies and multi-faceted eyes. He twirled his club before him, and almost every stroke was interrupted by an impact against a thinly armored body which collapsed with a spurting of reddish liquid.

An agonizing pain as of a red-hot iron struck upon Burl's

back. One of the stinging flies had thrust its sharp-tipped proboscis into Burl's flesh to suck the blood.

Burl uttered a cry and – ran full tilt into the thick stalk of a blackened and draggled toadstool. There was a curious crackling as of wet punk or brittle rotten wood. The toadstool collapsed upon itself with a strange splashing sound. Many flies had laid their eggs in the fungoid, and it was a teeming mass of corruption and ill-smelling liquid.

With the crash of the toadstool's "head" upon the ground, it fell into a dozen pieces, and the earth for yards around was spattered with a stinking liquid in which tiny, headless maggots twitched convulsively.

The buzzing of the flies took on a note of satisfaction, and they settled by hundreds about the edges of the ill-smelling pools, becoming lost in the ecstasy of feasting while Burl staggered to his feet and darted off again. This time he was but a minor attraction to the flies, and but one or two came near him. From every direction they were hurrying to the toadstool feast, to the banquet of horrible, liquefied fungus that lay spread upon the ground.

Burl ran on. He passed beneath the wide-spreading leaves of a giant cabbage. A great grasshopper crouched upon the ground, its tremendous jaws crunching the rank vegetation voraciously. Half a dozen great worms ate steadily from their resting-places among the leaves. One of them had slung itself beneath an overhanging leaf – which would have thatched a dozen homes for as many men – and was placidly anchoring itself in preparation for the spinning of a cocoon in which to sleep the sleep of metamorphosis.

A mile away, the great black tide of army ants was advancing relentlessly. The great cabbage, the huge grasshopper, and all the stupid caterpillars upon the wide leaves would soon be covered with the tiny biting insects. The cabbage would be reduced to a chewed and destroyed stump, the colossal, furry grubs would be torn into myriad mouthfuls and devoured by the black army ants, and the grasshopper would strike out with terrific, unguided strength, crushing its assailants by blows of its powerful hind legs and bites of its great jaws. But it would die, making terrible sounds of torment as the vicious mandibles of the army ants found crevices in its armor.

The clicking roar of the ants' advance overshadowed all other sounds, now. Burl was running madly, breath coming in great gasps, his eyes wide with panic. Alone of all the world about him, he knew the danger behind. The insects he passed were going about their business with that terrifying efficiency found only in the insect world.

# 13

There is something strangely daunting in the actions of an insect. It moves so directly, with such uncanny precision, with such utter indifference to anything but the end in view. Cannibalism is a rule, almost without exception. The paralysis of prey, so it may remain alive and fresh – though in agony – for weeks on end, is a common practice. The eating piecemeal of still living victims is a matter of course.

Absolute mercilessness, utter callousness, incredible inhumanity beyond anything known in the animal world is the natural and commonplace practice of the insects. And these vast cruelties are performed by armored, machine-like creatures with an abstraction and a routine air that suggests a horrible Nature behind them all.

Burl nearly stumbled upon a tragedy. He passed within a dozen yards of a space where a female dung-beetle was devouring the mate whose honeymoon had begun that same day and ended in that gruesome fashion. Hidden behind a clump of mushrooms, a great yellow-banded spider was coyly threatening a smaller male of her own species. He was discreetly ardent, but if he won the favor of the gruesome creature he was wooing, he would furnish an appetizing meal for her sometime within twenty-four hours.

Burl's heart was pounding madly. The breath whistled in his nostrils – and behind him, the wave of army ants was drawing nearer. They came upon the feasting flies. Some took to the air and escaped, but others were too engrossed in their delicious meal. The twitching little maggots, stranded upon the earth by the scattering of their soupy broth, were torn in pieces. The flies who were seized vanished into tiny maws. The serried ranks of black insects went on.

The tiny clickings of their limbs, the perpetual challenges and cross-challenges of crossed antennae, the stridulations of the creatures, all combined to make a high-pitched but deafening din. Now and then another sound pierced the noises made by the ants themselves. A cricket, seized by a thousand tiny jaws, uttered cries of agony. The shrill note of the crickets had grown deeply bass with the increase in size of the organs that uttered it.

There was a strange contrast between the ground before the advancing horde and that immediately behind it. Before, a busy world, teeming with life. Butterflies floating overhead on lazy wings, grubs waxing fat and huge upon the giant cabbages, crickets eating, great spiders sitting quietly in their lairs waiting with invincible patience for prey to draw near their trap doors or fall into their webs, colossal beetles lumbering heavily through the mushroom forests, seeking food, making love in monstrous, tragic fashion.

And behind the wide belt of army ants – chaos. The edible mushrooms gone. The giant cabbages left as mere stumps of unappetizing pulp, the busy life of the insect world completely wiped out save for the flying creatures that fluttered helplessly over an utterly changed landscape. Here and there little bands of stragglers moved busily over the denuded earth, searching for some fragment of food that might conceivably have been overlooked by the main body.

Burl was putting forth his last ounce of strength. His limbs trembled, his breathing was agony, sweat stood out upon his forehead. He ran a little, naked man with the disjointed fragment of a huge insect's limb in his hand, running for his insignificant life, running as if his continued existence among the million tragedies of that single day were the purpose for which the whole of the universe had been created.

He sped across an open space a hundred yards across. A thicket of beautifully golden mushrooms (*Agaricus caesareus*) barred his way. Beyond the mushrooms a range of strangely colored hills began, purple and green and black and gold, melting into each other, branching off from each other, inextricably tangled.

They rose to a height of perhaps sixty or seventy feet, and above them a little grayish haze had gathered. There seemed to be a layer of tenuous vapor upon their surfaces, which slowly rose and coiled, and gathered into a tiny cloudlet above their tips.

The hills, themselves, were but masses of fungus, mushrooms and fungoids of every description, yeasts, "musts," and every form of fungus growth which had grown within itself and about itself until this great mass of strangely colored, spongy stuff had gathered in a mass that undulated unevenly across the level earth for miles.

Burl burst through the golden thicket and attacked the ascent. His feet sank into the spongy sides of the hillock. Panting, gasping, staggering from exhaustion, he made his way up the top. He plunged into a little valley on the farther side, up another slope. For perhaps ten minutes he forced himself on, then collapsed. He lay, unable to move further, in a little hollow, his sharp-toothed club still clasped in his hands. Above him, a bright yellow butterfly with a thirty-foot spread of wing, fluttered lightly.

He lay motionless, breathing in great gasps, his limbs stubbornly refusing to lift him.

~ ~ ~

# 14

The sound of the army ants continued to grow near. At last, above the crest of the last hillock he had surmounted, two tiny antennae appeared, then the black glistening head of an army ant, the forerunner of its horde. It moved deliberately forward, waving its antennae ceaselessly. It made its way toward Burl, tiny clickings coming from the movements of its limbs.

A little wisp of tenuous vapor swirled toward the ant, a wisp of the same vapor that had gathered above the whole range of hills as a thin, low cloud. It enveloped the insect – and the ant seemed to be attacked by a strange convulsion. Its legs moved aimlessly. It threw itself desperately about. If it had been an animal, Burl would have watched with wondering eyes while it coughed and gasped, but it was an insect breathing through air-holes in its abdomen. It writhed upon the spongy fungus growth across which it had been moving.

Burl, lying in an exhausted, panting heap upon the purple mass of fungus, was conscious of a strange sensation. His body felt strangely warm. He knew nothing of fire or the heat of the sun, and the only sensation of warmth he had ever known was that caused when the members of his tribe had huddled together in their hiding place when the damp chill of the night had touched their soft-skinned bodies. Then the heat of their breaths and their bodies had kept out the chill.

This heat that Burl now felt was a hotter, fiercer heat. He moved his body with a tremendous effort, and for a moment the fungus was cool and soft beneath him. Then, slowly, the sensation of heat began again, and increased until Burl's skin was red and inflamed from the irritation.

The thin and tenuous vapor, too, made Burl's lungs smart and his eyes water. He was breathing in great, choking gasps, but the period of rest – short as it was – had enabled him to rise and stagger on. He crawled painfully to the top of the slope, and looked back.

The hill-crest on which he stood was higher than any of those he had passed in his painful run, and he could see clearly the whole of the purple range. Where he was, he was near the farther edge of the range, which was here perhaps half a mile wide.

It was a ceaseless, undulating mass of hills and hollows, ridges and spurs, all of them colored, purple and brown and golden-yellow, deepest black and dingy white. And from the tips of most of the pointed hills little wisps of vapor rose up.

A thin, dark cloud had gathered overhead. Burl could look to the right and left, and see the hills fading into the distance, growing fainter as the haze above them seemed to grow thicker. He saw, too, the advancing cohorts of the army ants, creeping over the tangled mass of fungus growth. They seemed to be feeding as they went, upon the fungus that had gathered into these incredible monstrosities.

The hills were living. They were not upheavals of the ground, they were festering heaps of insanely growing, festering mushrooms and fungus. Upon most of them a purple mold had spread itself so that they seemed a range of purple hills, but here and there patches of other vivid colors showed, and there was a large hill whose whole side was a brilliant golden hue. Another had tiny bright red spots of a strange and malignant mushroom whose properties Burl did not know, scattered all over the purple with which it was covered.

Burl leaned heavily upon his club and watched dully. He could run no more. The army ants were spreading everywhere over the mass of fungus. They would reach him soon.

Far to the right the vapor thickened. A column of smoke arose. What Burl did not know and would never know was that far down in the interior of that compressed mass of fungus, slow oxidization had been going on. The temperature of the interior had been raised. In the darkness and the dampness deep down in the hills, spontaneous combustion had begun.

Just as the vast piles of coal the railroad companies of thirty thousand years before had gathered together sometimes began to burn fiercely in their interiors, and just as the farmers' piles of damp straw suddenly burst into fierce flames from no cause, so these huge piles of tinder-like mushrooms had been burning slowly within themselves.

There had been no flames, because the surface remained intact and nearly air-tight. But when the army ants began to tear at the edible surfaces despite the heat they encountered, fresh air found its way to the smoldering masses of fungus. The slow combustion became rapid combustion. The dull heat became fierce flames. The slow trickle of thin smoke became a huge column of thick, choking, acrid stuff that set the army ants that breathed it into spasms of convulsive writhing.

From a dozen points the flames burst out. A dozen or more columns of blinding smoke rose to the heavens. A pall of fume-laden smoke gathered above the range of purple hills, while Burl watched apathetically. And the serried ranks of army ants marched on to the widening furnaces that awaited them.

They had recoiled from the river, because their instinct had warned them. Thirty thousand years without danger from fire, however, had let their racial fear of fire die out. They marched into the blazing orifices they had opened in the hills, snapping with their mandibles at the leaping flames, springing at the glowing tinder.

# 15

The blazing area widened, as the purple surface was undermined and fell in. Burl watched the phenomenon without comprehension and even without thankfulness. He stood, panting more and more slowly, breathing more and more easily, until the glow from the approaching flames reddened his skin and the acrid smoke made tears flow from his eyes.

Then he retreated slowly, leaning on his club and looking back. The black wave of the army ants was sweeping into the fire, sweeping into the incredible heat of that carbonized material burning with an open flame. At last there were only the little bodies of stragglers from the great ant-army, scurrying here and there over the ground their comrades had denuded of all living things. The bodies of the main army had vanished – burnt to crisp ashes in the furnace of the hills.

There had been agony in that flame, dreadful agony such as no man would like to dwell upon. The insane courage of the ants, attacking with their horny jaws the burning masses of fungus, rolling over and over with a flaming missile clutched in their mandibles, sounding their shrill war cry while cries of agony came from them – blinded, their antennae burnt off, their lidless eyes scorched by the licking flames, yet going madly forward on flaming feet to attack, ever attack this unknown and unknowable enemy.

Burl made his way slowly over the hills. Twice he saw small bodies of the army ants. They had passed between the widening surfaces their comrades had opened, and they were feeding voraciously upon the hills they trod on. Once Burl was spied, and a shrill war cry was sounded, but he moved on, and the ants were busily eating. A single ant rushed toward him. Burl brought down his club, and a writhing body remained to be eaten later by its comrades when they came upon it.

Again night fell. The skies grew red in the west, though the sun did not shine through the ever present cloud bank. Darkness spread across the sky. Utter blackness fell over the whole mad world, save where the luminous mushrooms shed their pale light upon the ground and fireflies the length of Burl's arm shed their fitful gleams upon an earth of fungus growths and monstrous insects.

Burl made his way across the range of mushroom hills, picking his path with his large blue eyes whose pupils expanded to great size. Slowly, from the sky, now a drop and then a drop, now a drop and then a drop, the nightly rain that would continue until daybreak began.

Burl found the ground hard beneath his feet. He listened keenly for sounds of danger. Something rustled heavily in a thicket of mushrooms a hundred yards away. There were sounds of preening, and of delicate feet placed lightly here and there upon the ground. Then the throbbing beat of huge wings began suddenly, and a body took to the air.

A fierce, down-coming current of air smote Burl, and he looked upward in time to catch the outline of a huge body – a moth – as it passed above him. He turned to watch the line of its flight, and saw a strange glow in the sky behind him. The mushroom hills were still burning.

He crouched beneath a squat toadstool and waited for the dawn, his club held tightly in his hands, and his ears alert for any sound of danger. The slow-dropping, sodden rain kept on. It fell with irregular, drum-like beats upon the tough top of the toadstool under which he had taken refuge.

Slowly, slowly, the sodden rainfall continued. Drop by drop, all the night long, the warm pellets of liquid came from the sky. They boomed upon the hollow heads of the toadstools, and splashed into the steaming pools that lay festering all over the fungus-covered earth.

And all the night long the great fires grew and spread in the mass of already half-carbonized mushroom. The flare at the horizon grew brighter and nearer. Burl, naked and hiding beneath a huge mushroom, watched it grow near him with wide eyes, wondering what this thing was. He had never seen a flame before.

The overhanging clouds were brightened by the flames. Over a stretch at least a dozen miles in length and from half a mile to three miles across, seething furnaces sent columns of dense smoke up to the roof of clouds, luminous from the glow below them, and spreading out and forming an intermediate layer below the cloudbanks.

It was like the glow of all the many lights of a vast city thrown against the sky – but the last great city had molded into fungus-covered rubbish thirty thousand years before. Like the flitting of airplanes above a populous city, too, was the flitting of fascinated creatures above the glow.

# 16

Moths and great flying beetles, gigantic gnats and midges grown huge with the passing of time, they fluttered and danced the dance of death above the flames. As the fire grew nearer to Burl, he could see them.

Colossal, delicately formed creatures swooped above the strange blaze. Moths with their riotously colored wings of thirty-foot spread beat the air with mighty strokes, and their huge eyes glowed like carbuncles as they stared with the frenzied gaze of intoxicated devotees into the glowing flames below them.

Burl saw a great peacock moth soaring above the burning mushroom hills. Its wings were all of forty feet across, and fluttered like gigantic sails as the moth gazed down at the flaming furnace below. The separate flames had united, now, and a single sheet of white-hot burning stuff spread across the country for miles, sending up its clouds of smoke, in which and through which the fascinated creatures flew.

Feathery antennae of the finest lace spread out before the head of the peacock moth, and its body was softest, richest velvet. A ring of snow-white down marked where its head began, and the red glow from below smote on the maroon of its body with a strange effect.

For one instant it was outlined clearly. Its eyes glowed more redly than any ruby's fire, and the great, delicate wings were poised in flight. Burl caught the flash of the flames upon two great iridescent spots upon the wide-spread wings. Shining purple and vivid red, the glow of opal and the sheen of pearl, all the glory of chalcedony and chrysoprase formed a single wonder in the red glare of burning fungus. White smoke compassed the great moth all about, dimming the radiance of its gorgeous dress.

Burl saw it dart straight into the thickest and brightest of the licking flames, flying madly, eagerly, into the searing, hellish heat as a willing, drunken sacrifice to the god of fire.

Monster flying beetles with their horny wing-cases stiffly stretched, blundered above the reeking, smoking pyre. In the red light from before them they shone like burnished metal, and their clumsy bodies with the spurred and fierce-toothed limbs darted like so many grotesque meteors through the luminous haze of ascending smoke.

Burl saw strange collisions and still stranger meetings. Male and female flying creatures circled and spun in the glare, dancing their dance of love and death in the wild radiance from the funeral pyre of the purple hills. They mounted higher than Burl could see, drunk with the ecstasy of living, then descended to plunge headlong to death in the roaring fires beneath them.

From every side the creatures came. Moths of brightest yellow with soft and furry bodies palpitant with life flew madly into the column of light that reached to the overhanging clouds, then moths of deepest black with gruesome symbols upon their wings came swiftly to dance, like motes in a bath of sunlight, above the glow.

And Burl sat crouched beneath an overshadowing toadstool and watched. The perpetual, slow, sodden raindrops fell. A continual faint hissing penetrated the sound of the fire – the raindrops being turned to steam. The air was alive with flying things. From far away, Burl heard a strange, deep bass muttering. He did not know the cause, but there was a vast swamp, of the existence of which he was ignorant, some ten or fifteen miles away, and the chorus of insect-eating giant frogs reached his ears even at that distance.

The night wore on, while the flying creatures above the fire danced and died, their numbers ever recruited by fresh arrivals. Burl sat tensely still, his wide eyes watching everything, his mind groping for an explanation of what he saw. At last the sky grew dimly gray, then brighter, and day came on. The flames of the burning hills grew faint as the fire died down, and after a long time Burl crept from his hiding place and stood erect.

A hundred yards from where he was, a straight wall of smoke rose from the still smoldering fungus, and Burl could see it stretching for miles in either direction. He turned to continue on his way, and saw the remains of one of the tragedies of the night.

A huge moth had flown into the flames, been horribly scorched, and floundered out again. Had it been able to fly, it would have returned to its devouring deity, but now it lay immovable upon the ground, its antennae seared hopelessly, one beautiful, delicate wing burned in gaping holes, its eyes dimmed by flame and its exquisitely tapering limbs broken and crushed by the force with which it had struck the ground. It lay helpless upon the earth, only the stumps of its antennae moving restlessly, and its abdomen pulsating slowly as it drew pain-racked breaths.

Burl drew near and picked up a stone. He moved on presently, a velvet cloak cast over his shoulders, gleaming with all the colors of the rainbow. A gorgeous mass of soft, blue moth fur was about his middle, and he had bound upon his forehead two yard-long, golden fragments of the moth's magnificent antennae. He strode on, slowly, clad as no man had been clad in all the ages.

After a little he secured a spear and took up his journey to Saya, looking like a prince of Ind upon a bridal journey – though no mere prince ever wore such raiment in days of greatest glory.

# 17

For many long miles Burl threaded his way through a single forest of thin-stalked toadstools. They towered three-man-heights high, and all about their bases were streaks and splashes of the rusts and molds that preyed upon them. Twice Burl came to open glades wherein open, bubbling pools of green slime festered in corruption, and once he hid himself fearfully as a monster scarabaeus beetle lumbered within three yards of him, moving heavily onward with a clanking of limbs as of some mighty machine.

Burl saw the mighty armor and the inward-curving jaws of the creature, and envied him his weapons. The time was not yet come, however, when Burl would smile at the great insect and hunt him for the juicy flesh contained in those armored limbs.

Burl was still a savage, still ignorant, still timid. His principal advance had been that whereas he had fled without reasoning, he now paused to see if he need flee. In his hands he bore a long, sharp-pointed chitinous spear. It had been the weapon of a huge, unnamed flying insect scorched to death in the burning of the purple hills, which had floundered out of the flames to die. Burl had worked for an hour before being able to detach the weapon he coveted. It was as long and longer than Burl himself.

He was a strange sight, moving slowly and cautiously through the shadowed lanes of the mushroom forest. A cloak of delicate velvet in which all the colors of the rainbow played in iridescent beauty hung from his shoulders. A mass of soft and beautiful moth fur was about his middle, and in the strip of sinew about his waist the fiercely toothed limb of a fighting beetle was thrust carelessly. He had bound to his forehead twin stalks of a great moth's feathery golden antennae.

Against the play of color that came from his borrowed plumage his pink skin showed in odd contrast. He looked like some proud knight walking slowly through the gardens of a goblin's castle. But he was still a fearful creature, no more than the monstrous creatures about him save in the possession of latent intelligence. He was weak – and therein lay his greatest promise. A hundred thousand years before him his ancestors had been forced by lack of claws and fangs to develop brains.

Burl was sunk as low as they had been, but he had to combat more horrifying enemies, more inexorable threatenings, and many times more crafty assailants. His ancestors had invented knives and spears and flying missiles. The creatures about Burl had knives and spears a thousand times more deadly than the weapons that had made his ancestors masters of the woods and forests.

Burl was in comparison vastly more weak than his forebears had been, and it was that weakness that in times to come would lead him and those who followed him to heights his ancestors had never known. But now –

He heard a discordant, deep bass bellow, coming from a spot not twenty yards away. In a flash of panic he darted behind a clump of mushrooms and hid himself, panting in sheer terror. He waited for an instant in frozen fear, motionless and tense. His wide, blue eyes were glassy.

The bellow came again, but this time with a querulous note. Burl heard a crashing and plunging as of some creature caught in a snare. A mushroom fell with a brittle snapping, and the spongy thud as it fell to the ground was followed by a tremendous commotion. Something was fighting desperately against something else, but Burl did not know what creature or creatures might be in combat.

He waited for a long time, and the noise gradually died away. Presently Burl's breath came more slowly, and his courage returned. He stole from his hiding place, and would have made away, but something held him back. Instead of creeping from the scene, he crept cautiously over toward the source of the noise.

He peered between two cream-colored toadstool stalks and saw the cause of the noise. A wide, funnel-shaped snare of silk was spread out before him, some twenty yards across and as many deep. The individual threads could be plainly seen, but in the mass it seemed a fabric of sheerest, finest texture. Held up by the tall mushrooms, it was anchored to the ground below, and drew away to a tiny point through which a hole gave on some yet unknown recess. And all the space of the wide snare was hung with threads, fine, twisted threads no more than half the thickness of Burl's finger.

This was the trap of a labyrinth spider. Not one of the interlacing threads was strong enough to hold the feeblest of prey, but the threads were there by thousands. A great cricket had become entangled in the maze of sticky lines. Its limbs thrashed out, smashing the snare-lines at every stroke, but at every stroke meeting and becoming entangled with a dozen more. It thrashed about mightily, emitting at intervals the horrible, deep bass cry that the chirping voice of the cricket had become with its increase in size.

# 18

**B**url breathed more easily, and watched with a fascinated curiosity. Mere death – even tragic death – as among insects held no great interest for him. It was a matter of such common and matter-of-fact occurrence that he was not greatly stirred. But a spider and his prey was another matter.

There were few insects that deliberately sought man. Most insects have their allotted victims, and will touch no others, but spiders have a terrifying impartiality. One great beetle devouring another was a matter of indifference to Burl. A spider devouring some luckless insect was but an example of what might happen to him. He watched alertly, his gaze traveling from the enmeshed cricket to the strange orifice at the rear of the funnel-shaped snare.

The opening darkened. Two shining, glistening eyes had been watching from the rear of the funnel. It drew itself into a tunnel there, in which the spider had been waiting. Now it swung out lightly and came toward the cricket. It was a gray spider (*Agelena labyrinthica*), with twin black ribbons upon its thorax, next the head, and with two stripes of curiously speckled brown and white upon its abdomen. Burl saw, too, two curious appendages like a tail.

It came nimbly out of its tunnel-like hiding place and approached the cricket. The cricket was struggling only feebly now, and the cries it uttered were but feeble, because of the confining threads that fettered its limbs. Burl saw the spider throw itself upon the cricket and saw the final, convulsive shudder of the insect as the spider's fangs pierced its tough armor. The sting lasted a long time, and finally Burl saw that the spider was really feeding. All the succulent juices of the now dead cricket were being sucked from its body by the spider. It had stung the cricket upon the haunch, and presently it went to the other leg and drained that, too, by means of its powerful internal suction-pump. When the second haunch had been sucked dry, the spider pawed the lifeless creature for a few moments and left it.

Food was plentiful, and the spider could afford to be dainty in its feeding. The two choicest titbits had been consumed. The remainder could be discarded.

A sudden thought came to Burl and quite took his breath away. For a second his knees knocked together in self-induced panic. He watched the gray spider carefully with growing determination in his eyes. He, Burl, had killed a hunting-spider upon the red-clay cliff. True, the killing had been an accident, and had nearly cost him his own life a few minutes later in the web-spider's snare, but he had killed a spider, and of the most deadly kind.

Now, a great ambition was growing in Burl's heart. His tribe had always feared spiders too much to know much of their habits, but they knew one or two things. The most important was that the snare-spiders never left their lairs to hunt – never! Burl was about to make a daring application of that knowledge.

He drew back from the white and shining snare and crept softly to the rear. The fabric gathered itself into a point and then continued for some twenty feet as a tunnel, in which the spider waited while dreaming of its last meal and waiting for the next victim to become entangled in the labyrinth in front. Burl made his way to a point where the tunnel was no more than ten feet away, and waited.

Presently, through the interstices of the silk, he saw the gray bulk of the spider. It had left the exhausted body of the cricket, and returned to its resting place. It settled itself carefully upon the soft walls of the tunnel, with its shining eyes fixed upon the tortuous threads of its trap. Burl's hair was standing straight up upon his head from sheer fright, but he was the slave of an idea.

He drew near and poised his spear, his new and sharp spear, taken from the body of an unknown flying creature killed by the burning purple hills. Burl raised the spear and aimed its sharp and deadly point at the thick gray bulk he could see dimly through the threads of the tunnel. He thrust it home with all his strength – and ran away at the top of his speed, glassy-eyed from terror.

A long time later he ventured near again, his heart in his mouth, ready to flee at the slightest sound. All was still. Burl had missed the horrible convulsions of the wounded spider, had not heard the frightful gnashings of its fangs as it tore at the piercing weapon, had not seen the silken threads of the tunnel ripped as the spider – hurt to death – had struggled with insane strength to free itself.

He came back beneath the overshadowing toadstools, stepping quietly and cautiously, to find a great rent in the silken tunnel, to find the great gray bulk lifeless and still, half-fallen through the opening the spear had first made. A little puddle of evil-smelling liquid lay upon the ground below the body, and from time to time a droplet fell from the spear into the puddle with a curious splash.

Burl looked at what he had done, saw the dead body of the creature he had slain, saw the ferocious mandibles, and the keen and deadly fangs. The dead eyes of the creature still stared at him malignantly, and the hairy legs were still braced as if further to enlarge the gaping hole through which it had partly fallen.

Exultation filled Burl's heart. His tribe had been but furtive vermin for thousands of years, fleeing from the mighty insects, hiding from them, and if overtaken but waiting helplessly for death, screaming shrilly in terror.

He, Burl, had turned the tables. He had slain one of the enemies of his tribe. His breast expanded. Always his tribesmen went quietly and fearfully, making no sound. But a sudden, exultant yell burst from Burl's lips – the first hunting cry from the lips of a man in three hundred centuries!

# 19

The next second his pulse nearly stopped in sheer panic at having made such a noise. He listened fearfully, but there was no sound. He drew near his prey and carefully withdrew his spear. The viscid liquid made it slimy and slippery, and he had to wipe it dry against a leathery toadstool. Then Burl had to conquer his illogical fear again before daring to touch the creature he had slain.

He moved off presently, with the belly of the spider upon his back and two of the hairy legs over his shoulders. The other limbs of the monster hung limp, and trailed upon the ground. Burl was now a still more curious sight as a gayly colored object with a cloak shining in iridescent colors, the golden antennae of a great moth rising from his forehead, and the hideous bulk of a gray spider for a burden.

He moved through the thin-stalked mushroom forest, and, because of the thing he carried, all creatures fled before him. They did not fear man – their instinct was slow-moving – but during all the millions of years that insects have existed, there have existed spiders to prey upon them. So Burl moved on in solemn state, a brightly clad man bent beneath the weight of a huge and horrible monster.

He came upon a valley full of torn and blackened mushrooms. There was not a single yellow top among them. Everyone had been infested with tiny maggots which had liquefied the tough meat of the mushroom and caused it to drip to the ground below. And all the liquid had gathered in a golden pool in the center of the small depression. Burl heard a loud humming and buzzing before he topped the rise that opened the valley for his inspection. He stopped a moment and looked down.

A golden-red lake, its center reflecting the hazy sky overhead. All about, blackened mushrooms, seeming to have been charred and burned by a fierce flame. A slow-flowing golden brooklet trickled slowly over a rocky ledge, into the larger pool. And all about the edges of the golden lake, in ranks and rows, by hundreds, thousands, and by millions, were ranged the green-gold, shining bodies of great flies.

They were small as compared with the other insects. They had increased in size but a fraction of the amount that the bees, for example, had increased; but it was due to an imperative necessity of their race.

The flesh-flies laid their eggs by hundreds in decaying carcasses. The others laid their eggs by hundreds in the mushrooms. To feed the maggots that would hatch, a relatively great quantity of food was needed, therefore the flies must remain comparatively small, or the body of a single grasshopper, say, would furnish food for but two or three grubs instead of the hundreds it must support.

Burl stared down at the golden pool. Bluebottles, greenbottles, and all the flies of metallic luster were gathered at the Lucullan feast of corruption. Their buzzing as they darted above the odorous pool of golden liquid made the sound Burl had heard. Their bodies flashed and glittered as they darted back and forth, seeking a place to alight and join in the orgy.

Those which clustered about the banks of the pool were still as if carved from metal. Their huge, red eyes glowed, and their bodies shone with an obscene fatness. Flies are the most disgusting of all insects. Burl watched them a moment, watched the interlacing streams of light as they buzzed eagerly above the pool, seeking a place at the festive board.

A drumming roar sounded in the air. A golden speck appeared in the sky, a slender, needle-like body with transparent, shining wings and two huge eyes. It grew nearer and became a dragonfly twenty feet and more in length, its body shimmering, purest gold. It poised itself above the pool and then darted down. Its jaws snapped viciously and repeatedly, and at each snapping the glittering body of a fly vanished.

A second dragonfly appeared, its body a vivid purple, and a third. They swooped and rushed above the golden pool, snapping in midair, turning their abrupt, angular turns, creatures of incredible ferocity and beauty. At the moment they were nothing more or less than slaughtering-machines. They darted here and there, their many-faceted eyes burning with blood-lust. In that mass of buzzing flies even the most voracious appetite must be sated, but the dragonflies kept on. Beautiful, slender, graceful creatures, they dashed here and there above the pond like avenging fiends or the mythical dragons for which they had been named.

# 20

**O**nly a few miles farther on Burl came upon a familiar landmark. He knew it well, but from a safe distance as always. A mass of rock had heaved itself up from the nearly level plain over which he was traveling, and formed an outjutting cliff. At one point the rock overhung a sheer drop, making an inverted ledge – a roof over nothingness – which had been pre-empted by a hairy creature and made into a fairylike dwelling. A white hemisphere clung tenaciously to the rock above, and long cables anchored it firmly.

Burl knew the place as one to be fearfully avoided. A Clotho spider (*Clotho Durandi, LATR*) had built itself a nest there, from which it emerged to hunt the unwary. Within that half-globe there was a monster, resting upon a cushion of softest silk. But if one went too near, one of the little inverted arches, seemingly firmly closed by a wall of silk, would open and a creature out of a dream of hell emerge, to run with fiendish agility toward its prey.

Surely, Burl knew the place. Hung upon the outer walls of the silken palace were stones and tiny boulders, discarded fragments of former meals, and the gutted armor from limbs of ancient prey. But what caused Burl to know the place most surely and most terribly was another decoration that dangled from the castle of this insect ogre. This was the shrunken, desiccated figure of a man, all its juices extracted and the life gone.

The death of that man had saved Burl's life two years before. They had been together, seeking a new source of edible mushrooms for food. The Clotho spider was a hunter, not a spinner of snares. It sprang suddenly from behind a great puff-ball, and the two men froze in terror. Then it came swiftly forward and deliberately chose its victim. Burl had escaped when the other man was seized. Now he looked meditatively at the hiding place of his ancient enemy. Some day –

But now he passed on. He went past the thicket in which the great moths hid during the day, and past the pool – a turgid thing of slime and yeast – in which a monster water snake lurked. He penetrated the little wood of the shining mushrooms that gave out light at night, and the shadowed place where the truffle-hunting beetles went chirping thunderously during the dark hours.

And then he saw Saya. He caught a flash of pink skin vanishing behind the thick stalk of a squat toadstool, and ran forward, calling her name. She appeared, and saw the figure with the horrible bulk of the spider upon its back. She cried out in horror, and Burl understood. He let his burden fall and then went swiftly toward her.

They met. Saya waited timidly until she saw who this man was, and then astonishment went over her face. Gorgeously attired, in an iridescent cloak from the whole wing of a great moth, with a strip of softest fur from a night-flying creature about his middle, with golden, feathery antennae bound upon his forehead, and a fierce spear in his hands – this was not the Burl she had known.

But then he moved slowly toward her, filled with a fierce delight at seeing her again, thrilling with joy at the slender gracefulness of her form and the dark richness of her tangled hair. He held out his hands and touched her shyly. Then, manlike, he began to babble excitedly of the things that had happened to him, and dragged her toward his great victim, the gray-bellied spider.

Saya trembled when she saw the furry bulk lying upon the ground, and would have fled when Burl advanced and took it upon his back. Then something of the pride that filled him came vicariously to her. She smiled a flashing smile, and Burl stopped short in his excited explanation. He was suddenly tongue-tied. His eyes became pleading and soft. He laid the huge spider at her feet and spread out his hands imploringly.

Thirty thousand years of savagery had not lessened the femininity in Saya. She became aware that Burl was her slave, that these wonderful things he wore and had done were as nothing if she did not approve. She drew away – saw the misery in Burl's face – and abruptly ran into his arms and clung to him, laughing happily. And quite suddenly Burl saw with extreme clarity that all these things he had done, even the slaying of a great spider, were of no importance whatever beside this most wonderful thing that had just happened, and told Saya so quite humbly, but holding her very close to him as he did so.

And so Burl came back to his tribe. He had left it nearly naked, with but a wisp of moth-wing twisted about his middle, a timid, fearful, trembling creature. He returned in triumph, walking slowly and fearlessly down a broad lane of golden mushrooms toward the hiding place of his people.

Upon his shoulders was draped a great and many-colored cloak made from the whole of a moth's wing. Soft fur was about his middle. A spear was in his hand and a fierce club at his waist. He and Saya bore between them the dead body of a huge spider – aforetime the dread of the pink-skinned, naked men. But to Burl the most important thing of all was that Saya walked beside him openly, acknowledging him before all the tribe.

THE END

# PLANET OF THE DAMNED

HARRY HARRISON

For my Mother and Father –
RIA AND LEO HARRISON

# I

*A man said to the universe:*
*"Sir, I exist!"*
*"However" replied the universe,*
*"The fact has not created in me*
*A sense of obligation."*

- Stephen Crane

**S**weat covered Brion's body, trickling into the tight loincloth that was the only garment he wore. The light fencing foil in his hand felt as heavy as a bar of lead to his exhausted muscles, worn out by a month of continual exercise. These things were of no importance. The cut on his chest, still dripping blood, the ache of his overstrained eyes – even the soaring arena around him with the thousands of spectators – were trivialities not worth thinking about. There was only one thing in his universe: the button-tipped length of shining steel that hovered before him, engaging his own weapon. He felt the quiver and scrape of its life, knew when it moved and moved himself to counteract it. And when he attacked, it was always there to beat him aside.

A sudden motion. He reacted – but his blade just met air. His instant of panic was followed by a small sharp blow high on his chest.

"*Touch!*" A world-shaking voice bellowed the word to a million waiting loudspeakers, and the applause of the audience echoed back in a wave of sound.

"One minute," a voice said, and the time buzzer sounded.

Brion had carefully conditioned the reflex in himself. A minute is not a very large measure of time and his body needed every fraction of it. The buzzer's whirr triggered his muscles into complete relaxation. Only his heart and lungs worked on at a strong, measured rate. His eyes closed and he was only distantly aware of his handlers catching him as he fell, carrying him to his bench. While they massaged his limp body and cleansed the wound, all of his attention was turned inward. He was in reverie, sliding along the borders of consciousness. The nagging memory of the previous night loomed up then, and he turned it over and over in his mind, examining it from all sides.

It was the very unexpectedness of the event that had been so unusual. The contestants in the Twenties needed undisturbed rest, therefore nights in the dormitories were as quiet as death. During the first few days, of course, the rule wasn't observed too closely. The men themselves were too keyed up and excited to rest easily. But as soon as the scores began to mount and eliminations cut into their ranks, there was complete silence after dark. Particularly so on this last night, when only two of the little cubicles were occupied, the thousands of others standing with dark, empty doors.

Angry words had dragged Brion from a deep and exhausted sleep. The words were whispered but clear – two voices, just outside the thin metal of his door. Someone spoke his name.

"... Brion Brandd. Of course not. Whoever said you could was making a big mistake and there is going to be trouble – "

"Don't talk like an idiot!" The other voice snapped with a harsh urgency, clearly used to command. "I'm here because the matter is of utmost importance, and Brandd is the one I must see. Now stand aside!"

"The Twenties – "

"I don't give a damn about your games, hearty cheers and physical exercises. This is *important*, or I wouldn't be here!"

The other didn't speak – he was surely one of the officials – and Brion could sense his outraged anger. He must have drawn his gun, because the intruder said quickly, "Put that away. You're being a fool!"

"Out!" was the single snarled word of the response. There was silence then and, still wondering, Brion was once more asleep.

"Ten seconds."

The voice chopped away Brion's memories and he let awareness seep back into his body. He was unhappily conscious of his total exhaustion. The month of continuous mental and physical combat had taken its toll. It would be hard to stay on his feet, much less summon the strength and skill to fight and win a touch.

"How do we stand?" he asked the handler who was kneading his aching muscles.

"Four-four. All you need is a touch to win!"

"That's all he needs too," Brion grunted, opening his eyes to look at the wiry length of the man at the other end of the long mat. No one who had reached the finals in the Twenties could possibly be a weak opponent, but this one, Irolg, was the pick of the lot. A red-haired mountain of a man, with an apparently inexhaustible store of energy. That was really all that counted now. There could be little art in this last and final round of fencing. Just thrust and parry, and victory to the stronger.

Brion closed his eyes again and knew the moment he had been hoping to avoid had arrived.

Every man who entered the Twenties had his own training tricks. Brion had a few individual ones that had helped him so far. He was a moderately strong chess player, but he had moved to quick victory in the chess rounds by playing incredibly unorthodox games. This was no accident, but the result of years of work. He had a standing order with off-planet agents for archaic chess books, the older the better. He had memorized thousands of these ancient games and openings. This was allowed. Anything was allowed that didn't involve drugs or machines. Self-hypnosis was an accepted tool.

It had taken Brion over two years to find a way to tap the sources of hysterical strength. Common as the phenomenon seemed to be in the textbooks, it proved impossible to duplicate. There appeared to be an immediate association with the death-trauma, as if the two were inextricably linked into one. Berserkers and juramentados continue to fight and kill though carved by scores of mortal wounds. Men with bullets in the heart or brain fight on, though already clinically dead. Death seemed an inescapable part of this kind of strength. But there was another type that could easily be brought about in any deep trance – hypnotic rigidity. The strength that enables someone in a trance to hold his body stiff and unsupported except at two points, the head and heels. This is physically impossible when conscious. Working with this as a clue, Brion had developed a self-hypnotic technique that allowed him to tap this reservoir of unknown strength – the source of "second wind," the survival strength that made the difference between life and death.

It could also kill – exhaust the body beyond hope of recovery, particularly when in a weakened condition as his was now. But that wasn't important. Others had died before during the Twenties, and death during the last round was in some ways easier than defeat.

Breathing deeply, Brion softly spoke the auto-hypnotic phrases that triggered the process. Fatigue fell softly from him, as did all sensations of heat, cold and pain. He could feel with acute sensitivity, hear, and see clearly when he opened his eyes.

With each passing second the power drew at the basic reserves of life, draining it from his body.

When the buzzer sounded he pulled his foil from his second's startled grasp, and ran forward. Irolg had barely time to grab up his own weapon and parry Brion's first thrust. The force of his rush was so great that the guards on their weapons locked, and their bodies crashed together. Irolg looked amazed at the sudden fury of the attack – then smiled. He thought it was a last burst of energy, he knew how close they both were to exhaustion. This must be the end for Brion.

They disengaged and Irolg put up a solid defense. He didn't attempt to attack, just let Brion wear himself out against the firm shield of his defense.

Brion saw something close to panic on his opponent's face when the man finally recognized his error. Brion wasn't tiring. If anything, he was pressing the attack. A wave of despair rolled out from Irolg – Brion sensed it and knew the fifth point was his.

Thrust – thrust – and each time the parrying sword a little slower to return. Then the powerful twist that thrust it aside. In and under the guard. The slap of the button on flesh and the arc of steel that reached out and ended on Irolg's chest over his heart.

Waves of sound – cheering and screaming – lapped against Brion's private world, but he was only remotely aware of their existence. Irolg dropped his foil, and tried to shake Brion's hand, but his legs suddenly gave way. Brion had an arm around him, holding him up, walking towards the rushing handlers. Then Irolg was gone and he waved off his own men, walking slowly by himself.

Except that something was wrong and it was like walking through warm glue. Walking on his knees. No, not walking, falling. At last. He was able to let go and fall.

# II

**I**hjel gave the doctors exactly one day before he went to the hospital. Brion wasn't dead, though there had been some doubt about that the night before. Now, a full day later, he was on the mend and that was all Ihjel wanted to know. He bullied and strong-armed his way to the new Winner's room, meeting his first stiff resistance at the door.

"You're out of order, Winner Ihjel," the doctor said. "And if you keep on forcing yourself in here, where you are not wanted, rank or no rank, I shall be obliged to break your head."

Ihjel had just begun to tell him, in some detail, just how slim his chances were of accomplishing that, when Brion interrupted them both. He recognized the newcomer's voice from the final night in the barracks.

"Let him in, Dr. Caulry," he said. "I want to meet a man who thinks there is something more important than the Twenties."

While the doctor stood undecided, Ihjel moved quickly around him and closed the door in his flushed face. He looked down at the Winner in the bed. There was a drip plugged into each one of Brion's arms. His eyes peered from sooty hollows; the eyeballs were a network of red veins. The silent battle he fought against death had left its mark. His square, jutting jaw now seemed all bone, as did his long nose and high cheekbones. They were prominent landmarks rising from the limp greyness of his skin. Only the erect bristle of his close-cropped hair was unchanged. He had the appearance of having suffered a long and wasting illness.

"You look like sin," Ihjel said. "But congratulations on your victory."

"You don't look so very good yourself – for a Winner," Brion snapped back. His exhaustion and sudden peevish anger at this man let the insulting words slip out. Ihjel ignored them.

But it was true; Winner Ihjel looked very little like a Winner, or even an Anvharian. He had the height and the frame all right, but it was draped in billows of fat – rounded, soft tissue that hung loosely from his limbs and made little limp rolls on his neck and under his eyes. There were no fat men on Anvhar, and it was incredible that a man so gross could ever have been a Winner. If there was muscle under the fat it couldn't be seen. Only his eyes appeared to still hold the strength that had once bested every man on the planet to win the annual games. Brion turned away from their burning stare, sorry now he had insulted the man without good reason. He was too sick, though, to bother about apologizing.

Ihjel didn't care either. Brion looked at him again and felt the impression of things so important that he himself, his insults, even the Twenties were of no more interest than dust motes in the air. It was only a fantasy of a sick mind, Brion knew, and he tried to shake the feeling off. The two men stared at each other, sharing a common emotion.

The door opened soundlessly behind Ihjel and he wheeled about, moving as only an athlete of Anvhar can move. Dr. Caulry was halfway through the door, off balance. Two men in uniform came close behind him. Ihjel's body pushed against them, his speed and the mountainous mass of his flesh sending them back in a tangle of arms and legs. He slammed the door and locked it in their faces.

"I have to talk to you," he said, turning back to Brion. "Privately," he added, bending over and ripping out the communicator with a sweep of one hand.

"Get out," Brion told him. "If I were able – "

"Well, you're not, so you're just going to have to lie there and listen. I imagine we have about five minutes before they decide to break the door down, and I don't want to waste any more of that. Will you come with me offworld? There's a job that must be done; it's my job, but I'm going to need help. You're the only one who can give me that help.

"Now refuse," he added as Brion started to answer.

"Of course I refuse," Brion said, feeling a little foolish and slightly angry, as if the other man had put the words into his mouth. "Anvhar is my planet – why should I leave? My life is here and so is my work. I also might add that I have just won the Twenties. I have a responsibility to remain."

"Nonsense. I'm a Winner, and I left. What you really mean is you would like to enjoy a little of the ego-inflation you have worked so hard to get. Off Anvhar no one even knows what a

Winner is – much less respects one. You will have to face a big universe out there, and I don't blame you for being a little frightened."

Someone was hammering loudly on the door.

"I haven't the strength to get angry," Brion said hoarsely. "And I can't bring myself to admire your ideas when they permit you to insult a man too ill to defend himself."

"I apologize," Ihjel said, with no hint of apology or sympathy in his voice. "But there are more desperate issues involved than your hurt feelings. We don't have much time now, so I want to impress you with an idea."

"An idea that will convince me to go offplanet with you? That's expecting a lot."

"No, this idea won't convince you – but thinking about it will. If you really *consider* it you will find a lot of your illusions shattered. Like everyone else on Anvhar, you're a scientific humanist, with your faith firmly planted in the Twenties. You accept both of these noble institutions without an instant's thought. All of you haven't a single thought for the past, for the untold billions who led the bad life as mankind slowly built up the good life for you to lead. Do you ever think of all the people who suffered and died in misery and superstition while civilization was clicking forward one more slow notch?"

"Of course I don't think about them," Brion retorted. "Why should I? I can't change the past."

"But you can change the future!" Ihjel said. "You owe something to the suffering ancestors who got you where you are today. If Scientific Humanism means anything more than just words to you, you must possess a sense of responsibility. Don't you want to try and pay off a bit of this debt by helping others who are just as backward and disease-ridden today as great-grandfather Troglodyte ever was?"

The hammering on the door was louder. This and the drug-induced buzzing in Brion's ear made thinking difficult. "Abstractly, I of course agree with you," he said haltingly. "But you know there is nothing I can do personally without being emotionally involved. A logical decision is valueless for action without personal meaning."

"Then we have reached the crux of the matter," Ihjel said gently. His back was braced against the door, absorbing the thudding blows of some heavy object on the outside. "They're knocking, so I must be going soon. I have no time for details, but I can assure you upon my word of honor as a Winner that there is something you can do. Only you. If you help me we might save seven million human lives. That is a fact."

The lock burst and the door started to open. Ihjel shouldered it back into the frame for a final instant.

"Here is the idea I want you to consider. Why is it that the people of Anvhar, in a galaxy filled with warring, hate-filled, backward planets, should be the only ones who base their entire existence on a complicated series of games?"

# III

This time there was no way to hold the door. Ihjel didn't try. He stepped aside and two men stumbled into the room. He walked out behind their backs without saying a word.

"What happened? What did he do?" the doctor asked, rushing in through the ruined door. He swept a glance over the continuous recording dials at the foot of Brion's bed. Respiration, temperature, heart, blood pressure – all were normal. The patient lay quietly and didn't answer him.

For the rest of that day, Brion had much to think about. It was difficult. The fatigue, mixed with the tranquilizers and other drugs, had softened his contact with reality. His thoughts kept echoing back and forth in his mind, unable to escape. What had Ihjel meant? What was that nonsense about Anvhar? Anvhar was that way because – well, it just was. It had come about naturally. Or had it?

The planet had a very simple history. From the very beginning there had never been anything of real commercial interest on Anvhar. Well off the interstellar trade routes, there were no minerals worth digging and transporting the immense distances to the nearest inhabited worlds. Hunting the winter beasts for their pelts was a profitable but very minor enterprise, never sufficient for mass markets. Therefore no organized attempt had ever been made to colonize the planet. In the end it had been settled completely by chance. A number of offplanet scientific groups had established observation and research stations, finding unlimited data to observe and record during Anvhar's unusual yearly cycle. The long-duration observations encouraged the scientific workers to bring their families and, slowly but steadily, small settlements grew up. Many of the fur hunters settled there as well, adding to the small population. This had been the beginning.

Few records existed of those early days, and the first six centuries of Anvharian history were more speculation than fact. The Breakdown occurred about that time, and in the galaxy-wide disruption Anvhar had to fight its own internal battle. When the Earth Empire collapsed it was the end of more than an era. Many of the observation stations found themselves representing institutions that no longer existed. The professional hunters no longer had markets for their furs, since Anvhar possessed no interstellar ships of its own. There had been no real physical hardship involved in the Breakdown as it affected Anvhar, since the planet was completely self-sufficient. Once they had made the mental adjustment to the fact that they were now a sovereign world, not a collection of casual visitors with various loyalties, life continued unchanged. Not easy – living on Anvhar is never easy – but at least without difference on the surface.

The thoughts and attitudes of the people were, however, going through a great transformation. Many attempts were made to develop some form of stable society and social relationship. Again, little record exists of these early trials, other than the fact of their culmination in the Twenties.

To understand the Twenties, you have to understand the unusual orbit that Anvhar tracks around its sun, 70 Ophiuchi. There are other planets in this system, all of them more or less conforming to the plane of the ecliptic. Anvhar is obviously a rogue, perhaps a captured planet of another sun. For the greatest part of its 780-day year it arcs far out from its primary, in a high-angled sweeping cometary orbit. When it returns there is a brief, hot summer of approximately eighty days before the long winter sets in once more. This severe difference in seasonal change has caused profound adaptations in the native life forms. During the winter most of the animals hibernate, the vegetable life lying dormant as spores or seeds. Some of the warm-blooded herbivores stay active in the snow-covered tropics, preyed upon by fur-insulated carnivores. Though unbelievably cold, the winter is a season of peace in comparison to the summer.

For summer is a time of mad growth. Plants burst into life with a strength that cracks rocks, growing fast enough for the motion to be seen. The snowfields melt into mud and within days a jungle stretches high into the air. Everything grows, swells, proliferates. Plants climb on top of plants, fighting for the life-energy of the sun. Everything is eat and be eaten, grow and thrive in that short season. Because when the first snow of winter falls again, ninety per cent of the year must pass until the next coming of warmth.

Mankind has had to adapt to the Anvharian cycle in order to stay alive. Food must be gathered and stored, enough to last out the long winter. Generation after generation had adapted until they look on the mad seasonal imbalance as something quite ordinary. The first thaw of the almost nonexistent spring triggers a wide-reaching metabolic change in the humans. Layers of subcutaneous fat vanish and half-dormant sweat glands come to life. Other changes are more subtle than the temperature adjustment, but equally important. The sleep center of the brain is depressed. Short naps or a night's rest every third or fourth day becomes enough. Life takes on a hectic and hysterical quality that is perfectly suited to the environment. By the time of the first frost, rapid-growing crops have been raised and harvested, sides of meat either preserved or frozen in mammoth lockers. With this supreme talent of adaptability mankind has become part of the ecology and guaranteed his own survival during the long winter.

Physical survival has been guaranteed. But what about mental survival? Primitive Earth Eskimos can fall into a long doze of half-conscious hibernation. Civilized men might be able to do this, but only for the few cold months of terrestrial midwinter. It would be impossible to do during a winter that is longer than an Earth year. With all the physical needs taken care of, boredom became the enemy of any Anvharian who was not a hunter. And even the hunters could not stay out on solitary trek all winter. Drink was one answer, and violence another. Alcoholism and murder were the twin terrors of the cold season, after the Breakdown.

It was the Twenties that ended all that. When they became a part of normal life the summer was considered just an interlude between games. The Twenties were more than just a contest – they became a way of life that satisfied all the physical, competitive and intellectual needs of this unusual planet. They were a decathlon – rather a double decathlon – raised to its highest power, where contests in chess and poetry composition held equal place with those in ski-jumping and archery. Each year there were two planet-wide contests held, one for men and one for women. This was not an attempt at sexual discrimination, but a logical facing of facts. Inherent differences prevented fair contests – for example, it is impossible for a woman to win a large chess tournament – and this fact was recognized. Anyone could enter for any number of years. There were no scoring handicaps.

When the best man won he was really the best man. A complicated series of playoffs and eliminations kept contestants and observers busy for half the winter. They were only preliminary to the final encounter that lasted a month, and picked a single winner. That was the title he was awarded. Winner. The man – and woman – who had bested every other contestant on the entire planet and who would remain unchallenged until the following year.

Winner. It was a title to take pride in. Brion stirred weakly on his bed and managed to turn so he could look out of the window. Winner of Anvhar. His name was already slated for the history books, one of the handful of planetary heroes. School children would be studying *him* now, just as he had read of the Winners of the past. Weaving daydreams and imaginary adventures around Brion's victories, hoping and fighting to equal them someday. To be a Winner was the greatest honor in the universe.

Outside, the afternoon sun shimmered weakly in a dark sky. The endless icefields soaked up the dim light, reflecting it back as a colder and harsher illumination. A single figure on skis cut a line across the empty plain; nothing else moved. The depression of the ultimate fatigue fell on Brion and everything changed, as if he looked in a mirror at a previously hidden side.

He saw suddenly – with terrible clarity – that to be a Winner was to be absolutely nothing. Like being the best flea, among all the fleas on a single dog.

What was Anvhar after all? An ice-locked planet, inhabited by a few million human fleas, unknown and unconsidered by the rest of the galaxy. There was nothing here worth fighting for; the wars after the Breakdown had left them untouched. The Anvharians had always taken pride in this – as if being so unimportant that no one else even wanted to come near you could possibly be a source of pride. All the other worlds of man grew, fought, won, lost, changed. Only on Anvhar did life repeat its sameness endlessly, like a loop of tape in a player....

Brion's eyes were moist; he blinked. *Tears!* Realization of this incredible fact wiped the maudlin pity from his mind and replaced it with fear. Had his mind snapped in the strain of the last match? These thoughts weren't his. Self-pity hadn't made him a Winner –

why was he feeling it now? Anvhar was his universe – how could he even imagine it as a tag-end planet at the outer limb of creation? What had come over him and induced this inverse thinking?

As he thought the question, the answer appeared at the same instant. Winner Ihjel. The fat man with the strange pronouncements and probing questions. Had he cast a spell like some sorcerer – or the devil in *Faust*? No, that was pure nonsense. But he had done something. Perhaps planted a suggestion when Brion's resistance was low. Or used subliminal vocalization like the villain in *Cerebrus Chained*. Brion could find no adequate reason on which to base his suspicions. But he knew, with sure positiveness, that Ihjel was responsible.

He whistled at the sound-switch next to his pillow and the repaired communicator came to life. The duty nurse appeared in the small screen.

"The man who was here today," Brion said, "Winner Ihjel. Do you know where he is? I must contact him."

For some reason this flustered her professional calm. The nurse started to answer, excused herself, and blanked the screen. When it lit again a man in guard's uniform had taken her place.

"You made an inquiry," the guard said, "about Winner Ihjel. We are holding him here in the hospital, following the disgraceful way in which he broke into your room."

"I have no charges to make. Will you ask him to come and see me at once?"

The guard controlled his shock. "I'm sorry, Winner – I don't see how we can. Dr. Caulry left specific orders that you were not to be – "

"The doctor has no control over my personal life." Brion interrupted. "I'm not infectious, nor ill with anything more than extreme fatigue. I want to see that man. At once."

The guard took a deep breath, and made a quick decision. "He is on the way up now," he said, and rung off.

"What did you do to me?" Brion asked as soon as Ihjel had entered and they were alone. "You won't deny that you have put alien thoughts in my head?"

"No, I won't deny it. Because the whole point of my being here is to get those 'alien' thoughts across to you."

"Tell me how you did it," Brion insisted. "I must know."

"I'll tell you – but there are many things you should understand first, before you decide to leave Anvhar. You must not only hear them, you will have to believe them. The primary thing, the clue to the rest, is the true nature of your life here. How do you think the Twenties originated?"

Before he answered, Brion carefully took a double dose of the mild stimulant he was allowed. "I don't think," he said; "I know. It's a matter of historical record. The founder of the games was Giroldi, the first contest was held in 378 A.B. The Twenties have been held every year since then. They were strictly local affairs in the beginning, but were soon well established on a planet-wide scale."

"True enough," Ihjel said. "But you're describing *what* happened. I asked you *how* the Twenties originated. How could any single man take a barbarian planet, lightly inhabited by half-mad hunters and alcoholic farmers, and turn it into a smooth-running social machine built around the artificial structure of the Twenties? It just couldn't be done."

"But it *was* done!" Brion insisted. "You can't deny that. And there is nothing artificial about the Twenties. They are a logical way to live a life on a planet like this."

Ihjel laughed, a short ironic bark. "Very logical," he said; "but how often does logic have anything to do with the organization of social groups and governments? You're not thinking. Put yourself in founder Giroldi's place. Imagine that you have glimpsed the great idea of the Twenties and you want to convince others. So you walk up to the nearest louse-ridden, brawling, superstitious, booze-embalmed hunter and explain clearly. How a program of his favorite sports – things like poetry, archery and chess – can make his life that much more interesting and virtuous. You do that. But keep your eyes open at the same time, and be ready for a fast draw."

Even Brion had to smile at the absurdity of the suggestion. Of course it couldn't happen that way. Yet, since it had happened, there must be a simple explanation.

"We can beat this back and forth all day," Ihjel told him, "and you won't get the right idea unless – " He broke off suddenly, staring at the communicator. The operation light had come on, though the screen stayed dark. Ihjel reached down a meaty hand and pulled loose the recently connected wires. "That doctor of yours is very curious – and he's going to stay that way. The truth behind the Twenties is none of his business. But it's going to be yours. You must come to realize that the life you lead here is a complete and artificial construction, developed by Societics experts and put into application by skilled field workers."

"Nonsense!" Brion broke in. "Systems of society can't be dreamed up and forced on people like that. Not without bloodshed and violence."

"Nonsense, yourself," Ihjel told him. "That may have been true in the dawn of history, but not anymore. You have been reading too many of the old Earth classics; you imagine that we still live in the Ages of Superstition. Just because fascism and communism were once forced on reluctant populations, you think this holds true for all time. Go back to your books. In exactly the same era democracy and self-government were adapted by former colonial states, like India and the Union of North Africa, and the only violence was between local religious groups. Change is the lifeblood of mankind. Everything we today accept as normal was at one time an innovation. And one of the most recent innovations is the attempt to guide the societies of mankind into something more consistent with the personal happiness of individuals."

"The God complex," Brion said; "forcing human lives into a mold whether they want to be fitted into it or not."

"Societies can be that," Ihjel agreed. "It was in the beginning, and there were some disastrous results of attempts to force populations into a political climate where they didn't belong. They weren't all failures – Anvhar here is a striking example of how good the technique can be when correctly applied. It's not done this way anymore, though. As with all of the other sciences, we have found out that the more we know, the more there is to know. We no longer attempt to guide cultures towards what we consider a beneficial goal. There are too many goals, and from our limited vantage point it is hard to tell the good ones from the bad ones. All we do now is try to protect the growing cultures, give a little jolt to the stagnating ones – and bury the dead ones. When the work was first done here on Anvhar the theory hadn't progressed that far. The understandably complex equations that determine just where in the scale from a Type I to a Type V a culture is, had not yet been completed. The technique then was to work out an artificial culture that would be most beneficial for a planet, then bend it into the mold."

"How can that be done?" Brion asked. "How was it done here?"

"We've made some progress – you're finally asking 'how.' The technique here took a good number of agents, and a great deal of money. Personal honor was emphasized in order to encourage dueling, and this led to a heightened interest in the technique of personal combat. When this was well intrenched Giroldi was brought in, and he showed how organized competitions could be more interesting than haphazard encounters. Tying the intellectual aspects onto the framework of competitive sports was a little more difficult, but not overwhelmingly so. The details aren't important; all we are considering now is the end product. Which is you. You're needed very much."

"Why me?" Brion asked. "Why am I special? Because I won the Twenties? I can't believe that. Taken objectively, there isn't that much difference between myself and the ten runners-up. Why don't you ask one of them? They could do your job as well as I."

"No, they couldn't. I'll tell you later why you are the only man I can use. Our time is running out and I must convince you of some other things first." Ihjel glanced at his watch. "We have less than three hours to dead-deadline. Before that time I must explain enough of our work to you to enable you to decide voluntarily to join us."

"A very tall order," Brion said. "You might begin by telling me just who this mysterious 'we' is that you keep referring to."

"The Cultural Relationships Foundation. A non-governmental body, privately endowed, existing to promote peace and ensure the sovereign welfare of independent planets, so that all will prosper from the good will and commerce thereby engendered."

"Sounds as if you're quoting," Brion told him. "No one could possibly make up something that sounds like that on the spur of the moment."

"I *was* quoting, from our charter of organization. Which is all very fine in a general sense, but I'm talking specifically now. About you. You are the product of a tightly knit and very advanced society. Your individuality has been encouraged by your growing up in a society so small in population that a mild form of government control is necessary. The normal Anvharian education is an excellent one, and participation in the Twenties has given you a general and advanced education second to none in the galaxy. It would be a complete waste of your entire life if you now took all this training and wasted it on some rustic farm."

"You give me very little credit. I plan to teach – "

"Forget Anvhar!" Ihjel cut him off with a chop of his hand. "This world will roll on quite successfully whether you are here or not. You must forget it, think of its relative unimportance on a galactic scale, and consider instead the existing, suffering hordes of mankind. You must think what you can do to help them."

"But what can I do – as an individual? The day is long past when a single man, like Caesar or Alexander, could bring about world-shaking changes."

"True – but not true," Ihjel said. "There are key men in every conflict of forces, men who act like catalysts applied at the right instant to start a chemical reaction. You might be one of these men, but I must be honest and say that I can't prove it yet. So in order to save time and endless discussion, I think I will have to spark your personal sense of obligation."

"Obligation to whom?"

"To mankind, of course, to the countless billions of dead who kept the whole machine rolling along that allows you the full, long and happy life you enjoy today. What they gave to you, you must pass on to others. This is the keystone of humanistic morals."

"Agreed. And a very good argument in the long run. But not one that is going to tempt me out of this bed within the next three hours."

"A point of success," Ihjel said. "You agree with the general argument. Now I apply it specifically to you. Here is the statement I intend to prove. There exists a planet with a population of seven million people. Unless I can prevent it, this planet will be completely destroyed. It is my job to stop that destruction, so that is where I am going now. I won't be able to do the job alone. In addition to others, I need you. Not anyone like you – but you, and you alone."

"You have precious little time left to convince me of all that," Brion told him, "so let me make the job easier for you. The work you do, this planet, the imminent danger of the people there – these are all facts that you can undoubtedly supply. I'll take a chance that this whole thing is not a colossal bluff, and admit that given time, you could verify them all. This brings the argument back to me again. How can you possibly prove that I am the only person in the galaxy who can help you?"

"I can prove it by your singular ability, the thing I came here to find."

"Ability? I am different in no way from the other men on my planet."

"You're wrong," Ihjel said. "You are the embodied proof of evolution. Rare individuals with specific talents occur constantly in any species, man included. It has been two generations since an empathetic was last born on Anvhar, and I have been watching carefully most of that time."

"What in blazes is an empathetic – and how do you recognize it when you have found it?" Brion chuckled, this talk was getting preposterous.

"I can recognize one because I'm one myself – there is no other way. As to how projective empathy works, you had a demonstration of that a little earlier, when you felt those strange thoughts about Anvhar. It will be a long time before you can master that, but receptive empathy is your natural trait. This is mentally entering into the feeling, or what could be called the spirit of another person. Empathy is not thought perception; it might better be described as the sensing of someone else's emotional makeup, feelings and attitudes. You can't lie to a trained empathetic, because he can sense the real attitude behind the verbal lies. Even your undeveloped talent has proved immensely useful in the Twenties. You can outguess your opponent because you know his movements even as his body tenses to make them. You accept this without ever questioning it."

"How do you know?" This was Brion's understood, but never voiced secret.

Ihjel smiled. "Just guessing. But I won the Twenties too, remember, also without knowing a thing about empathy at the time. On top of our normal training, it's a wonderful trait to have. Which brings me to the proof we mentioned a minute ago. When you said you would be convinced if I could prove you were the only person who could help me. I *believe* you are – and that is one thing I cannot lie about. It's possible to lie about a belief verbally, to have a falsely based belief, or to change a belief. But you can't lie about it to yourself.

"Equally important – you can't lie about a belief to an empathetic. Would you like to see how I feel about this? 'See' is a bad word – there is no vocabulary yet for this kind of thing. Better, would you join me in my feelings? Sense my attitudes, memories and emotions just as I do?"

Brion tried to protest, but he was too late. The doors of his senses were pushed wide and he was overwhelmed.

"Dis ..." Ihjel said aloud. "Seven million people ... hydrogen bombs ... Brion Brandd." These were just key words, landmarks of association. With each one Brion felt the rushing wave of the other man's emotions.

There could be no lies here – Ihjel was right in that. This was the raw stuff that feelings are made of, the basic reactions to the things and symbols of memory.

*DIS ... DIS ... DIS ... it was a word it was a planet and the word thundered like a drum a drum the sound of its thunder surrounded and was a wasteland a planet of death a planet where living was dying and dying was very better than living crude barbaric backward miserable dirty beneath-consideration planet hot burning scorching wasteland of sands and sands and sands and sands that burned had burned will burn forever the people of this planet so crude dirty miserable barbaric sub-human in-human less-than-human DIS but they were going to be DEAD and DEAD they would be seven million blackened corpses that would blacken your dreams all dreams dreams forever because those H Y D R O G E N B O M B S were waiting to kill them unless ... unless ... unless ... you Ihjel stopped it you Ihjel (DEATH) you (DEATH) you (DEATH) alone couldn't do it you (DEATH) must have BRION BRANDD wet-behind-the-ears-raw-untrained- Brion-Brandd-to-help-you he was the only one in the galaxy who could finish the job ....*

As the flow of sensation died away, Brion realized he was sprawled back weakly on his pillows, soaked with sweat, washed with the memory of the raw emotion. Across from him Ihjel sat with his face bowed in his hands. When he lifted his head Brion saw within his eyes a shadow of the blackness he had just experienced.

"Death," Brion said. "That terrible feeling of death. It wasn't just the people of Dis who would die. It was something more personal."

"Myself," Ihjel said, and behind this simple word were the repeated echoes of night that Brion had been made aware of with his newly recognized ability. "My own death, not too far away. This is the wonderfully terrible price you must pay for your talent. *Angst* is an inescapable part of empathy. It is a part of the whole unknown field of psi phenomena that seems to be independent of time. Death is so traumatic and final that it reverberates back along the time line. The closer I get, the more aware of it I am. There is no exact feeling of date, just a rough location in time. That is the horror of it. I *know* I will die soon after I get to Dis – and long before the work there is finished. I know the job to be done there, and I know the men who have already failed at it. I also know you are the only person who can possibly complete the work I have started. Do you agree now? Will you come with me?"

"Yes, of course," Brion said. "I'll go with you."

# IV

"I've never seen anyone quite as angry as that doctor," Brion said.

"Can't blame him." Ihjel shifted his immense weight and grunted from the console, where he was having a coded conversation with the ship's brain. He hit the keys quickly, and read the answer from the screen. "You took away his medical moment of glory. How many times in his life will he have a chance to nurse back to rugged smiling health the triumphantly exhausted Winner of the Twenties?"

"Not many, I imagine. The wonder of it is how you managed to convince him that you and the ship here could take care of me as well as his hospital could."

"I could never convince him of that," Ihjel said. "But I and the Cultural Relationships Foundation have some powerful friends on Anvhar. I'm forced to admit I brought a little pressure to bear." He leaned back and read the course tape as it streamed out of the printer. "We have a little time to spare, but I would rather spend it waiting at the other end. We'll blast as soon as I have you tied down in a stasis field."

The completeness of the stasis field leaves no impressions on the body or mind. In it there is no weight, no pressure, no pain – no sensation of any kind. Except for a stasis of very long duration, there is no sensation of time. To Brion's consciousness, Ihjel flipped the switch off with a continuation of the same motion that had turned it on. The ship was unchanged, only outside of the port was the red-shot blankness of jump-space.

"How do you feel?" Ihjel asked.

Apparently, the ship was wondering the same thing. Its detector unit, hovering impatiently just outside of Brion's stasis field, darted down and settled on his bare forearm. The doctor back on Anvhar had given the medical section of the ship's brain a complete briefing. A quick check of a dozen factors of Brion's metabolism was compared to the expected norm. Apparently, everything was going well, because the only reaction was the expected injection of vitamins and glucose.

"I can't say I'm feeling wonderful yet," Brion answered, levering himself higher on the pillows. "But every day it's a bit better – steady progress."

"I hope so, because we have about two weeks before we get to Dis. Do you think you'll be back in shape by that time?"

"No promises," Brion said, giving a tentative squeeze to one bicep. "It should be enough time, though. Tomorrow I start mild exercise and that will tighten me up again. Now – tell me more about Dis and what you have to do there."

"I'm not going to do it twice, so just save your curiosity awhile. We're heading for a rendezvous point now to pick up another operator. This is going to be a three-man team, you, me and an exobiologist. As soon as he is aboard I'll do a complete briefing for you both at the same time. What you can do now is get your head into the language box and start working on your Disan. You'll want to speak it perfectly by the time we touchdown."

With an autohypno for complete recall, Brion had no difficulty in mastering the grammar and vocabulary of Disan. Pronunciation was a different matter altogether. Almost all the word endings were swallowed, muffled or gargled. The language was rich in glottal stops, clicks and guttural strangling sounds. Ihjel stayed in a different part of the ship when Brion used the voice mirror and analysis scope, claiming that the awful noises interfered with his digestion.

Their ship angled through jump-space along its calculated course. It kept its fragile human cargo warm, fed them and supplied breathable air. It had orders to worry about Brion's health, so it did, checking constantly against its recorded instructions and noting his steady progress. Another part of the ship's brain counted microseconds with moronic fixation, finally closing a relay when a predetermined number had expired in its heart. A light flashed and a buzzer hummed gently but insistently.

Ihjel yawned, put away the report he had been reading, and started for the control room. He shuddered when he passed the room where Brion was listening to a playback of his Disan efforts.

"Turn off that dying brontosaurus and get strapped in," he called through the thin door. "We're coming to the point of optimum possibility and we'll be dropping back into normal space soon."

The human mind can ponder the incredible distances

between the stars, but cannot possibly contain within itself a real understanding of them. Marked out on a man's hand an inch is a large unit of measure. In interstellar space a cubical area with sides a hundred thousand miles long is a microscopically fine division. Light crosses this distance in a fraction of a second. To a ship moving with a relative speed far greater than that of light, this measuring unit is even smaller. Theoretically, it appears impossible to find a particular area of this size. Technologically, it was a repeatable miracle that occurred too often to even be interesting.

Brion and Ihjel were strapped in when the jump-drive cut off abruptly, lurching them back into normal space and time. They didn't unstrap, but just sat and looked at the dimly distant pattern of stars. A single sun, apparently of fifth magnitude, was their only neighbor in this lost corner of the universe. They waited while the computer took enough star sights to triangulate a position in three dimensions, muttering to itself electronically while it did the countless calculations to find their position. A warning bell chimed and the drive cut on and off so quickly that the two acts seemed simultaneous. This happened again, twice, before the brain was satisfied it had made as good a fix as possible and flashed a NAVIGATION POWER OFF light. Ihjel unstrapped, stretched, and made them a meal.

Ihjel had computed their passage time with precise allowances. Less than ten hours after they arrived a powerful signal blasted into their waiting receiver. They strapped in again as the NAVIGATION POWER ON signal blinked insistently.

A ship had paused in flight somewhere relatively near in the vast volume of space. It had entered normal space just long enough to emit a signal of radio query on an assigned wave length. Ihjel's ship had detected this and instantly responded with a verifying signal. The passenger spacer had accepted this assurance and gracefully laid a ten-foot metal egg in space. As soon as this had cleared its jump field the parent ship vanished towards its destination, light years away.

Ihjel's ship climbed up the signal it had received. This signal had been recorded and examined minutely. Angle, strength and Doppler movement were computed to find course and distance. A few minutes of flight were enough to get within range of the far weaker transmitter in the drop-capsule. Homing on this signal was so simple, a human pilot could have done it himself. The shining sphere loomed up, then vanished out of sight of the viewports as the ship rotated to bring the spacelock into line. Magnetic clamps cut in when they made contact.

"Go down and let the bug-doctor in," Ihjel said. "I'll stay and monitor the board in case of trouble."

"What do I have to do?"

"Get into a suit and open the outer lock. Most of the drop sphere is made of inflatable metallic foil, so don't bother to look for the entrance. Just cut a hole in it with the oversize can-opener you'll find in the tool box. After Dr. Morees gets aboard jettison the thing. Only get the radio and locator unit out first – it gets used again."

The tool did look like a giant can-opener. Brion carefully felt the resilient metal skin that covered the lock entrance, until he was sure there was nothing on the other side. Then he jabbed the point through and cut a ragged hole in the thin foil. Dr. Morees boiled out of the sphere, knocking Brion aside.

"What's the matter?" Brion asked.

There was no radio on the other's suit; he couldn't answer. But he did shake his fist angrily. The helmet ports were opaque, so there was no way to tell what expressions went with the gesture. Brion shrugged and turned back to salvaging the equipment pack, pushing the punctured balloon free and sealing the lock. When pressure was pumped back to ship-normal, he cracked his helmet and motioned the other to do the same.

"You're a pack of dirty lying dogs!" Dr. Morees said when the helmet came off. Brion was completely baffled. Dr. Lea Morees had long dark hair, large eyes, and a delicately shaped mouth now taut with anger. Dr. Morees was a woman.

"Are you the filthy swine responsible for this atrocity?" Dr. Morees asked menacingly.

"In the control room," Brion said quickly, knowing when cowardice was preferable to valor. "A man named Ihjel. There's a lot of him to hate, you can have a good time doing it. I just joined up myself ...." He was talking to her back as she stormed from the room. Brion hurried after her, not wanting to miss the first human spark of interest in the trip to date.

"Kidnapped! Lied to, and forced against my will! There is no court in the galaxy that won't give you the maximum sentence, and

I'll scream with pleasure as they roll your fat body into solitary – "

"They shouldn't have sent a woman," Ihjel said, completely ignoring her words. "I asked for a highly qualified exobiologist for a difficult assignment. Someone young and tough enough to do field work under severe conditions. So the recruiting office sends me the smallest female they can find, one who'll melt in the first rain."

"I will not!" Lea shouted. "Female resiliency is a well-known fact, and I'm in far better condition than the average woman. Which has nothing to do with what I'm telling you. I was hired for a job in the university on Moller's World and signed a contract to that effect. Then this bully of an agent tells me the contract has been changed – read subparagraph 189-C or some such nonsense – and I'll be transhipping. He stuffed me into that suffocating basketball without a by-your-leave and they threw me overboard. If that is not a violation of personal privacy."

"Cut a new course, Brion," Ihjel broke in. "Find the nearest settled planet and head us there. We have to drop this woman and find a man for this job. We are going to what is undoubtedly the most interesting planet an exobiologist ever conceived of, but we need a man who can take orders and not faint when it gets too hot."

Brion was lost. Ihjel had done all the navigating and Brion had no idea how to begin a search like this.

"Oh, no you don't," Lea said. "You don't get rid of me that easily. I placed first in my class, and most of the five hundred other students were male. This is only a man's universe because the men say so. What is the name of this garden planet where we are going?"

"Dis. I'll give you a briefing as soon as I get this ship on course." He turned to the controls and Lea slipped out of her suit and went into the lavatory to comb her hair. Brion closed his mouth, aware suddenly it had been open for a long time. "Is that what you call applied psychology?" he asked.

"Not really. She was going to go along with the job in the end – since she did sign the contract even if she didn't read the fine print – but not until she had exhausted her feelings. I just shortened the process by switching her onto the male-superiority hate. Most women who succeed in normally masculine fields have a reflexive antipathy there; they have been hit on the head with it so much."

He fed the course tape into the console and scowled. "But there was a good chunk of truth in what I said. I wanted a young, fit and highly qualified biologist from recruiting. I never thought they would find a female one – and it's too late to send her back now. Dis is no place for a woman."

"Why?" Brion asked, as Lea appeared in the doorway.

"Come inside, and I'll show you both," Ihjel said.

# V

"Dis," Ihjel said, consulting a thick file, "third planet out from its primary, Epsilon Eridani. The fourth planet is Nyjord – remember that, because it is going to be very important. Dis is a place you need a good reason to visit and no reason at all to leave. Too hot, too dry; the temperature in the temperate zones rarely drops below a hundred Fahrenheit. The planet is nothing but scorched rock and burning sand. Most of the water is underground and normally inaccessible. The surface water is all in the form of briny, chemically saturated swamps – undrinkable without extensive processing. All the facts and figures are here in the folder and you can study them later. Right now I want you just to get the idea that this planet is as loathsome and inhospitable as they come. So are the people. This is a solido of a Disan."

Lea gasped at the three-dimensional representation on the screen. Not at the physical aspects of the man; as a biologist trained in the specialty of alien life she had seen a lot stranger sights. It was the man's pose, the expression on his face – tensed to leap, his lips drawn back to show all of his teeth.

"He looks as if he wanted to kill the photographer," she said.

"He almost did – just after the picture was taken. Like all Disans, he has an overwhelming hatred and loathing of offworlders. Not without good reason, though. His planet was settled completely by chance during the Breakdown. I'm not sure of the details, but the overall picture is clear, since the story of their desertion forms the basis of all the myths and animistic religions on Dis.

"Apparently there were large-scale mining operations carried on there once; the world is rich enough in minerals and mining them is very simple. But water came only from expensive extraction processes and I imagine most of the food came from offworld. Which was good enough until the settlement was forgotten, the way a lot of other planets were during the Breakdown. All the records were destroyed in the fighting, and the ore carriers were pressed into military service. Dis was on its own.

What happened to the people there is a tribute to the adaptation possibilities of homo sapiens. Individuals died, usually in enormous pain, but the race lived. Changed a good deal, but still human. As the water and food ran out and the extraction machinery broke down, they must have made heroic efforts to survive. They couldn't do it mechanically, but by the time the last machine collapsed, enough people were adjusted to the environment to keep the race going.

"Their descendants are still there, completely adapted to the environment. Their body temperatures are around a hundred and thirty degrees. They have specialized tissue in the gluteal area for storing water. These are minor changes, compared to the major ones they have done in fitting themselves for this planet. I don't know the exact details, but the reports are very enthusiastic about symbiotic relationships. They assure us that this is the first time homo sapiens has been an active part of either commensalism or inquilinism other than in the role of host."

"Wonderful!" Lea exclaimed.

"Is it?" Ihjel scowled. "Perhaps from the abstract scientific point of view. If you can keep notes perhaps you might write a book about it some time. But I'm not interested. I'm sure all these morphological changes and disgusting intimacies will fascinate you, Dr. Morees. But while you are counting blood types and admiring your thermometers, I hope you will be able to devote a little time to a study of the Disans' obnoxious personalities. We must either find out what makes these people tick – or we are going to have to stand by and watch the whole lot blown up!"

"Going to do what!" Lea gasped. "Destroy them? Wipe out this fascinating genetic pool? Why?

"Because they are so incredibly loathsome, that's why!" Ihjel said. "These aboriginal hotheads have managed to lay their hands on some primitive cobalt bombs. They want to light the fuse and drop these bombs on Nyjord, the next planet. Nothing said or done can convince them differently. They demand unconditional surrender, or else. This is impossible for a lot of reasons – most important, because the Nyjorders would like to keep their planet for their very own. They have tried every kind of compromise but none of them works. The Disans are out to commit racial suicide. A Nyjord fleet is now over Dis and the deadline has almost expired for the surrender of the cobalt bombs. The Nyjord ships carry enough H-bombs to turn the entire planet into an atomic pile. That is what we must stop."

Brion looked at the solido on the screen, trying to make some judgment of the man. Bare, horny feet. A bulky, ragged length of cloth around the waist was the only garment. What looked like a piece of green vine was hooked over one shoulder. From a plaited belt were suspended a number of odd devices made of hand-beaten metal, drilled stone and looped leather. The only recognizable item was a thin knife of unusual design. Loops of piping, flared bells, carved stones tied in senseless patterns of thonging gave the rest of the collection a bizarre appearance. Perhaps they had some religious significance. But the well-worn and handled look of most of them gave Brion an uneasy sensation. If they were used – what in the universe could they be used *for*?

"I can't believe it," he finally concluded. "Except for the exotic hardware, this lowbrow looks as if he has sunk back into the Stone Age. I don't see how his kind can be any real threat to another planet."

"The Nyjorders believe it, and that's good enough for me," Ihjel said. "They are paying our Cultural Relationships Foundation a good sum to try and prevent this war. Since they are our employers, we must do what they ask." Brion ignored this large lie, since it was obviously designed as an explanation for Lea. But he made a mental note to query Ihjel later about the real situation.

"Here are the tech reports." Ihjel dropped them on the table. "Dis has some spacers as well as the cobalt bombs – though these aren't the real threat. A tramp trader was picked up *leaving* Dis. It had delivered a jump-space launcher that can drop those bombs on Nyjord while anchored to the bedrock of Dis. While essentially a peaceful and happy people, the Nyjorders were justifiably annoyed at this and convinced the tramp's captain to give them some more information. It's all here. Boiled down, it gives a minimum deadline by which time the launcher can be set up and start throwing bombs."

"When is that deadline?" Lea asked.

"In ten more days. If the situation hasn't been changed drastically by then, the Nyjorders are going to wipe all life from the face of Dis. I assure you they don't want to do it. But they will drop the bombs in order to assure their own survival."

"What am I supposed to do?" Lea asked, flipping the pages of the report. "I don't know a thing about nucleonics or jump-space. I'm an exobiologist, with a supplementary degree in anthropology. What help could I possibly be?"

Ihjel looked down at her, stroking his jaw, fingers sunk deep into the rolls of flesh. "My faith in our recruiters is restored," he said. "That's a combination that is probably rare – even on Earth. You're as scrawny as an underfed chicken, but young enough to survive if we keep a close eye on you." He cut off Lea's angry protest with a raised hand. "No more bickering. There isn't time. The Nyjorders must have lost over thirty agents trying to find the bombs. Our foundation has had six people killed – including my late predecessor in charge of the project. He was a good man, but I think he went at this problem the wrong way. I think it is a cultural one, not a physical one."

"Run it through again with the power turned up," Lea said, frowning. "All I hear is static."

"It's the old problem of genesis. Like Newton and the falling apple, Levy and the hysteresis in the warp field. Everything has a beginning. If we can find out why these people are so hell-bent on suicide we might be able to change the reasons. Not that I intend to stop looking for the bombs or the jump-space generator either. We are going to try anything that will avert this planetary murder."

"You're a lot brighter than you look," Lea said, rising and carefully stacking the sheets of the report. "You can count on me for complete cooperation. Now I'll study all this in bed if one of you overweight gentlemen will show me to a room with a strong lock on the inside of the door. Don't call me; I'll call you when I want breakfast."

Brion wasn't sure how much of her barbed speech was humor and how much was serious, so he said nothing. He showed her to an empty cabin – she did lock the door – then looked for Ihjel. The Winner was in the galley adding to his girth with an immense gelatin dessert that filled a good-sized tureen.

"Is she short for a native Terran?" Brion asked. "The top of her head is below my chin."

"That's the norm. Earth is a reservoir of tired genes. Weak backs, vermiform appendixes, bad eyes. If they didn't have the universities and the trained people we need I would never use them."

"Why did you lie to her about the Foundation?"

"Because it's a secret – isn't that reason enough?" Ihjel rumbled angrily, scraping the last dregs from the bowl. "Better eat something. Build up the strength. The Foundation has to maintain its undercover status if it is going to accomplish anything. If she returns to Earth after this it's better that she should know nothing of our real work. If she joins up, there'll be time enough to tell her. But I doubt if she will like the way we operate. Particularly since I plan to drop some H-bombs on Dis myself – if we can't turn off the war."

"I don't believe it!"

"You heard me correctly. Don't bulge your eyes and look moronic. As a last resort I'll drop the bombs myself rather than let the Nyjorders do it. That might save them."

"Save them – they'd all be radiated and dead!" Brion's voice rose in anger.

"Not the Disans. I want to save the Nyjorders. Stop clenching your fists and sit down and have some of this cake. It's delicious. The Nyjorders are all that counts here. They have a planet blessed by the laws of chance. When Dis was cut off from outside contact, the survivors turned into a gang of swamp-crawling homicidals. It did the opposite for Nyjord. You can survive there just by pulling fruit off a tree. The population was small, educated, intelligent. Instead of sinking into an eternal siesta they matured into a vitally different society. Not mechanical – they weren't even using the wheel when they were rediscovered. They became sort of cultural specialists, digging deep into the philosophical aspects of interrelationship – the thing that machine societies never have had time for. Of course this was ready-made for the Cultural Relationships Foundation, and we have been working with them ever since. Not guiding so much as protecting them from any blows that might destroy this growing idea. But we've fallen down on the job. Nonviolence is essential to these people – they have vitality without needing destruction. But if they are forced to blow up Dis for their own survival – against every one of their basic tenets – their philosophy won't endure. Physically they'll live on, as just one more dog-eat-dog planet with an A-bomb for any of the competition who drop behind."

"Sounds like paradise now."

"Don't be smug. It's just another worldful of people with the same old likes, dislikes and hatreds. But they are evolving a way of living together, without violence, that may someday form the key to mankind's survival. They are worth looking after. Now get below and study your Disan and read the reports. Get it all pat before we land."

# VI

"Identify yourself, please." The quiet words from the speaker in no way appeared to coincide with the picture on the screen. The spacer that had matched their orbit over Dis had recently been a freighter. A quick conversion had tacked the hulking shape of a primary weapons turret on top of her hull. The black disc of the immense muzzle pointed squarely at them. Ihjel switched open the ship-to-ship communication channel.

"This is Ihjel. Retinal pattern 490-BJ4-67 – which is also the code that is supposed to get me through your blockade. Do you want to check that pattern?"

"There will be no need, thank you. If you will turn on your recorder I have a message relayed to you from Prime-four."

"Recording and out," Ihjel said. "Damn! Trouble already, and four days to blowup. Prime-four is our headquarters on Dis. This ship carries a cover cargo so we can land at the spaceport. This is probably a change of plan and I don't like the smell of it."

There was something behind Ihjel's grumbling this time, and without conscious effort Brion could sense the chilling touch of the other man's *angst*. Trouble was waiting for them on the planet below. When the message was typed by the decoder Ihjel hovered over it, reading each word as it appeared on the paper. When it was finished he only snorted and went below to the galley. Brion pulled the message out of the machine and read it.

IHJEL IHJEL IHJEL SPACEPORT LANDING DANGER NIGHT LANDING PREFERABLE COORDINATES MAP 46 J92 MN75 REMOTE YOUR SHIP VION WILL MEET END END END

Dropping into the darkness was safe enough. It was done on instruments, and the Disans were thought to have no detection apparatus. The altimeter dials spun backwards to zero and a soft vibration was the only indication they had landed. All of the cabin lights were off except for the fluorescent glow of the instruments. A white-speckled grey filled the infra-red screen, radiation from the still warm sand and stone. There were no moving blips on it, not the characteristic shape of a shielded atomic generator.

"We're here first," Ihjel said, opaqueing the ports and turning on the cabin lights. They blinked at each other, faces damp with perspiration.

"Must you have the ship this hot?" Lea asked, patting her forehead with an already sodden kerchief. Stripped of her heavier clothing, she looked even tinier to Brion. But the thin cloth tunic – reaching barely halfway to her knees – concealed very little. Small she may have appeared to him: unfeminine she was not. Her breasts were full and high, her waist tiny enough to offset the outward curve of her hips.

"Shall I turn around so you can stare at the back too?" she asked Brion. Five days' experience had taught him that this type of remark was best ignored. It only became worse if he tried to make an intelligent answer.

"Dis is hotter than this cabin," he said, changing the subject. "By raising the interior temperature we can at least prevent any sudden shock when we go out – "

"I know the theory – but it doesn't stop me from sweating," she said curtly.

"Best thing you can do is sweat." Ihjel said. He looked like a glistening captive balloon in shorts. Finishing a bottle of beer, he took another from the freezer. "Have a beer."

"No, thank you. I'm afraid it would dissolve the last shreds of tissue and my kidneys would float completely away. On Earth we never – "

"Get Professor Morees' luggage for her," Ihjel interrupted. "Vion's coming, there's his signal. I'm sending this ship up before any of the locals spot it."

When he cracked the outer port the puff of air struck them like the exhaust from a furnace, dry and hot as a tongue of flame. Brion heard Lea's gasp in the darkness. She stumbled down the ramp and he followed her slowly, careful of the weight of packs and equipment he carried. The sand, still hot from the day, burned through his boots. Ihjel came last, the remote-control unit in his hand. As soon as they were clear he activated it and the ramp slipped back like a giant tongue. As soon as the lock had swung shut, the ship lifted and drifted upwards silently towards its orbit, a shrinking darkness against the stars.

There was just enough starlight to see the sandy wastes around them, as wave-filled as a petrified sea. The dark shape of a sand car drew up over a dune and hummed to a stop. When the door opened Ihjel stepped towards it and everything happened at once.

Ihjel broke into a blue nimbus of crackling flame, his skin blackening, charred. He was dead in an instant. A second pillar of flame bloomed next to the car, and a choking scream was cut off at the moment it began. Ihjel died silently.

Brion was diving even as the electrical discharges still crackled in the air. The boxes and packs dropped from him and he slammed against Lea, knocking her to the ground. He hoped she had the sense to stay there and be quiet. This was his only conscious thought; the rest was reflex. He was rolling over and over as fast as he could.

The spitting electrical flames flared again, playing over the bundles of luggage he had dropped. This time Brion was expecting it, pressed flat on the ground a short distance away. He was facing the darkness away from the sand car and saw the brief, blue glow of the ion-rifle discharge. His own gun was in his hand. When Ihjel had given him the missile weapon he had asked no questions, but had just strapped it on. There had been no thought that he would need it this quickly. Holding it firmly before him in both hands, he let his body aim at the spot where the glow had been. A whiplash of explosive slugs ripped the night air. They found their target and something thrashed voicelessly and died.

In the brief instant after he fired, a jarring weight landed on his back and a line of fire circled his throat. Normally he fought with a calm mind, with no thoughts other than of the contest. But Ihjel, a friend, a man of Anvhar, had died a few seconds before, and Brion found himself welcoming this physical violence and pain.

There are many foolish and dangerous things that can be done, such as smoking next to high-octane fuel and putting fingers into electrical sockets. Just as dangerous, and equally deadly, is physically attacking a Winner of the Twenties.

Two men hit Brion together, though this made very little difference. The first died suddenly as hands like steel claws found his neck and in a single spasmodic contraction did such damage to the large blood vessels there that they burst and tiny hemorrhages filled his brain. The second man had time for a single scream, though he died just as swiftly when those hands closed on his larynx.

Running in a crouch, partially on his knuckles, Brion swiftly made a circle of the area, gun ready. There were no others. Only when he touched the softness of Lea's body did the blood anger seep from him. He was suddenly aware of the pain and fatigue, the sweat soaking his body and the breath rasping in his throat. Holstering the gun, he ran light fingers over her skull, finding a bruised spot on one temple. Her chest was rising and falling regularly. She had struck her head when he pushed her. It had undoubtedly saved her life.

Sitting down suddenly, he let his body relax, breathing deeply. Everything was a little better now, except for the pain at his throat. His fingers found a thin strand on the side of his neck with a knobby weight on the end. There was another weight on his other shoulder and a thin line of pain across his neck. When he pulled on them both, the strangler's cord came away in his hand. It was thin fiber, strong as a wire. When it had been pulled around his neck it had sliced the surface skin and flesh like a knife, halted only by the corded bands of muscle below. Brion threw it from him, into the darkness where it had come from.

He could think again, and he carefully kept his thoughts from the men he had killed. Knowing it was useless, he went to Ihjel's body. A single touch of the scorched flesh was enough. Behind him Lea moaned with returning consciousness and he hurried on to the sand car, stepping over the charred body outside the door. The driver slumped, dead, killed perhaps by the same strangling cord that had sunk into Brion's throat. He laid the man gently on the sand and closed the lids over the staring horror of the eyes. There was a canteen in the car and he brought it back to Lea.

"My head – I've hurt my head," she said groggily.

"Just a bruise," he reassured her. "Drink some of this water and you'll soon feel better. Lie back. Everything's over for the moment and you can rest."

"Ihjel's dead!" Lea said with sudden shocked memory. "They've killed him! What's happened?" she tensed, tried to rise, and he pressed her back gently.

"I'll tell you everything. Just don't try to get up yet. There was an ambush and they killed Vion and the driver of the sand car, as well as Ihjel. Three men did it and they're all dead now too. I don't think there are any more around, but if there are I'll hear them coming. We're just going to wait a few minutes until you feel better, then we're getting out of here in the car."

"Bring the ship down!" There was a thin note of hysteria in her voice. "We can't stay here alone. We don't know where to go or what to do. With Ihjel dead, the whole thing's spoiled. We have to get out ...."

There are some things that can't sound gentle, no matter how gently they are said. This was one of them. "I'm sorry, Lea, but the ship is out of our reach right now. Ihjel was killed with an ion gun and it fused the control unit into a solid lump. We must take the car and get to the city. We'll do it now. See if you can stand up – I'll help you."

She rose, not saying anything, and as they walked towards the car a single, reddish moon cleared the hills behind them. In its light Brion saw a dark line bisecting the rear panel of the sand car. He stopped abruptly. "What's the matter?" Lea asked.

The unlocked engine cover could have only one significance and he pushed it open, knowing in advance what he would see. The attackers had been very thorough and fast. In the short time available to them they had killed the driver and the car as well. Ruddy light shone on torn wires, ripped out connections. Repair would be impossible.

"I think we'll have to walk," he told her, trying to keep the gloom out of his voice. "This spot is roughly a hundred and fifty kilometers from the city of Hovedstad, where we have to go. We should be able to – "

"We're going to die. We can't walk anywhere. This whole planet is a death trap. Let's get back in the ship!" The shrillness of hysteria was at the edge of her voice, as well as a subtle slurring of sounds.

Brion didn't try to reason with her or bother to explain. She had a concussion from the blow, that much was obvious. He had her sit and rest while he made what preparations he could for the long walk.

Clothing first. With each passing minute the desert air was growing colder as the day's heat ebbed away. Lea was beginning to shiver, and he took some heavier clothing from her charred bag and made her pull it on over her light tunic. There was little else that was worth carrying – the canteen from the car and a first-aid kit he found in one of the compartments. There were no maps and no radio. Navigation was obviously done by compass on this almost featureless desert. The car was equipped with an electrically operated gyrocompass, of no use to him now. But he did use it to check the direction of Hovedstad, as he remembered it from the map, and found it lined up perfectly with the tracks the car had cut into the sand. It had come directly from the city. They could find their way by back-tracking.

Time was slipping away. He would have liked to bury Ihjel and the men from the car, but the night hours were too valuable to be wasted. The best he could do was put the three corpses in the car, for protection from the Disan animals. He locked the door and threw the key as far as he could into the blackness. Lea had slipped into a restless sleep and he carefully shook her awake.

"Come," Brion said. "We have a little walking to do."

# VII

With the cool air and firmly packed sand under foot, walking should have been easy. Lea spoiled that. The concussion seemed to have temporarily cut off the reasoning part of her brain, leaving a direct connection to her vocal cords. As she stumbled along, only half conscious, she mumbled all of her darkest fears that were better left unvoiced. Occasionally there was relevancy in her complaints. They would lose their way, never find the city, die of thirst, freezing, heat or hunger. Interspersed and entwined with these were fears from her past that still floated, submerged in the timeless ocean of her subconscious. Some Brion could understand, though he tried not to listen. Fears of losing credits, not getting the highest grade, falling behind, a woman alone in a world of men, leaving school, being lost, trampled among the nameless hordes that struggled for survival in the crowded city-states of Earth.

There were other things she was afraid of that made no sense to a man of Anvhar. Who were the alkians that seemed to trouble her? Or what was canceri? Daydle and haydle? Who was Manstan, whose name kept coming up, over and over, each time accompanied by a little moan?

Brion stopped and picked her up in both arms. With a sigh she settled against the hard width of his chest and was instantly asleep. Even with the additional weight he made better time now, and he stretched to his fastest, kilometer-consuming stride to make good use of these best hours.

Somewhere on a stretch of gravel and shelving rock he lost the track of the sand car. He wasted no time looking for it. By carefully watching the glistening stars rise and set he had made a good estimate of the geographic north. Dis didn't seem to have a pole star; however, a boxlike constellation turned slowly around the invisible point of the pole. Keeping this positioned in line with his right shoulder guided him on the westerly course he needed.

When his arms began to grow tired he lowered Lea gently to the ground; she didn't wake. Stretching for an instant, before taking up his burden again, Brion was struck by the terrible loneliness of the desert. His breath made a vanishing mist against the stars; all else was darkness and silence. How distant he was from his home, his people, his planet! Even the constellations of the night sky were different. He was used to solitude, but this was a loneliness that touched some deep-buried instinct. A shiver that wasn't from the desert cold touched lightly along his spine, prickling at the hairs on his neck.

It was time to go on. He shrugged the disquieting sensations off and carefully tied Lea into the jacket he had been wearing. Slung like a pack on his back, it made the walking easier. The gravel gave way to sliding dunes of sand that seemed to continue to infinity. It was a painful, slipping climb to the top of each one, then an equally difficult descent to the black-pooled hollow at the foot of the next.

With the first lightening of the sky in the east he stopped, breath rasping in his chest, to mark his direction before the stars faded. One line scratched in the sand pointed due north, a second pointed out the course they should follow. When they were aligned to his satisfaction he washed his mouth out with a single swallow of water and sat on the sand next to the still form of the girl.

Gold fingers of fire searched across the sky, wiping out the stars. It was magnificent; Brion forgot his fatigue in appreciation. There should be some way of preserving it. A quatrain would be best. Short enough to be remembered, yet requiring attention and skill to compact everything into it. He had scored high with his quatrains in the Twenties. This would be a special one. Taind, his poetry mentor, would have to get a copy.

"What are you mumbling about?" Lea asked, looking up at the craggy blackness of his profile against the reddening sky.

"Poem," he said. "Shhh. Just a minute."

It was too much for Lea, coming after the tension and dangers of the night. She began to laugh, laughing even harder when he scowled at her. Only when she heard the tinge of growing hysteria did she make an attempt to break off the laughter. The sun cleared the horizon, washing a sudden warmth over them. Lea gasped.

"Your throat's been cut! You're bleeding to death!"

"Not really," he said, touching his fingertips lightly against the blood-clotted wound that circled his neck. "Just superficial."

Depression sat on him as he suddenly remembered the battle

and death of the previous night. Lea didn't notice his face; she was busy digging in the pack he had thrown down. He had to use his fingers to massage and force away the grimace of pain that twisted his mouth. Memory was more painful than the wound. How easily he had killed! Three men. How close to the surface of the civilized man the animal dwelled! In countless matches he had used those holds, always drawing back from the exertion of the full killing power. They were part of a game, part of the Twenties. Yet when his friend had been killed he had become a killer himself. He believed in nonviolence and the sanctity of life – until the first test, when he had killed without hesitation. More ironic was the fact he really felt no guilt, even now. Shock at the change, yes. But no more than that.

"Lift your chin," Lea said, brandishing the antiseptic applicator she had found in the medicine kit. He lifted his chin obligingly and the liquid drew a cool, burning line across his neck. Antibio pills would do a lot more good, since the wound was completely clotted by now, but he didn't speak his thoughts aloud. For the moment Lea had forgotten herself in taking care of him. He put some of the antiseptic on her scalp bruise and she squeaked, pulling back. They both swallowed the pills.

"That sun is hot already," Lea said, peeling off her heavy clothing. "Let's find a nice cool cave or an air-cooled saloon to crawl into for the day."

"I don't think there are any here. Just sand. We have to walk – "

"I know we have to walk," she interrupted. "There's no need for a lecture about it. You're as seriously cubical as the Bank of Terra. Relax. Count ten and start again." Lea was making empty talk while she listened to the memory of hysteria tittering at the fringes of her brain.

"No time for that. We have to keep going." Brion climbed slowly to his feet after stowing everything in the pack. When he sighted along his marker at the western horizon he saw nothing to mark their course, only the marching dunes. He helped Lea to her feet and began walking slowly towards them.

"Just hold on a second," Lea called after him. "Where do you think you're going?"

"In that direction," he said, pointing. "I hoped there would be some landmarks, but there aren't. We'll have to keep on by dead reckoning. The sun will keep us pretty well on course. If we aren't there by night the stars will be a better guide."

"All this on an empty stomach? How about breakfast? I'm hungry – and thirsty."

"No food." He shook the canteen that gurgled emptily. It had been only partly filled when he found it. "The water's low and we'll need it later."

"I need it now," she said shortly. "My mouth tastes like an unemptied ashtray and I'm dry as paper."

"Just a single swallow," he said after the briefest hesitation. "This is all we have."

Lea sipped at it with her eyes closed in appreciation. Then he sealed the top and returned it to the pack without taking any himself. They were sweating as they started up the first dune.

The desert was barren of life; they were the only things moving under that merciless sun. Their shadows pointed the way ahead of them, and as the shadows shortened the heat rose. It had an intensity Lea had never experienced before, a physical weight that pushed at her with a searing hand. Her clothing was sodden with perspiration, and it trickled burning into her eyes. The light and heat made it hard to see, and she leaned on the immovable strength of Brion's arm. He walked on steadily, apparently ignoring the heat and discomfort.

"I wonder if those things are edible – or store water?" Brion's voice was a harsh rasp. Lea blinked and squinted at the leathery shape on the summit of the dune. Plant or animal, it was hard to tell. It was the size of a man's head, wrinkled and grey as dried-out leather, knobbed with thick spikes. Brion pushed it up with his toe and they had a brief glimpse of a white roundness, like a shiny taproot, going down into the dune. Then the thing contracted, pulling itself lower into the sand. At the same instant something thin and sharp lashed out through a fold in the skin, striking at Brion's boot and withdrawing. There was a scratch on the hard plastic, beaded with drops of green liquid.

"Probably poison," he said, digging his toe into the sand. "This thing is too mean to fool with – without a good reason. Let's keep going."

It was before noon when Lea fell down. She really wanted to go on, but her body wouldn't obey. The thin soles of her shoes were no protection against the burning sand and her feet were lumps of raw pain. Heat hammered down, poured up from the sand and swirled her in an oven of pain. The air she gasped in was molten metal that dried and cracked her mouth. Each pulse of her heart throbbed blood to the wound in her scalp until it seemed her skull would burst with the agony. She had stripped down to the short tunic – in spite of Brion's insistence that she keep her body protected from the sun – and that clung to her, soaked with sweat. She tore at it in a desperate effort to breathe. There was no escape from the unending heat.

Though the baked sand burned torture into her knees and hands, she couldn't rise. It took all her strength not to fall further. Her eyes closed and everything swirled in immense circles.

Brion, blinking through slitted eyes, saw her go down. He lifted her, and carried her again as he had the night before. The hot touch of her body shocked his bare arms. Her skin was flushed pink. The tunic was torn open and one pointed breast rose and fell unevenly with the irregularity of her breathing. Wiping his palm free of sweat and sand, he touched her skin and felt the ominous hot dryness.

Heat-shock, all the symptoms. Dry, flushed skin, the ragged breathing. Her temperature rising quickly as her body stopped fighting the heat and succumbed.

There was nothing he could do here to protect her from the heat. He measured a tiny portion of the remaining water into her mouth and she swallowed convulsively. Her thin clothing was little protection from the sun. He could only take her in his arms and keep on towards the horizon. An outcropping of rock threw a tiny patch of shade and he walked towards it.

The ground here, shielded from the direct rays of the sun, felt almost cool by contrast. Lea opened her eyes when he put her down, peering up at him through a haze of pain. She wanted to apologize to him for her weakness, but no words came from the dried membrane of her throat. His body above her seemed to swim back and forth in the heat waves, swaying like a tree in a high wind.

Shock drove her eyes open, cleared her mind for an instant. He really was swaying. Suddenly she realized how much she had come to depend on the unending solidity of his strength – and now it was failing. All over his body the corded muscles contracted in ridges, striving to keep him erect. She saw his mouth pulled open by the taut cords of his neck, and the gaping, silent scream was more terrible than any sound. Then she herself screamed as his eyes rolled back, leaving only the empty white of the eyeballs staring terribly at her. He went over, back, down, like a felled tree, thudding heavily on the sand. Unconscious or dead, she couldn't tell. She pulled limply at his leg, but couldn't drag his immense weight into the shade.

Brion lay on his back in the sun, sweating. Lea saw this and knew that he was still alive. Yet what was happening? She groped for memory in the red haze of her mind, but could remember nothing from her medical studies that would explain this. On every square inch of his body the sweat glands seethed with sudden activity. From every pore oozed great globules of oily liquid, far thicker than normal perspiration. Brion's arms rippled with motion and Lea gaped, horrified as the hairs there writhed and stirred as though endowed with separate life. His chest rose and fell rapidly, deep, gasping breaths racking his body. Lea could only stare through the dim redness of unreality and wonder if she was going mad before she died.

A coughing fit broke the rhythm of his rasping breath, and when it was over his breathing was easier. The perspiration still covered his body, the individual beads touching and forming tiny streams that trickled down his body and vanished in the sand. He stirred and rolled onto his side, facing her. His eyes were open and normal now as he smiled.

"Didn't mean to frighten you. It caught me suddenly coming at the wrong season and everything. It was a bit of a jar to my system. I'll get you some water now – there's still a bit left."

"What happened? When you looked like that, when you fell ...."

"Take two swallows, no more," he said, holding the open canteen to her mouth. "Just summer change, that's all. It happens to us every year on Anvhar – only not that violently, of course. In the winter our bodies store a layer of fat under the skin for insulation, and sweating almost ceases completely. There are a lot of internal changes too. When the weather warms up the process is reversed. The fat is metabolized and the sweat glands enlarge and begin working overtime as the body prepares for two months of hard work, heat and little sleep. I guess the heat here triggered off the summer change early."

"You mean – you've adapted to this terrible planet?"

"Just about. Though it does feel a little warm. I'll need a lot more water soon, so we can't remain here. Do you think you can stand the sun if I carry you?"

"No, but I won't feel any better staying here." She was light-headed, scarcely aware of what she said. "Keep going, I guess. Keep going."

As soon as she was out of the shadow of the rock the sunlight burst over her again in a wave of hot pain. She fell unconscious at once. Brion picked her up and staggered forward. After a few yards, he began to feel the pull of the sand. He knew he was reaching the end of his strength. He went more slowly and each dune seemed a bit higher than the one before. Giant, sand-scoured rocks pushed through the dunes here and he had to stumble around them. At the base of the largest of these monoliths was a straggling clump of knotted vegetation. He passed it by – then stopped as something tried to penetrate his heat-crazed mind. What was it? A difference. Something about these plants that he hadn't noticed in any of the others he had passed during the day.

It was almost like defeat to turn and push his clumsy feet backwards in his own footprints; to stand blinking helplessly at the plants. Yet they were important. Some of them had been cut off close to the sand. Not broken by any natural cause, but cut sharply and squarely by a knife or blade of some sort. The cut plants were long dried and dead, but a tiny hope flared up in him. This was the first sign that other people were actually alive on this heat-blasted planet. And whatever the plants had been cut for, they might be of aid to him. Food – perhaps drink. His hands trembled at the thought as he dropped Lea heavily into the shade of the rock. She didn't stir.

His knife was sharp, but most of the strength was gone from his hands. Breath rasping in his dried throat, he sawed at the tough stem, finally cutting it through. Raising up the shrub, he saw a thick liquid dripping from the severed end. He braced his hand against his leg, so it wouldn't shake and spill, until his cupped palm was full of sap.

It was wet, even a little cool as it evaporated. Surely it was mostly life-giving water. He had a moment's misgiving as he raised it to his lips, and instead of drinking it merely touched it with the tip of his tongue.

At first nothing – then a searing pain. It stabbed deep into his throat and choked him. His stomach heaved and he vomited bitter bile. On his knees, fighting the waves of pain, he lost body fluid he vitally needed.

Despair was worse than the pain. The plant juice must have some use; there must be a way of purifying it or neutralizing it. But Brion, a stranger on this planet, would be dead long before he found out how to do this.

Weakened by the cramps that still tore at him, he tried not to realize how close to the end he was. Getting the girl on his back seemed an impossible task, and for an instant he was tempted to leave her there. Yet even as he considered this he shouldered her leaden weight and once more went on. Each footstep an effort, he followed his own track up the dune. Painfully he forced his way to the top, and looked at the Disan standing a few feet away.

They were both too surprised by the sudden encounter to react at once. For a breath of time they stared at each other, unmoving. When they reacted it was the same defense of fear. Brion dropped the girl, bringing the gun up from the holster in the return of the same motion. The Disan jerked a belled tube from his waistband and raised it to his mouth.

Brion didn't fire. A dead man had taught him how to train his empathetic sense, and to trust it. In spite of the fear that wanted him to jerk the trigger, a different sense read the unvoiced emotions of the native Disan. There was fear there, and hatred. Welling up around these was a strong desire not to commit violence, this time, to communicate instead. Brion felt and recognized all this in a fraction of a second. He had to act instantly to avoid a tragic happening. A jerk of his wrist threw the gun to one side.

As soon as it was gone he regretted its loss. He was gambling their lives on an ability he still was not sure of. The Disan had the tube to his mouth when the gun hit the ground. He held the pose, unmoving, thinking. Then he accepted Brion's action and thrust the tube back into his waistband.

"Do you have any water?" Brion asked, the guttural Disan words hurting his throat.

"I have water," the man said. He still didn't move. "Who are you? What are you doing here?"

"We're from offplanet. We had ... an accident. We want to go to the city. The water."

The Disan looked at the unconscious girl and made his decision. Over one shoulder he wore one of the green objects that Brion remembered from the solido. He pulled it off and the thing writhed slowly in his hands. It was alive – a green length a meter long, like a noduled section of a thick vine. One end flared out into a petal-like formation. The Disan took a hook-shaped object from his waist and thrust it into the petaled orifice. When he turned the hook in a quick motion the length of green writhed and curled around his arm. He pulled something small and dark out and threw it to the ground, extending the twisting green shape towards Brion. "Put your mouth to the end and drink," he said.

Lea needed the water more, but he drank first, suspicious of the living water source. A hollow below the writhing petals was filling with straw-colored water from the fibrous, reedy interior. He raised it to his mouth and drank. The water was hot and tasted swampy. Sudden sharp pains around his mouth made him jerk the thing away. Tiny glistening white barbs projected from the petals pink-tipped now with his blood. Brion swung towards the Disan angrily – and stopped when he looked at the other man's face. His mouth was surrounded by many small white scars.

"The *vaede* does not like to give up its water, but it always does," the man said.

Brion drank again, then put the vaede to Lea's mouth. She moaned without regaining consciousness, her lips seeking reflexively for the life-saving liquid. When she was satisfied Brion gently drew the barbs from her flesh and drank again. The Disan hunkered down on his heels and watched them expressionlessly. Brion handed back the vaede, then held some of the clothes so that Lea was in their shade. He settled to the same position as the native and looked closely at him.

Squatting immobile on his heels, the Disan appeared perfectly comfortable under the flaming sun. There was no trace of perspiration on his naked, browned skin. Long hair fell to his shoulders, and startlingly blue eyes stared back at Brion from deep-set sockets. The heavy kilt around his loins was the only garment he wore. Once more the vaede rested over his shoulder, still stirring unhappily. Around his waist was the same collection of leather, stone and brass objects that had been in the solido. Two of them now had meaning to Brion: the tube-and-mouthpiece, a blowgun of some kind; and the specially shaped hook for opening the vaede. He wondered if the other strangely formed things had equally practical functions. If you accepted them as artifacts with a purpose – not barbaric decorations – you had to accept their owner as something more than the crude savage he resembled.

"My name is Brion. And you – "

"You may not have my name. Why are you here? To kill my people?"

Brion forced away the memory of last night. Killing was just what he had done. Some expectancy in the man's manner, some sensed feeling of hope prompted Brion to speak the truth.

"I'm here to stop your people from being killed. I believe in the end of the war."

"Prove it."

"Take me to the Cultural Relationships Foundations in the city and I'll prove it. I can do nothing here in the desert. Except die."

For the first time there was emotion on the Disan's face. He frowned and muttered something to himself. There was a fine beading of sweat above his eyebrows now as he fought an internal battle. Coming to a decision, he rose, and Brion stood too.

"Come with me. I'll take you to Hovedstad. But first you will tell me – are you from Nyjord?"

"No."

The nameless Disan merely grunted and turned away. Brion shouldered Lea's unconscious body and followed him. They walked for two hours, the Disan setting a cruel pace, before they reached a wasteland of jumbled rock. The native pointed to the highest tower of sand-eroded stone. "Wait near this," he said. "Someone will come for you." He watched while Brion placed the girl's still body in the shade, and passed over the vaede for the last time. Just before leaving he turned back, hesitating.

"My name is ... Ulv," he said. Then he was gone.

Brion did what he could to make Lea comfortable, but it was very little. If she didn't get medical attention soon she would be dead. Dehydration and shock were uniting to destroy her.

Just before sunset he heard clanking, and the throbbing whine of a sand car's engine coming from the west.

# VIII

With each second the noise grew louder, coming their way. The tracks squeaked as the car turned around the rock spire, obviously seeking them out. A large carrier, big as a truck, it stopped before them in a cloud of its own dust and the driver kicked the door open.

"Get in here – and fast!" the man shouted. "You're letting in all the heat." He gunned the engine, ready to kick in the gears, and looked at them irritatedly.

Ignoring the driver's nervous instructions, Brion carefully placed Lea on the rear seat before he pulled the door shut. The car surged forward instantly, a blast of icy air pouring from the air-cooling vents. It wasn't cold in the vehicle – but the temperature was at least forty degrees lower than the outer air. Brion covered Lea with all their extra clothing to prevent any further shock to her system. The driver, hunched over the wheel and driving with an intense speed, hadn't said a word to them since they had entered.

Brion looked up as another man stepped from the engine compartment in the rear of the car. He was thin, harried-looking. And he was pointing a gun.

"Who are you?" he said, without a trace of warmth in his voice.

It was a strange reception, but Brion was beginning to realize that Dis was a strange planet. The other man chewed at his lip nervously while Brion sat, relaxed and unmoving. He didn't want to startle him into pulling the trigger, and he kept his voice pitched low as he answered.

"My name is Brandd. We landed from space two nights ago and have been walking in the desert ever since. Now don't get excited and shoot the gun when I tell you this – but both Vion and Ihjel are dead."

The man with the gun gasped, his eyes widened. The driver threw a single frightened look over his shoulder, then turned quickly back to the wheel. Brion's probe had hit its mark. If these men weren't from the Cultural Relationships Foundation they at least knew a lot about it. It seemed safe to assume they were C.R.F. men.

"When they were shot the girl and I escaped. We were trying to reach the city and contact you. You are from the Foundation, aren't you?"

"Yes. Of course," the man said, lowering the gun. He stared glassy-eyed into space for a moment, nervously working his teeth against his lip. Startled at his own inattention, he raised the gun again.

"If you're Brandd, there's something I want to know." Rummaging in his breast pocket with his free hand, he brought out a yellow message form. He moved his lips as he reread the message. "Now answer me – if you can – what are the last three events in the ..." He took a quick look at the paper again. "... in the Twenties?"

"Chess finals, rifle prone position, and fencing playoffs. Why?"

The man grunted and slid the pistol back into its holder, satisfied. "I'm Faussel," he said, and waved the message at Brion. "This is Ihjel's last will and testament, relayed to us by the Nyjord blockade control. He thought he was going to die and he sure was right. Passed on his job to you. You're in charge. I was Mervv's second-in-command, until he was poisoned. I was supposed to work for Ihjel, and now I guess I'm yours. At least until tomorrow, when we'll have everything packed and get off this hell planet."

"What do you mean, tomorrow?" Brion asked. "It's three days to deadline and we still have a job to do."

Faussel had dropped heavily into one of the seats and he sprang to his feet again, clutching the seat back to keep his balance in the swaying car.

"Three days, three weeks, three minutes – what difference does it make?" His voice rose shrilly with each word, and he had to make a definite effort to master himself before he could go on. "Look. You don't know anything about this. You just arrived and that's your bad luck. My bad luck is being assigned to this death trap and watching the depraved and filthy things the natives do. And trying to be polite to them even when they are killing my friends, and those Nyjord bombers up there with their hands on the triggers. One of those bombardiers is going to start thinking about home and about the cobalt bombs down here and he's going to press that button, deadline or no deadline."

"Sit down, Faussel. Sit down and take a rest." There was sympathy in Brion's voice – but also the firmness of an order. Faussel swayed for a second longer, then collapsed. He sat with his cheek against the window, eyes closed. A pulse throbbed visibly in his temple and his lips worked. He had been under too much tension for too long a time.

This was the atmosphere that hung heavily in the air at the C.R.F. building when they arrived. Despair and defeat. The doctor was the only one who didn't share this mood as he bustled Lea off to the clinic with prompt efficiency. He obviously had enough patients to keep his mind occupied. With the others the feeling of depression was unmistakable. From the instant they had driven through the automatic garage door, Brion had swum in this miasma of defeat. It was omnipresent and hard to ignore.

As soon as he had eaten he went with Faussel into what was to have been Ihjel's office. Through the transparent walls he could see the staff packing the records, crating them for shipment. Faussel seemed less nervous now that he was no longer in command. Brion rejected any idea he had of letting the man know that he himself was only a novice in the foundation. He was going to need all the authority he could muster, since they would undoubtedly hate him for what he was going to do.

"Better take notes of this, Faussel, and have it typed. I'll sign it." The printed word always carried more weight. "All preparations for leaving are to be stopped at once. Records are to be returned to the files. We are going to stay here just as long as we have clearance from the Nyjorders. If this operation is unsuccessful we will all leave together when the time expires. We will take whatever personal baggage we can carry by hand; everything else stays here. Perhaps you don't realize we are here to save a planet – not file cabinets full of papers."

Out of the corner of his eye he saw Faussel flush with anger. "As soon as that is typed bring it back. And all the reports as to what has been accomplished on this project. That will be all for now."

Faussel stamped out, and a minute later Brion saw the shocked, angry looks from the workers in the outer office. Turning his back to them, he opened the drawers in the desk, one after another. The top drawer was empty, except for a sealed envelope. It was addressed to Winner Ihjel.

Brion looked at it thoughtfully, then ripped it open. The letter inside was handwritten.

*Ihjel:*

*I've had the official word that you are on the way to relieve me and I am forced to admit I feel only an intense satisfaction. You've had the experience on these outlaw planets and can get along with the odd types. I have been specializing in research for the last twenty years, and the only reason I was appointed planetary supervisor on Nyjord was because of the observation and application facilities. I'm the research type, not the office type; no one has ever denied that.*

*You're going to have trouble with the staff, so you had better realize that they are all compulsory volunteers. Half are clerical people from my staff. The others a mixed bag of whoever was close enough to be pulled in on this crash assignment. It developed so fast we never saw it coming. And I'm afraid we've done little or nothing to stop it. We can't get access to the natives here, not in the slightest. It's frightening! They don't fit! I've done Poisson Distributions on a dozen different factors and none of them can be equated. The Pareto Extrapolations don't work. Our field men can't even talk to the natives and two have been killed trying. The ruling class is unapproachable and the rest just keep their mouths shut and walk away.*

*I'm going to take a chance and try to talk to Lig-magte, perhaps I can make him see sense. I doubt if it will work and there is a chance he will try violence with me. The nobility here are very prone to violence. If I get back all right you won't see this note. Otherwise – good-by, Ihjel. Try to do a better job than I did.*

*Aston Mervv*

*P.S. There is a problem with the staff. They are supposed to be saviors, but without exception they all loathe the Disans. I'm afraid I do too.*

Brion ticked off the relevant points in the letter. He had to find some way of discovering what Pareto Extrapolations were – without uncovering his own lack of knowledge. The staff would vanish in five minutes if they knew how new he was at the job. Poisson Distribution made more sense. It was used in physics as the unchanging probability of an event that would be true at all times. Such as the numbers of particles that would be given off by a lump of radioactive matter during a short period. From the way Mervv used it in his letter it looked as if the societics people had found measurable applications in societies and groups. At least on other planets. None of the rules seemed to be working on Dis. Ihjel had admitted that, and Mervv's death had proven it. Brion wondered who this Lig-magte was who appeared to have killed Mervv.

A forged cough broke through Brion's concentration, and he realized that Faussel had been standing in front of his desk for some minutes. Brion looked up and mopped perspiration from his face.

"Your air conditioner seems to be out of order," Faussel said. "Should I have the mechanic look at it?"

"There's nothing wrong with the machine; I'm just adapting to Dis's climate. What else do you want, Faussel?"

The assistant had a doubting look that he didn't succeed in hiding. He also had trouble believing the literal truth. He placed the small stack of file folders on the desk.

"These are the reports to date, everything we have uncovered about the Disans. It's not very much; but considering the anti-social attitudes on this lousy world it is the best we could do." A sudden thought hit him, and his eyes narrowed slyly. "It can't be helped, but some of the staff have been wondering out loud about that native that contacted us. How did you get him to help you? We've never gotten to first base with these people, and as soon as you land you have one working for you. You can't stop people from thinking about it, you being a newcomer and a stranger. After all, it looks a little odd – " He broke off in midsentence as Brion looked at him in cold fury.

"I can't stop people from thinking about it – but I can stop them from talking. Our job is to contact the Disans and stop this suicidal war. I have done more in one day than you all have done since you arrived. I have accomplished this because I am better at my work than the rest of you. That is all the information any of you are going to receive. You are dismissed."

White with anger, Faussel turned on his heel and stamped out – to spread the word about what a slave-driver the new director was. They would then all hate him passionately, which was just the way he wanted it. He couldn't risk exposure as the tyro he was. And perhaps a new emotion, other than disgust and defeat, might jar them into a little action. They certainly couldn't do any worse than they had been doing.

It was a tremendous amount of responsibility. For the first time since setting foot on this barbaric planet Brion had time to stop and think. He was taking an awful lot upon himself. He knew nothing about this world, nor about the powers involved in the conflict. Here he sat pretending to be in charge of an organization he had first heard about only a few weeks earlier. It was a frightening situation. Should he slide out from under?

There was just one possible answer, and that was *no*. Until he found someone else who could do better, he seemed to be the one best suited for the job. And Ihjel's opinion had to count for something. Brion had felt the surety of the man's conviction that Brion was the only one who might possibly succeed in this difficult spot.

Let it go at that. If he had any qualms it would be best to put them behind him. Aside from everything else, there was a primary bit of loyalty involved. Ihjel had been an Anvharian and a Winner. Maybe it was a provincial attitude to hold in this big universe – Anvhar was certainly far enough away from here – but honor is very important to a man who must stand alone. He had a debt to Ihjel, and he was going to pay it off.

Once the decision had been made, he felt easier. There was an intercom on the desk in front of him and he leaned with a heavy thumb on the button labeled *Faussel*.

"Yes?" Even through the speaker the man's voice was cold with ill-concealed hatred.

"Who is Lig-magte? And did the former director ever return from seeing him?"

"Magte is a title that means roughly noble or lord. Lig-magte is the local overlord. He has an ugly stoneheap of a building just outside the city. He seems to be the mouthpiece for the group of magter that are pushing this idiotic war. As to your second question, I have to answer yes and no. We found Director Mervv's head outside the door next morning with all the skin gone. We knew who it was because the doctor identified the bridgework in his mouth. *Do you understand?*"

All pretense of control had vanished, and Faussel almost shrieked the last words. They were all close to cracking up, if he was any example. Brion broke in quickly.

"That will be all, Faussel. Just get word to the doctor that I would like to see him as soon as I can." He broke the connection and opened the first of the folders. By the time the doctor called he had skimmed the reports and was reading the relevant ones in greater detail. Putting on his warm coat, he went through the outer office.

The few workers still on duty turned their backs in frigid silence.

Doctor Stine had a pink and shiny bald head that rose above a thick black beard. Brion had liked him at once. Anyone with enough firmness of mind to keep a beard in this climate was a pleasant exception after what he had met so far.

"How's the new patient, Doctor?"

Stine combed his beard with stubby fingers before answering. "Diagnosis: heat-syncope. Prognosis: complete recovery. Condition fair, considering the dehydration and extensive sunburn. I've treated the burns, and a saline drip is taking care of the other. She just missed going into heat-shock. I have her under sedation now."

"I'd like to have her up and helping me tomorrow morning. Could she do this – with stimulants or drugs?"

"She could – but I don't like it. There might be side factors, perhaps long-standing debilitation. It's a chance."

"A chance we will have to take. In less than seventy hours this planet is due for destruction. In attempting to avert that tragedy I'm expendable, as is everyone else here. Agreed?"

The doctor grunted deep in his beard and looked Brion's immense frame up and down. "Agreed," he said, almost happily. "It is a distinct pleasure to see something besides black defeat around here. I'll go along with you."

"Well, you can help me right now. I checked the personnel roster and discovered that out of the twenty-eight people working here there isn't a physical scientist of any kind – other than yourself."

"A scruffy bunch of button-pushers and theoreticians. Not worth a damn for field work, the whole bunch of them!" The doctor toed the floor switch on a waste receptacle and spat into it with feeling.

"Then I'm going to depend on you for some straight answers," Brion said. "This is an un-standard operation, and the standard techniques just don't begin to make sense. Even Poisson Distributions and Pareto Extrapolations don't apply here." Stine nodded agreement and Brion relaxed a bit. He had just relieved himself of his entire knowledge of societics, and it had sounded authentic. "The more I look at it the more I believe that this is a physical problem, something to do with the exotic and massive adjustments the Disans have made to this hellish environment. Could this tie up in any way with their absolutely suicidal attitude towards the cobalt bombs?"

"Could it? Could it?" Dr. Stine paced the floor rapidly on his stocky legs, twining his fingers behind his back. "You are bloody well right it could. Someone is thinking at last and not just punching bloody numbers into a machine and sitting and scratching his behind while waiting for the screen to light up with the answers. Do you know how Disans exist?" Brion shook his head. "The fools here think it disgusting but I call it fascinating. They have found ways to join a symbiotic relationship with the life forms on this planet. Even a parasitic relationship. You must realize that living organisms will do anything to survive. Castaways at sea will drink their own urine in their need for water. Disgust at this is only the attitude of the overprotected who have never experienced extreme thirst or hunger. Well, here on Dis you have a planet of castaways."

Stine opened the door of the pharmacy. "This talk of thirst makes me dry." With economically efficient motions he poured grain alcohol into a beaker, thinned it with distilled water and flavored it with some crystals from a bottle. He filled two glasses and handed Brion one. It didn't taste bad at all.

"What do you mean by parasitic, Doctor? Aren't we all parasites of the lower life forms? Meat animals, vegetables and such?"

"No, no – you miss the point! I speak of parasitic in the exact meaning of the word. You must realize that to a biologist there is no real difference between parasitism, symbiosis, mutualism, biontergasy, commensalism – "

"Stop, stop!" Brion said. "Those are just meaningless sounds to me. If that is what makes this planet tick I'm beginning to see why the rest of the staff has that lost feeling."

"It is just a matter of degree of the same thing. Look. You have a kind of crustacean living in the lakes here, very much like an ordinary crab. It has large claws in which it holds anemones, tentacled sea animals with no power of motion. The crustacean waves these around to gather food, and eats the pieces they capture that are too big for them. This is biontergasy, two creatures living and working together, yet each capable of existing alone.

"Now, this same crustacean has a parasite living under its shell, a degenerated form of a snail that has lost all powers of movement. A true parasite that takes food from its host's body and gives nothing in return. Inside this snail's gut there is a protozoan that lives off the snail's ingested food. Yet this little organism is not a parasite, as you might think at first, but a symbiote. It takes food from the snail, but at the same time it secretes a chemical that aids the snail's digestion of the food. Do you get the picture? All these life forms exist in a complicated interdependence."

Brion frowned in concentration, sipping at the drink. "It's making some kind of sense now. Symbiosis, parasitism and all the rest are just ways of describing variations of the same basic process of living together. And there is probably a grading and shading between some of these that make the exact relationship hard to define."

"Precisely. Existence is so difficult on this world that the competing forms have almost died out. There are still a few left, preying off the others. It was the cooperating and interdependent life forms that really won out in the race for survival. I say life forms with intent. The creatures here are mostly a mixture of plant and animal, like the lichens you have elsewhere. The Disans have a creature they call a "vaede" that they use for water when traveling. It has rudimentary powers of motion from its animal part, yet uses photosynthesis and stores water like a plant. When the Disans drink from it the thing taps their blood streams for food elements."

"I know," Brion said wryly. "I drank from one. You can see my scars. I'm beginning to comprehend how the Disans fit into the physical pattern of their world, and I realize it must have all kinds of psychological effects on them. Do you think this has any effect on their social organization?"

"An important one. But maybe I'm making too many suppositions now. Perhaps your researchers upstairs can tell you better; after all, this is their field."

Brion had studied the reports on the social setup and not one word of them made sense. They were a solid maze of unknown symbols and cryptic charts. "Please continue, Doctor," he insisted. "The societics reports are valueless so far. There are factors missing. You are the only one I have talked to so far who can give me any intelligent reports or answers."

"All right then – be it on your own head. The way I see it, you've got no society here at all, just a bunch of rugged individualists. Each one for himself, getting nourishment from the other life forms of the planet. If they have a society, it is orientated towards the rest of the planetary life – instead of towards other human beings. Perhaps that's why your figures don't make sense. They are set up for the human societies. In their relations with each other, these people are completely different."

"What about the magter, the upper-class types who build castles and are causing all this trouble?"

"I have no explanation," Dr. Stine admitted. "My theories hold water and seem logical enough up to this point. But the magter are the exception, and I have no idea why. They are completely different from the rest of the Disans. Argumentative, blood-thirsty, looking for planetary conquest instead of peace. They aren't rulers, not in the real sense. They hold power because nobody else wants it. They grant mining concessions to offworlders because they are the only ones with a sense of property. Maybe I'm going out on a limb. But if you can find out *why* they are so different you may be onto the clue to our difficulties."

For the first time since his arrival Brion began to feel a touch of enthusiasm. Plus a sense of the remote possibility that there might even be a solution to the deadly problem. He drained his glass and stood up.

"I hope you'll wake your patient early, Doctor. You might be as interested in talking to her as I am. If what you told me is true, she could well be our key to the answer. She is Professor Lea Morees, and she is just out from Earth with degrees in exobiology and anthropology, and has a head stuffed with vital facts."

"Wonderful!" Stine said. "I shall take care of the head, not only because it is so pretty but because of its knowledge. Though we totter on the edge of atomic destruction I have a strange feeling of optimism – for the first time since I landed on this planet."

# IX

The guard inside the front entrance of the Foundation building jumped at the thunderous noise and reached for his gun. He dropped his hand sheepishly when he realized it was only a sneeze – though a gargantuan one. Brion came up, sniffling, huddling down into his coat. "I'm going out before I catch pneumonia," he said. The guard saluted dumbly, and after checking his proximity detector screens he slipped out and the heavy portal thudded shut behind him. The street was still warm from the heat of the day and he sighed happily and opened his coat.

This was partly a reconnaissance trip – and partly a way of getting warmed up. There was little else he could do in the building; the staff had long since retired. He had slept for a half an hour, and had waked refreshed and ready to work. All of the reports he could understand had been read and reread until they were memorized. He could use the time now, while the rest of them were asleep, to get better acquainted with the main city of Dis.

As he walked the dark streets he realized how alien the Disan way of life was to everything he knew. This city – Hovedstad – literally meant "main place" in the native language. And that's all it was. It was only the presence of the offworlders that made it into a city. Building after building, standing deserted, bore the names of mining companies, traders, space transporters. None of them was occupied now. Some still had lights burning, switched on by automatic apparatus, others were as dark as the Disan structures. There weren't many of these native constructions and they seemed out of place among the rammed earth and prefab offworld buildings. Brion examined one that was dimly illuminated by the light on the corner of VEGAN SMELTERS, LTD.

It consisted of a single large room, resting right on the ground. There were no windows, and the whole thing appeared to have been constructed of some sort of woven material plastered with stone-hard mud. Nothing was blocking the door and he was thinking seriously of going in when he became aware that he was being followed.

It was only a slight noise, almost lost in the night. Normally it would never have been noticed, but tonight Brion was listening with his entire body. Someone was behind him, swallowed up in the pools of darkness. Brion shrank back against the wall. There was very little chance this could be anyone but a Disan. He had a sudden memory of Mervv's severed head as it had been discovered outside the door.

Ihjel had helped him train his empathetic sense and he reached out with it. It was difficult working in the dark; he could be sure of nothing. Was he getting a reaction – or just wishing for one? Why did it have a ring of familiarity to it? A sudden idea struck him.

"Ulv," he said, very softly. "This is Brion." He crouched, ready for any attack.

"I know," a voice said softly in the night. "Do not talk. Walk in the direction you were going before."

Asking questions now would accomplish nothing. Brion turned instantly and did as he was bidden. The buildings grew further apart until he realized from the sand underfoot that he was back in the planet-wide desert. It could be a trap – he hadn't recognized the voice behind the whisper – yet he had to take this chance. A darker shape appeared in the dark night near him, and a burning hot hand touched his arm lightly.

"I will walk ahead. Follow close behind me." The words were louder and this time Brion recognized the voice.

Without waiting for an answer, Ulv turned and his dimly seen shape vanished into the darkness. Brion moved swiftly after him, until they walked side by side over the rolling hills of sand. The sand merged into hard-baked ground, became cracked and scarred with rock-filled gullies. They followed a deepening gulley that grew into a good-sized ravine. When they turned an angle of the ravine Brion saw a weak yellow light coming from an opening in the hard dirt wall.

Ulv dropped on all fours and vanished through the shoulder-wide hole. Brion followed him, trying to ignore the growing tension and unease he felt. Crawling like this, head down, he was terribly vulnerable. He tried to shrug off the feeling, mentally blaming it on tense nerves.

The tunnel was short and opened into a larger chamber. A

sudden scuffle of feet sounded at the same instant that a wave of empathetic hatred struck him. It took vital seconds to fight his way out of the trapping tunnel, to roll clear and bring his gun up. During those seconds he should have died. The Disan poised above him had the short-handled stone hammer raised to strike a skull-crushing blow.

Ulv was clutching the man's wrist, fighting silently to keep the hammer from falling. Neither combatant said a word, the rasp of their calloused feet on the sand the only sound. Brion backed away from the struggling men, his gun centered on the stranger. The Disan followed him with burning eyes, and dropped the hammer as soon as it was obvious the attack had failed.

"Why did you bring him here?" he growled at Ulv. "Why didn't you kill him?"

"He is here so we can listen to what he says, Gebk. He is the one I told you of, that I found in the desert."

"We listen to what he says and then we kill him," Gebk said with a mirthless grin. The remark wasn't meant to be humorous, but was made in all seriousness. Brion recognized this and knew that there was no danger for the present moment. He slid the gun away, and for the first time looked around the chamber.

It was domed in shape and was still hot from the heat of the day. Ulv took off the length of cloth he had wrapped around his body against the chill, and refolded it as a kilt, strapping it on under his belt artifacts. He grunted something unintelligible and when a muttered answer came, Brion for the first time became aware of the woman and the child.

The two sat against the far wall, squatting on either side of a heap of fibrous plants. Both were nude, clothed only in the matted hair that fell below their shoulders. The belt of strange tools could not be classified as clothing. Even the child wore a tiny replica of her mother's. Putting down a length of plant she had been chewing, the woman shuffled over to the tiny fire that illuminated the room. A clay pot stood over it, and from this she ladled three bowls of food for the men. It smelled atrocious, and Brion tried not to taste or smell the sickening mixture while he ate it. He used his fingers, as did the other men, and did not talk while he ate. There was no way to tell if the silence was ritual or habit. It gave him a chance for a closer look at the Disan way of living.

The cave was obviously hand-made; tool marks could be

clearly seen in the hard clay of the walls, except in the portion opposite the entrance. This was covered with a network of roots, rising out of the floor and vanishing into the roof of earth above. Perhaps this was the reason for the cave's existence. The thin roots had been carefully twisted and plaited together until they formed a single swollen root in the center, as thick as a man's arm. From this hung four of the vaedes: Ulv had placed his there before he sat down. The teeth must have instantly sunk in, for it hung unsupported – another link in the Disan life cycle. This appeared to be the source of the vaede's water that nourished the people.

Brion was aware of eyes upon him and turned and smiled at the little girl. She couldn't have been over six years old, but she was already a Disan in every way. She neither returned his smile nor changed her expression, unchildlike in its stolidity. Her hands and jaw never stopped as she worked on the lengths of fibrous plant her mother had placed before her. The child split them with a small tool and removed a pod of some kind. This was peeled – partially by scraping with a different tool, and partially by working between her teeth. It took long minutes to remove the tough rind; the results seemed scarcely worth it. A tiny wriggling object was finally disclosed which the girl instantly swallowed. She then began working on the next pod.

Ulv put down his clay bowl and belched. "I brought you to the city as I told you I would," he said. "Have you done as you said you would?"

"What did he promise?" Gebk asked.

"That he would stop the war. Have you stopped it?"

"I am trying to stop it," Brion said. "But it is not that easy. I'll need some help. It is your life that needs saving – yours and your families'. If you would help me – "

"What is the truth?" Ulv broke in savagely. "All I hear is difference, and there is no longer any way to tell truth. For as long as always we have done as the magter say. We bring them food and they give us the metal and sometimes water when we need it. As long as we do as they ask they do not kill us. They live the wrong way, but I have had bronze from them for my tools. They have told us that they are getting a world for us from the sky people, and that is good."

"It has always been known that the sky people are evil in every way, and only good can come from killing them," Gebk said.

Brion stared back at the two Disans and their obvious hatred. "Then why didn't you kill me, Ulv?" he asked. "That first time in the desert, or tonight when you stopped Gebk?"

"I could have. But there was something more important. What is the truth? Can we believe as we have always done? Or should we listen to this?"

He threw a small sheet of plastic to Brion, no bigger than the palm of his hand. A metal button was fastened to one corner of the wafer, and a simple drawing was imbedded in the wafer. Brion held it to the light and saw a picture of a man's hand squeezing the button between thumb and forefinger. It was a subminiaturized playback; mechanical pressure on the case provided enough current to play the recorded message. The plastic sheet vibrated, acting as a loudspeaker.

Though the voice was thin and scratchy, the words were clearly audible. It was an appeal for the Disan people not to listen to the magter. It explained that the magter had started a war that could have only one ending – the destruction of Dis. Only if the magter were thrown down and their weapons discovered could there be any hope.

"Are these words true?" Ulv asked.

"Yes," Brion said.

"They are perhaps true," Gebk said, "but there is nothing that we can do. I was with my brother when these word-things fell out of the sky and he listened to one and took it to the magter to ask them. They killed him, as he should have known they would do. The magter kill us if they know we listen to the words."

"And the words tell us we will die if we listen to the magter!" Ulv shouted, his voice cracking. Not with fear, but with frustration at the attempt to reconcile two opposite points of view. Up until this time his world had consisted of black and white values, with very few shadings of difference in between.

"There are things you can do that will stop the war without hurting yourself or the magter," Brion said, searching for a way to enlist their aid.

"Tell us," Ulv grunted.

"There would be no war if the magter could be contacted, made to listen to reason. They are killing you all. You could tell me how to talk to the magter, how I could understand them – "

"No one can talk to the magter," the woman broke in. "If you say something different they will kill you as they killed Gebk's brother. So they are easy to understand. That is the way they are. They do not change." She put the length of plant she had been softening for the child back into her mouth. Her lips were deeply grooved and scarred from a lifetime of this work, her teeth at the sides worn almost to the bone.

"Mor is right," Ulv said. "You do not talk to magter. What else is there to do?"

Brion looked at the two men before he spoke, and shifted his weight. The motion brought his fingertips just a few inches from his gun. "The magter have bombs that will destroy Nyjord – this is the next planet, a star in your sky. If I can find where the bombs are, I will have them taken away and there will be no war."

"You want to aid the devils in the sky against our own people!" Gebk shouted, half rising. Ulv pulled him back to the ground, but there was no more warmth in his voice as he spoke.

"You are asking too much. You will leave now."

"Will you help me, though? Will you help stop the war?" Brion asked, aware he had gone too far, but unable to stop. Their anger was making them forget the reasons for his being there.

"You ask too much," Ulv said again. "Go back now. We will talk about it."

"Will I see you again? How can I reach you?"

"We will find you if we wish to talk to you," was all Ulv said. If they decided he was lying he would never see them again. There was nothing he could do about it.

"I have made up my mind," Gebk said, rising to his feet and drawing his cloth up until it covered his shoulders. "You are lying and this is all a lie of the sky people. If I see you again I will kill you." He stepped to the tunnel and was gone.

There was nothing more to be said. Brion went out next – checking carefully to be sure that Gebk really had left – and Ulv guided him to the spot where the lights of Hovedstad were visible. He did not speak during their return journey and vanished without a word. Brion shivered in the night chill of the air and wrapped his coat more tightly around himself. Depressed, he walked back towards the warmer streets of the city.

It was dawn when he reached the Foundation building; a new guard was at the front entrance. No amount of hammering or threats could convince the man to open until Faussel came down, yawning and blinking with sleep. He was starting some complaint when Brion cut him off curtly and ordered him to finish dressing and report for work at once. Still feeling elated, Brion hurried into his office and cursed the overly efficient character who had turned on his air conditioner to chill the room again. When he turned it off this time he removed enough vital parts to keep it out of order for the duration.

When Faussel came in he was still yawning behind his fist – obviously a low morning-sugar type. "Before you fall on your face, go out and get some coffee," Brion said. "Two cups. I'll have a cup too."

"That won't be necessary," Faussel said, drawing himself up stiffly. "I'll call the canteen if you wish some." He said it in the iciest tone he could manage this early in the morning.

In his enthusiasm Brion had forgotten the hate campaign he had directed against himself. "Suit yourself," he said shortly, getting back into the role. "But the next time you yawn there'll be a negative entry in your service record. If that's clear – you can brief me on this organization's visible relations with the Disans. How do they take us?"

Faussel choked and swallowed a yawn. "I believe they look on the C.R.F. people as some species of simpleton, sir. They hate all offworlders; memory of their desertion has been passed on verbally for generations. So by their one-to-one logic we should either hate back or go away. We stay instead. And give them food, water, medicine and artifacts. Because of this they let us remain on sufferance. I imagine they consider us do-gooder idiots, and as long as we cause no trouble they'll let us stay." He was struggling miserably to suppress a yawn, so Brion turned his back and gave him a chance to get it out.

"What about the Nyjorders? How much do they know of our work?" Brion looked out the window at dusty buildings, outlined in purple against the violent colors of the desert sunrise.

"Nyjord is a cooperating planet, and has full knowledge at all executive levels. They are giving us all the aid they can."

"Well, now is the time to ask for more. Can I contact the commander of the blockading fleet?"

"There is a scrambler connection right through to him. I'll set it up." Faussel bent over the desk and punched a number into the phone controls. The screen flowed with the black and white patterns of the scrambler.

"That's all, Faussel," Brion said. "I want privacy for this talk. What's the commander's name?"

"Professor Krafft – he's a physicist. They have no military men at all, so they called him in for the construction of the bombs and energy weapons. He's still in charge." Faussel yawned extravagantly as he went out the door.

The Professor-Commander was very old, with wispy grey hair and a network of wrinkles surrounding his eyes. His image shimmered, then cleared as the scrambler units aligned.

"You must be Brion Brandd," he said. "I have to tell you how sorry we all are that your friend Ihjel and the two others – had to die, after coming so far to help us. I'm sure you are very happy to have had a friend like that."

"Why ... yes, of course," Brion said, reaching for the scattered fragments of his thought processes. It took an effort to remember the first conflict, now that he was worrying about the death of a planet. "It's very kind of you to mention it. But I would like to find out a few things from you, if I could."

"Anything at all; we are at your disposal. Before we begin, though, I shall pass on the thanks of our council for your aid in joining us. Even if we are eventually forced to drop the bombs, we shall never forget that your organization did everything possible to avert the disaster."

Once again Brion was caught off balance. For an instant he wondered if Krafft was being insincere, then recognized the baseness of this thought. The completeness of the man's humanity was obvious and compelling. The thought passed through Brion's mind that now he had an additional reason for wanting the war ended without destruction on either side. He very much wanted to visit Nyjord and see these people on their home grounds.

Professor Krafft waited, patiently and silently, while Brion pulled his thoughts together and answered. "I still hope that this thing can be stopped in time. That's what I wanted to talk to you about. I want to see Lig-magte and I thought it would be better if I had a legitimate reason. Are you in contact with him?"

Krafft shook his head. "No, not really in contact. When this trouble started I sent him a transceiver so we could talk directly. But he has delivered his ultimatum, speaking for the magter. The only terms he will hear are unconditional surrender. His receiver is on, but he has said that is the only message he will answer."

"Not much chance of him ever being told that," Brion said.

"There was – at one time. I hope you realize, Brion, that the decision to bomb Dis was not easily arrived at. A great many people – myself included – voted for unconditional surrender. We lost the vote by a very small margin."

Brion was getting used to these philosophical body blows and he rolled with the punches now. "Are there any of your people left on this planet? Or do you have any troops I can call on for help? This is still a remote possibility, but if I do find out where the bombs or the launchers are, a surprise raid would knock them out."

"We have no people left in Hovedstad now – all the ones who weren't evacuated were killed. But there are commando teams standing by here to make a landing if the weapons are detected. The Disans must depend on secrecy to protect their armament, since we have both the manpower and the technology to reach any objective. We also have technicians and other volunteers looking for the weapon sites. They have not been successful as yet, and most of them were killed soon after landing."

Krafft hesitated for a moment. "There is another group you should know about; you will need all the factors. Some of our people are in the desert outside of Hovedstad. We do not officially approve of them, though they have a good deal of popular support. They are mostly young men, operating as raiders, killing and destroying with very little compunction. They are attempting to uncover the weapons by sheer strength of arms."

This was the best news yet. Brion controlled his voice and kept his expression calm when he spoke. "I don't know how far I can stretch your cooperation – but could you possibly tell me how to get in touch with them?"

Kraft allowed himself a small smile. "I'll give you the wave length on which you can reach their radio. They call themselves the 'Nyjord army.' When you talk to them you can do me a favor. Pass on a message. Just to prove things aren't bad enough, they've become a little worse. One of our technical crews has detected jump-space energy transmissions in the planetary crust. The Disans are apparently testing their projector, sooner than we had estimated. Our deadline has been revised by one day. I'm afraid there are only two days left before you must evacuate." His eyes were large with compassion. "I'm sorry. I know this will make your job that much harder."

Brion didn't want to think about the loss of a full day from his already close deadline. "Have you told the Disans this yet?"

"No," Krafft told him. "The decision was reached a few minutes before your call. It is going on the radio to Lig-magte now."

"Can you cancel the transmission and let me take the message in person?"

"I can do that." Krafft thought for a moment. "But it would surely mean your death at their hands. They have no hesitation in killing any of our people. I would prefer to send it by radio."

"If you do that you will be interfering with my plans, and perhaps destroying them under the guise of saving my life. Isn't my life my own – to dispose of as I will?"

For the first time Professor Krafft was upset. "I'm sorry, terribly sorry. I'm letting my concern and worry wash over into my public affairs. Of course you may do as you please; I could never think of stopping you." He turned and said something inaudible offscreen. "The call is cancelled. The responsibility is yours. All our wishes for success go with you. End of transmission."

"End of transmission," Brion said, and the screen went dark.

"Faussel!" he shouted into the intercom. "Get me the best and fastest sand car we have, a driver who knows his way around, and two men who can handle a gun and know how to take orders. We're going to get some positive action at last."

# X

"**It**'s suicide," the taller guard grumbled.

"Mine, not yours, so don't worry about it," Brion barked at him. "Your job is to remember your orders and keep them straight. Now – let's hear them again."

The guard rolled his eyes up in silent rebellion and repeated in a toneless voice: "We stay here in the car and keep the motor running while you go inside the stone pile there. We don't let anybody in the car and we try and keep them clear of the car – short of shooting them, that is. We don't come in, no matter what happens or what it looks like, but wait for you here. Unless you call on the radio, in which case we come in with the automatics going and shoot the place up, and it doesn't matter who we hit. This will be done only as a last resort."

"See if you can't arrange that last resort thing," the other guard said, patting the heavy blue barrel of his weapon.

"I meant that *last* resort," Brion said angrily. "If any guns go off without my permission you will pay for it, and pay with your necks. I want that clearly understood. You are here as a rear guard and a base for me to get back to. This is my operation and mine alone – unless I call you in. Understood?"

He waited until all three men had nodded in agreement, then checked the charge on his gun – it was fully loaded. It would be foolish to go in unarmed, but he had to. One gun wouldn't save him. He put it aside. The button radio on his collar was working and had a strong enough signal to get through any number of walls. He took off his coat, threw open the door and stepped out into the searing brilliance of the Disan noon.

There was only the desert silence, broken by the steady throb of the car's motor behind him. Stretching away to the horizon in every direction was the eternal desert of sand. The keep stood nearby, solitary, a massive pile of black rock. Brion plodded closer, watching for any motion from the walls. Nothing stirred. The high-walled, irregularly shaped construction sat in a ponderous silence. Brion was sweating now, only partially from the heat.

He circled the thing, looking for a gate. There wasn't one at ground level. A slanting cleft in the stone could be climbed easily, but it seemed incredible that this might be the only entrance. A complete circuit proved that it was. Brion looked unhappily at the slanting and broken ramp, then cupped his hands and shouted loudly.

"I'm coming up. Your radio doesn't work any more. I'm bringing the message from Nyjord that you have been waiting to hear." This was a slight bending of the truth without fracturing it. There was no answer – just the hiss of wind-blown sand against the rock and the mutter of the car in the background. He started to climb.

The rock underfoot was crumbling and he had to watch where he put his feet. At the same time he fought a constant impulse to look up, watching for anything falling from above. Nothing happened. When he reached the top of the wall he was breathing hard; sweat moistened his body. There was still no one in sight. He stood on an unevenly shaped wall that appeared to circle the building. Instead of having a courtyard inside it, the wall was the outer face of the structure, the domed roof rising from it. At varying intervals dark openings gave access to the interior. When Brion looked down, the sand car was just a dun-colored bump in the desert, already far behind him.

Stooping, he went through the nearest door. There was still no one in sight. The room inside was something out of a madman's funhouse. It was higher than it was wide, irregular in shape, and more like a hallway than a room. At one end it merged into an incline that became a stairwell. At the other it ended in a hole that vanished in darkness below. Light of sorts filtered in through slots and holes drilled into the thick stone wall. Everything was built of the same crumble-textured but strong rock. Brion took the stairs. After a number of blind passages and wrong turns he saw a stronger light ahead, and went on. There was food, metal, even artifacts of the unusual Disan design in the different rooms he passed through. Yet no people. The light ahead grew stronger, and the last passageway opened and swelled out until it led into the large central chamber.

This was the heart of the strange structure. All the rooms, passageways and halls existed just to give form to this gigantic chamber. The walls rose sharply, the room being circular in cross section and growing narrower towards the top. It was a truncated cone, since there was no ceiling; a hot blue disk of sky cast light on the floor below.

On the floor stood a knot of men who stared at Brion.

Out of the corner of his eyes, and with the very periphery of his consciousness, he was aware of the rest of the room – barrels, stores, machinery, a radio transceiver, various bundles and heaps that made no sense at first glance. There was no time to look closer. Every fraction of his attention was focused on the muffled and hooded men.

He had found the enemy.

Everything that had happened to him so far on Dis had been preparation for this moment. The attack in the desert, the escape, the dreadful heat of sun and sand. All this had tempered and prepared him. It had been nothing in itself. Now the battle would begin in earnest.

None of this was conscious in his mind. His fighter's reflexes bent his shoulders, curved his hands before him as he walked softly in balance, ready to spring in any direction. Yet none of this was really necessary. All the danger so far was nonphysical. When he did give conscious thought to the situation he stopped, startled. What was wrong here? None of the men had moved or made a sound. How could he even know they were men? They were so muffled and wrapped in cloth that only their eyes were exposed.

No doubt, however, existed in Brion's mind. In spite of muffled cloth and silence, he knew them for what they were. The eyes were empty of expression and unmoving, yet were filled with the same negative emptiness as those of a bird of prey. They could look on life, death, and the rending of flesh with the same lack of interest and compassion. All this Brion knew in an instant of time, without words being spoken. Between the time he lifted one foot and walked a step he understood what he had to face. There could be no doubt, not to an empathetic.

From the group of silent men poured a frost-white wave of unemotion. An empathetic shares what other men feel. He gets his knowledge of their reaction by sensing lightly their emotions, the surges of interest, hate, love, fear, desire, the sweep of large and small sensations that accompany all thought and action. The empathetic is always aware of this constant and silent surge, whether he makes the effort to understand it or not. He is like a man glancing across the open pages of a tableful of books. He can see that the type, words, paragraphs, thoughts are there, even without focusing his attention to understand any of it.

Then how does the man feel when he glances at the open books and sees only blank pages? The books are there – the words are not. He turns the pages of one, of the others, flipping the pages, searching for meaning. There is no meaning. All of the pages are blank.

This was the way in which the magter were blank, without emotions. There was a barely sensed surge and return that must have been neural impulses on a basic level – the automatic adjustments of nerve and muscle that keep an organism alive. Nothing more. Brion reached for other sensations, but there was nothing there to grasp. Either these men were without emotions, or they were able to block them from his detection; it was impossible to tell which.

Very little time had passed while Brion made these discoveries. The knot of men still looked at him, silent and unmoving. They weren't expectant, their attitude could not have been called one of interest. But he had come to them and now they waited to find out why. Any questions or statements they spoke would be superfluous, so they didn't speak. The responsibility was his.

"I have come to talk with Lig-magte. Who is he?" Brion didn't like the tiny sound his voice made in the immense room.

One of the men gave a slight motion to draw attention to himself. None of the others moved. They still waited.

"I have a message for you," Brion said, speaking slowly to fill the silence of the room and the emptiness of his thoughts. This had to be handled right. But what was right? "I'm from the Foundation in the city, as you undoubtedly know. I've been talking to the people of Nyjord. They have a message for you."

The silence grew longer. Brion had no intention of making this a monologue. He needed facts to operate, to form an opinion. Looking at the silent forms was telling him nothing. Time stretched taut, and finally Lig-magte spoke.

"The Nyjorders are going to surrender."

It was an impossibly strange sentence. Brion had never realized before how much of the content of speech was made up of emotion. If the man had given it a positive emphasis, perhaps said it with enthusiasm, it would have meant, "Success! The enemy is going to surrender!" This wasn't the meaning.

With a rising inflection on the end it would have been a question. "Are they going to surrender?" It was neither of these. The sentence carried no other message than that contained in the simplest meanings of the separate words. It had intellectual connotations, but these could only be gained from past knowledge, not from the sound of the words. There was only one message they were prepared to receive from Nyjord. Therefore Brion was bringing the message. If that was not the message Brion was bringing the men here were not interested.

This was the vital fact. If they were not interested he could have no further value to them. Since he came from the enemy, he was the enemy. Therefore he would be killed. Because this was vital to his existence, Brion took the time to follow the thought through. It made logical sense – and logic was all he could depend on now. He could be talking to robots or alien creatures, for all the human response he was receiving.

"You can't win this war – all you can do is hurry your own deaths." He said this with as much conviction as he could, realizing at the same time that it was wasted effort. No flicker of response stirred in the men before him. "The Nyjorders know you have the cobalt bombs, and they have detected your jump-space projector. They can't take any more chances. They have pushed the deadline closer by an entire day. There are one and a half days left before the bombs fall and you are all destroyed. Do you realize what that means – "

"Is that the message?" Lig-magte asked.

"Yes," Brion said.

Two things saved his life then. He had guessed what would happen as soon as they had his message, though he hadn't been sure. But even the suspicion had put him on his guard. This, combined with the reflexes of a Winner of the Twenties, was barely enough to enable him to survive.

From frozen mobility Lig-magte had catapulted into headlong attack. As he leaped forward he drew a curved, double-edged blade from under his robes. It plunged unerringly through the spot where Brion's body had been an instant before.

There had been no time to tense his muscles and jump, just the space of time to relax them and fall to one side. His reasoning mind joined the battle as he hit the floor. Lig-magte plunged by him, turning and bringing the knife down at the same time. Brion's foot lashed out and caught the other man's leg, sending him sprawling.

They were both on their feet at the same instant, facing each other. Brion now had his hands clasped before him in the unarmed man's best defense against a knife, the two arms protecting the body, the two hands joined to beat aside the knife arm from whichever direction it came. The Disan hunched low, flipped the knife quickly from hand to hand, then thrust it again at Brion's midriff.

Only by the merest fractional margin did Brion evade the attack for the second time. Lig-magte fought with utter violence. Every action was as intense as possible, deadly and thorough. There could be only one end to this unequal contest if Brion stayed on the defensive. The man with the knife had to win.

With the next charge Brion changed tactics. He leaped inside the thrust, clutching for the knife arm. A burning slice of pain cut across his arm, then his fingers clutched the tendoned wrist. They clamped down hard, grinding shut, compressing with the tightening intensity of a closing vise.

It was all he could do simply to hold on. There was no science in it, just his greater strength from exercise and existence on a heavier planet. All of this strength went to his clutching hand, because he held his own life in that hand, forcing away the knife that wanted to terminate it forever. Nothing else mattered – neither the frightening force of the knees that thudded into his body nor the hooked fingers that reached for his eyes to tear them out. He protected his face as well as he could, while the nails tore furrows through his flesh and the cut on his arm bled freely. These were only minor things to be endured. His life depended on the grasp of the fingers of his right hand.

There was a sudden immobility as Brion succeeded in clutching Lig-magte's other arm. It was a good grip, and he could hold the arm immobilized. They had reached stasis, standing knee to knee, their faces only a few inches apart. The muffling cloth had fallen from the Disan's face during the struggle, and empty, frigid eyes stared into Brion's. No flicker of emotion crossed the harsh planes of the other man's face. A great puckered white scar covered one cheek and pulled up a corner of the mouth in a cheerless grimace. It was false; there was still no expression here, even when the pain must be growing more intense.

Brion was winning – if none of the watchers broke the impasse. His greater weight and strength counted now. The Disan would have to drop the knife before his arm was dislocated at the shoulder. He didn't do it. With sudden horror, Brion realized that he wasn't going to drop it – no matter what happened.

A dull, hideous snap jerked through the Disan's body and the arm hung limp and dead. No expression crossed the man's face. The knife was still locked in the fingers of the paralyzed hand. With his other hand Lig-magte reached across and started to pry the blade loose, ready to continue the battle one-handed. Brion raised his foot and kicked the knife free, sending it spinning across the room.

Lig-magte made a fist of his good hand and crashed it into Brion's groin. He was still fighting, as if nothing had changed. Brion backed slowly away from the man. "Stop it," he said. "You can't win now. It's impossible." He called to the other men who were watching the unequal battle with expressionless immobility. No one answered him.

With a terrible sinking sensation Brion then realized what would happen and what he had to do. Lig-magte was as heedless of his own life as he was of the life of his planet. He would press the attack no matter what damage was done to him. Brion had an insane vision of him breaking the man's other arm, fracturing both his legs, and the limbless broken creature still coming forward. Crawling, rolling, teeth bared, since they were the only remaining weapon.

There was only one way to end it. Brion feinted and the Lig-magte's arm moved clear of his body. The engulfing cloth was thin and through it Brion could see the outlines of the Disan's abdomen and rib cage, the clear location of the great nerve ganglion.

It was the death blow of karate. Brion had never used it on a man. In practice he had broken heavy boards, splintering them instantly with the short, precise stroke. The stiffened hand moving forward in a sudden surge, all the weight and energy of his body concentrated in his joined fingertips. Plunging deep into the other's flesh.

Killing, not by accident or in sudden anger. Killing because this was the only way the battle could possibly end.

Like a ruined tower of flesh, the Disan crumpled and fell.

Dripping blood, exhausted, Brion stood over the body of Ligmagte and stared at the dead man's allies.

Death filled the room.

# XI

Facing the silent Disans, Brion's thoughts hurtled about in sweeping circles. There would be no more than an instant's tick of time before the magter avenged themselves bloodily and completely. He felt a fleeting regret for not having brought his gun, then abandoned the thought. There was no time for regrets – what could he do *now*?

The silent watchers hadn't attacked instantly, and Brion realized that they couldn't be positive yet that Lig-magte had been killed. Only Brion himself knew the deadliness of that blow. Their lack of knowledge might buy him a little more time.

"Lig-magte is unconscious, but he will revive quickly," Brion said, pointing at the huddled body. As the eyes turned automatically to follow his finger, he began walking slowly towards the exit. "I did not want to do this, but he forced me to, because he wouldn't listen to reason. Now I have something else to show you, something that I hoped it would not be necessary to reveal."

He was saying the first words that came into his head, trying to keep them distracted as long as possible. He must appear to be only going across the room, that was the feeling he must generate. There was even time to stop for a second and straighten his rumpled clothing and brush the sweat from his eyes. Talking easily, walking slowly towards the hall that led out of the chamber.

He was halfway there when the spell broke and the rush began. One of the magter knelt and touched the body, and shouted a single word:

"Dead!"

Brion hadn't waited for the official announcement. At the first movement of feet, he dived headlong for the shelter of the exit. There was a spatter of tiny missiles on the wall next to him and he had a brief glimpse of raised blowguns before the wall intervened. He went up the dimly lit stairs three at a time.

The pack was just behind him, voiceless and deadly. He could not gain on them – if anything, they were closing the distance as he pushed his already tired body to the utmost. There was no subtlety or trick he could use now, just straightforward flight back the way he had come. A single slip on the irregular steps and it would be all over.

There was someone ahead of him. If the woman had waited a few seconds more he would certainly have been killed; but instead of slashing at him as he went by the doorway, she made the mistake of rushing to the center of the stairs, the knife ready to impale him as he came up. Without slowing, Brion fell onto his hands and easily dodged under the blow. As he passed he twisted and seized her around the waist, picking her from the ground.

When her legs lifted from under her the woman screamed – the first human sound Brion had heard in this human anthill. His pursuers were just behind him, and he hurled the woman into them with all his strength. They fell in a tangle, and Brion used the precious seconds gained to reach the top of the building.

There must have been other stairs and exits, because one of the magter stood between Brion and the way down out of this trap – armed and ready to kill him if he tried to pass.

As he ran towards the executioner, Brion flicked on his collar radio and shouted into it. "I'm in trouble here. Can you – "

The guards in the car must have been waiting for this message. Before he had finished there was the thud of a high-velocity slug hitting flesh and the Disan spun and fell, blood soaking his shoulder. Brion leaped over him and headed for the ramp.

"The next one is me – hold your fire!" he called.

Both guards must have had their telescopic sights zeroed on the spot. They let Brion pass, then threw in a hail of semi-automatic fire that tore chunks from the stone and screamed away in noisy ricochets. Brion didn't try to see if anyone was braving this hail of covering fire; he concentrated his energies on making as quick and erratic a descent as he could. Above the sounds of the firing he heard the car motor howl as it leaped forward. With their careful aim spoiled, the gunners switched to full automatic and unleashed a hailstorm of flying metal that bracketed the top of the tower.

"Cease ... firing!" Brion gasped into the radio as he ran. The driver was good, and timed his arrival with exactitude. The car reached the base of the tower at the same instant Brion did, and he burst through the door while it was still moving. No orders were necessary. He fell headlong onto a seat as the car swung in a dust-raising turn and ground into high gear, back to the city.

Reaching over carefully, the tall guard gently extracted a bit of pointed wood and fluff from a fold of Brion's pants. He cracked open the car door, and just as delicately threw it out.

"I knew that thing didn't touch you," he said, "since you are still among the living. They've got a poison on those blowgun darts that takes all of twelve seconds to work. Lucky."

Lucky! Brion was beginning to realize just how lucky he was to be out of the trap alive. And with information. Now that he knew more about the magter, he shuddered at his innocence in walking alone and unarmed into the tower. Skill had helped him survive – but better than average luck had been necessary. Curiosity had gotten him in, brashness and speed had taken him out. He was exhausted, battered and bloody – but cheerfully happy. The facts about the magter were arranging themselves into a theory that might explain their attempt at racial suicide. It just needed a little time to be put into shape.

A pain cut across his arm and he jumped, startled, pieces of his thoughts crashing into ruin around him. The gunner had cracked the first-aid box and was swabbing his arm with antiseptic. The knife wound was long, but not deep. Brion shivered while the bandage was going on, then quickly slipped into his coat. The air conditioner whined industriously, bringing down the temperature.

There was no attempt to follow the car. When the black tower had dropped over the horizon the guards relaxed, ran cleaning rods through their guns and compared marksmanship. All of their antagonism towards Brion was gone; they actually smiled at him. He had given them the first chance to shoot back since they had been on this planet.

The ride was uneventful, and Brion was scarcely aware of it. A theory was taking form in his mind. It was radical and startling – yet it seemed to be the only one that fitted the facts. He pushed at it from all sides, but if there were any holes he couldn't find them. What it needed was dispassionate proving or disproving. There was only one person on Dis who was qualified to do this.

Lea was working in the lab when he came in, bent over a low-power binocular microscope. Something small, limbless and throbbing was on the slide. She glanced up when she heard his footsteps, smiling warmly when she recognized him. Fatigue and pain had drawn her face; her skin, glistening with burn ointment, was chapped and peeling.

"I must look a wreck," she said, putting the back of her hand to her cheek. "Something like a well-oiled and lightly cooked piece of beef." She lowered her arm suddenly and took his hand in both of hers. Her palms were warm and slightly moist.

"Thank you, Brion," was all she could say. Her society on Earth was highly civilized and sophisticated, able to discuss any topic without emotion and without embarrassment. This was fine in most circumstances, but made it difficult to thank a person for saving your life. However you tried to phrase it, it came out sounding like a last-act speech from a historical play. There was no doubt, however, as to what she meant. Her eyes were large and dark, the pupils dilated by the drugs she had been given. They could not lie, nor could the emotions he sensed. He did not answer, just held her hand an instant longer.

"How do you feel," he asked, concerned. His conscience twinged as he remembered that he was the one who had ordered her out of bed and back to work today.

"I should be feeling terrible," she said, with an airy wave of her hand. "But I'm walking on top of the world. I'm so loaded with pain-killers and stimulants that I'm high as the moon. All the nerves to my feet feel turned off – it's like walking on two balls of fluff. Thanks for getting me out of that awful hospital and back to work."

Brion was suddenly sorry for having driven her from her sick bed.

"Don't be sorry!" Lea said, apparently reading his mind, but really seeing only his sudden ashamed expression. "I'm feeling no pain. Honestly. I feel a little light-headed and foggy at times, nothing more. And this is the job I came here to do. In fact ... well, it's almost impossible to tell you just how fascinating it all is! It was almost worth getting baked and parboiled for."

She swung back to the microscope, centering the specimen with a turn of the stage adjustment screw. "Poor Ihjel was right when he said this planet was exobiologically fascinating. This is a gastropod, a lot like *Odostomia*, but it has parasitical morphological changes so profound that – "

"There's something else I remember," Brion said, interrupting her enthusiastic lecture, only half of which he could understand. "Didn't Ihjel also hope that you would give some study to the natives as well as their environment? The problem is with the Disans – not with the local wild life."

"But I *am* studying them," Lea insisted. "The Disans have attained an incredibly advanced form of commensalism. Their lives are so intimately connected and integrated with the other life forms that they must be studied in relation to their environment. I doubt if they show as many external physical changes as little eating-foot *Odostomia* on the slide here, but there will surely be a number of psychological changes and adjustments that will crop up. One of these might be the explanation of their urge for planetary suicide."

"That may be true – but I don't think so," Brion said. "I went on a little expedition this morning and found something that has more immediate relevancy."

For the first time Lea became aware of his slightly battered condition. Her drug-grooved mind could only follow a single idea at a time and had over-looked the significance of the bandage and dirt.

"I've been visiting," Brion said, forestalling the question on her lips. "The magter are the ones who are responsible for causing the trouble, and I had to see them up close before I could make any decisions. It wasn't a very pleasant thing, but I found out what I wanted to know. They are different in every way from the normal Disans. I've compared them. I've talked to Ulv – the native who saved us in the desert – and I can understand him. He is not like us in many ways – he certainly couldn't be, living in this oven – but he is still undeniably human. He gave us drinking water when we needed it, then brought help. The magter, the upper-class lords of Dis, are the direct opposite. As cold-blooded and ruthless a bunch of murderers as you can possibly imagine. They tried to kill me when they met me, without reason. Their clothes, habits, dwellings, manners – everything about them differs from that of the normal Disan. More important, the magter are as coldly efficient and inhuman as a reptile. They have no emotions, no love, no hate, no anger, no fear – nothing. Each of them is a chilling bundle of thought processes and reactions, with all the emotions removed."

"Aren't you exaggerating?" Lea asked. "After all, you can't be sure. It might just be part of their training not to reveal any emotional state. Everyone must experience emotional states, whether they like it or not."

"That's my main point. Everyone does – except the magter. I can't go into all the details now, so you'll just have to take my word for it. Even at the point of death they have no fear or hatred. It may sound impossible, but it is true."

Lea tried to shake the knots from her drug-hazed mind. "I'm dull today," she said. "You'll have to excuse me. If these rulers had no emotional responses, that might explain their present suicidal position. But an explanation like this raises more new problems than it supplies answers to the old ones. How did they get this way! It doesn't seem humanly possible to be without emotions of some kind."

"Just my point. Not *humanly* possible. I think these ruling class Disans aren't human at all, like the other Disans. I think they are alien creatures – robots or androids – anything except men. I think they are living in disguise among the normal human dwellers."

At first Lea started to smile, then her feeling changed when she saw his face. "You are serious?" she asked.

"Never more so. I realize it must sound as if I've had my brains bounced around too much this morning. Yet this is the only idea I can come up with that fits all of the facts. Look at the evidence yourself. One simple thing stands out clearly, and must be considered first if any theory is to hold up. That is the magters' complete indifference to death – their own or anyone else's. Is that normal to mankind?"

"No – but I can find a couple of explanations that I would rather explore first, before dragging in an alien life form. There may have been a mutation or an inherited disease that has deformed or warped their minds."

"Wouldn't that be sort of self-eliminating?" Brion asked. "Anti-survival? People who die before puberty would find it a little difficult to pass on a mutation to their children. But let's not beat this one point to death – it's the totality of these people that I find so hard to accept. Any one thing might be explained away, but not the collection of them. What about their complete lack of emotion? Or their manner of dress and their secrecy in general? The ordinary Disan wears a cloth kilt, while the magter cover themselves as completely as possible. They stay in their black towers and never go out except in groups. Their dead are always removed so they can't be examined. In every way they act like a race apart – and I think they are."

"Granted for the moment that this outlandish idea might be true, how did they get here? And why doesn't anyone know about it besides them?"

"Easily enough explained," Brion insisted. "There are no written records on this planet. After the Breakdown, when the handful of survivors were just trying to exist here, the aliens could have landed and moved in. Any interference could have been wiped out. Once the population began to grow, the invaders found they could keep control by staying separate, so their alien difference wouldn't be noticed."

"Why should that bother them?" Lea asked. "If they are so indifferent to death, they can't have any strong thoughts on public opinion or alien body odor. Why would they bother with such a complex camouflage? And if they arrived from another planet, what has happened to the scientific ability that brought them here?"

"Peace," Brion said. "I don't know enough to be able even to guess at answers to half your questions. I'm just trying to fit a theory to the facts. And the facts are clear. The magter are so inhuman they would give me nightmares – if I were sleeping these days. What we need is more evidence."

"Then get it," Lea said with finality. "I'm not telling you to turn murderer – but you might try a bit of grave-digging. Give me a scalpel and one of your friends stretched out on a slab and I'll quickly tell you what he is or is not." She turned back to the microscope and bent over the eyepiece.

That was really the only way to hack the Gordian knot. Dis had only thirty-six more hours to live, so individual deaths shouldn't be of any concern. He had to find a dead magter, and if none was obtainable in the proper condition he had to get one of them by violence. For a planetary savior, he was personally doing in an awful lot of the citizenry.

He stood behind Lea, looking down at her thought fully while she worked. The back of her neck, lightly covered with gently curling hair, was turned toward him. With one of the about-face shifts the mind is capable of, his thoughts flipped from death to life, and he experienced a strong desire to caress this spot lightly, to feel the yielding texture of female flesh ....

Plunging his hands deep into his pockets, he walked quickly to the door. "Get some rest soon," he called to her. "I doubt if those bugs will give you the answer. I'm going now to see if I can get the full-sized specimen you want."

"The truth could be anywhere. I'll stay on these until you come back," she said, not looking up from the microscope.

Up under the roof was a well-equipped communications room. Brion had taken a quick look at it when he had first toured the building. The duty operator had earphones on – though only one of the phones covered an ear – and was monitoring through the bands. His shoeless feet were on the edge of the table, and he was eating a thick sandwich held in his free hand. His eyes bulged when he saw Brion in the doorway and he jumped into a flurry of action.

"Hold the pose," Brion told him; "it doesn't bother me. And if you make any sudden moves you are liable to break a phone, electrocute yourself, or choke to death. Just see if you can set the transceiver on this frequency for me." Brion wrote the number on a scratch pad and slid it over to the operator. It was the frequency Professor-Commander Krafft had given him for the radio of the illegal terrorists – the Nyjord army.

The operator plugged in a handset and gave it to Brion. "Circuit open," he mumbled around a mouthful of still unswallowed sandwich.

"This is Brandd, director of the C.R.F. Come in, please." He went on repeating this for more than ten minutes before he got an answer.

"*What do you want?*"

"I have a message of vital urgency for you – and I would also like your help. Do you want any more information on the radio?

"*No. Wait there – we'll get in touch with you after dark.*" The carrier wave went dead.

Thirty-five hours to the end of the world – and all he could do was wait.

# XII

On Brion's desk when he came in, were two neat piles of paper. As he sat down and reached for them he was conscious of an arctic coldness in the air, a frigid blast. It was coming from the air-conditioner grill, which was now covered by welded steel bars. The control unit was sealed shut. Someone was either being very funny or very efficient. Either way, it was cold. Brion kicked at the cover plate until it buckled, then bent it aside. After a careful look into the interior he disconnected one wire and shorted it to another. He was rewarded by a number of sputtering cracks and a quantity of smoke. The compressor moaned and expired.

Faussel was standing in the door with more papers, a shocked expression on his face. "What do you have there?" Brion asked.

Faussel managed to straighten out his face and brought the folders to the desk, arranging them on the piles already there. "These are the progress reports you asked for, from all units. Details to date, conclusions, suggestions, et cetera."

"And the other pile?" Brion pointed.

"Offplanet correspondence, commissary invoices, requisitions." He straightened the edges of the stack while he answered. "Daily reports, hospital log ...." His voice died away and stopped as Brion carefully pushed the stack off the edge of the desk into the wastebasket.

"In other words, red tape," Brion said. "Well, it's all filed."

One by one the progress reports followed the first stack into the basket, until the desk was clear. Nothing. It was just what he had expected. But there had always been the off chance that one of the specialists could come up with a new approach. They hadn't; they were all too busy specializing.

Outside the sky was darkening. The front entrance guard had been told to let in anyone who came asking for the director. There was nothing else Brion could do until the Nyjord rebels made contact. Irritation bit at him. At least Lea was doing something constructive; he could look in on her.

He opened the door to the lab with a feeling of pleasant

anticipation. It froze and shattered instantly. Her microscope was hooded and she was gone. *She's having dinner,* he thought, or – *she's in the hospital.* The hospital was on the floor below, and he went there first.

"Of course she's here!" Dr. Stine grumbled. "Where else should a girl in her condition be? She was out of bed long enough today. Tomorrow's the last day, and if you want to get any more work out of her before the deadline, you had better let her rest tonight. Better let the whole staff rest. I've been handing out tranquilizers like aspirin all day. They're falling apart."

"The world's falling apart. How is Lea doing?"

"Considering her shape, she's fine. Go in and see for yourself if you won't take my word for it. I have other patients to look at."

"Are you that worried, Doctor?"

"Of course I am! I'm just as prone to the weakness of the flesh as the rest of you. We're sitting on a ticking bomb and I don't like it. I'll do my job as long as it is necessary, but I'll also be damned glad to see the ships land to pull us out. The only skin that I really feel emotionally concerned about right now is my own. And if you want to be let in on a public secret – the rest of your staff feels the same way. So don't look forward to too much efficiency."

"I never did," Brion said to the retreating back.

Lea's room was dark, illuminated only by the light of Dis's moon slanting in through the window. Brion let himself in and closed the door behind him. Walking quietly, he went over to the bed. Lea was sleeping soundly, her breathing gentle and regular. A night's sleep now would do as much good as all the medication.

He should have gone then; instead, he sat down in the chair placed next to the head of the bed. The guards knew where he was – he could wait here just as well as any place else.

It was a stolen moment of peace on a world at the brink of destruction. He was grateful for it. Everything looked less harsh in the moonlight, and he rubbed some of the tension from his eyes. Lea's face was ironed smooth by the light, beautiful and young, a direct contrast to everything else on this poisonous world. Her hand was outside of the covers and he took it in his own, obeying a sudden impulse. Looking out of the window at the desert in the distance, he let the peace wash over him, forcing himself to forget for the moment that in one more day life would be stripped from this planet.

Later, when he looked back at Lea he saw that her eyes were open, though she hadn't moved. How long had she been awake? He jerked his hand away from hers, feeling suddenly guilty.

"Is the boss-man looking after the serfs, to see if they're fit for the treadmills in the morning?" she asked. It was the kind of remark she had used with such frequency in the ship, though it didn't sound quite as harsh now. And she was smiling. Yet it reminded him too well of her superior attitude towards rubes from the stellar sticks. Here he might be the director, but on ancient Earth he would be only one more gaping, lead-footed yokel.

"How do you feel?" he asked, realizing and hating the triteness of the words, even as he said them.

"Terrible. I'll be dead by morning. Reach me a piece of fruit from that bowl, will you? My mouth tastes like an old boot heel. I wonder how fresh fruit ever got here. Probably a gift to the working classes from the smiling planetary murderers on Nyjord."

She took the apple Brion gave her and bit into it. "Did you ever think of going to Earth?"

Brion was startled. This was too close to his own thoughts about planetary backgrounds. There couldn't possibly be a connection though. "Never," he told her. "Up until a few months ago I never even considered leaving Anvhar. The Twenties are such a big thing at home that it is hard to imagine that anything else exists while you are still taking part in them."

"Spare me the Twenties," she pleaded. "After listening to you and Ihjel, I know far more about them than I shall ever care to know. But what about Anvhar itself? Do you have big city-states as Earth does?"

"Nothing like that. For its size, it has a very small population. No big cities at all. I guess the largest centers of population are around the schools, packing plants, things like that."

"Any exobiologists there?" Lea asked, with a woman's eternal ability to make any general topic personal.

"At the universities, I suppose, though I wouldn't know for sure. And you must realize that when I say no big cities, I also mean no little cities. We aren't organized that way at all. I imagine the basic physical unit is the family and the circle of friends. Friends get important quickly, since the family breaks up when children are still relatively young. Something in the genes, I suppose – we all enjoy being alone. I suppose you might call it an inbred survival trait."

"Up to a point," she said, biting delicately into the apple. "Carry that sort of thing too far and you end up with no population at all. A certain amount of proximity is necessary for that."

"Of course it is. And there must be some form of recognized relationship or control – that or complete promiscuity. On Anvhar the emphasis is on personal responsibility, and that seems to take care of the problem. If we didn't have an adult way of looking at ... things, our kind of life would be impossible. Individuals are brought together either by accident or design, and with this proximity must be some certainty of relations...."

"You're losing me," Lea protested. "Either I'm still foggy from the dope, or you are suddenly unable to speak a word of less than four syllables. You know – whenever this happens with you, I get the distinct impression that you are trying to cover up something. For Occam's sake, be specific! Bring me together two of these hypothetical individuals and tell me what happens."

Brion took a deep breath. He was in over his head and far from shore. "Well – take a bachelor like myself. Since I like cross-country skiing I make my home in this big house our family has, right at the edge of the Broken Hills. In summer I looked after a drumtum herd, but after slaughtering my time was my own all winter. I did a lot of skiing, and used to work for the Twenties. Sometimes I would go visiting. Then again, people would drop in on me – houses are few and far between on Anvhar. We don't even have locks on our doors. You accept and give hospitality without qualification. Whoever comes. Male ... female ... in groups or just traveling alone...."

"I get the drift. Life must be dull for a single girl on your iceberg planet. She must surely have to stay home a lot."

"Only if she wants to. Otherwise she can go wherever she wishes and be welcomed as another individual. I suppose it is out of fashion in the rest of the galaxy – and would probably raise a big laugh on Earth – but a platonic, disinterested friendship between man and woman is an accepted thing on Anvhar."

"Sounds exceedingly dull. If you are all such cool and distant friends, how do babies get made?"

Brion felt his ears reddening, not sure if he was being teased or not. "The same damn way they get made any place else! But it's not just a reflexive process like a couple of rabbits that happen to meet under the same bush. It's the woman's choice to indicate if she is interested in marriage."

"Is marriage the only thing your women are interested in?"

"Marriage or ... anything else. That's up to the girl. We have a special problem on Anvhar – probably the same thing occurs on every planet where the human race has made a massive adaptation. Not all unions are fertile and there is always a large percentage of miscarriages. A large number of births are conceived by artificial insemination. Which is all right when you can't have babies normally. But most women have an emotional bias towards having their husband's children. And there is only one way to find out if this is possible."

Lea's eyes widened. "Are you suggesting that your girls see if a man can father children *before* considering marriage?"

"Of course. Otherwise Anvhar would have been depopulated centuries ago. Therefore the woman does the choosing. If she is interested in a man, she says so. If she is not interested, the man would never think of suggesting anything. It's a lot different from other planets, but so is our planet Anvhar. It works well for us, which is the only test that applies."

"Just about the opposite of Earth," Lea told him, dropping the apple core into a dish and carefully licking the tips of her fingers. "I guess you Anvharians would describe Earth as a planetary hotbed of sexuality. The reverse of your system, and going full blast all the time. There are far too many people there for comfort. Birth control came late and is still being fought – if you can possibly imagine that. There are just too many of the archaic religions still around, as well as crackbrained ideas that have been long entrenched in custom. The world's overcrowded. Men, women, children, a boiling mob wherever you look. And all of the physically mature ones seem to be involved in the Great Game of Love. The male is always the aggressor. Not physically – at least not often – and women take the most outrageous kinds of flattery for granted. At parties there are always a couple of hot breaths of passion fanning your neck. A girl has to keep her spike heels filed sharp."

"She has to *what*?"

"A figure of speech, Brion. Meaning you fight back all the time, if you don't want to be washed under by the flood."

"Sounds rather" – Brion weighed the word before he said it,

but could find none other suitable – "repellent."

"From your point of view, it would be. I'm afraid we get so used to it that we even take it for granted. Sociologically speaking ...." She stopped and looked at Brion's straight back and almost rigid posture. Her eyes widened and her mouth opened in an unspoken *oh* of sudden realization.

"I'm being a fool," she said. "You weren't speaking generally at all! You had a very specific subject in mind. Namely *me*!"

"Please, Lea, you must understand ...."

"But I do!" She laughed. "All the time I thought you were being a frigid and hard-hearted lump of ice, you were really being very sweet. Just playing the game in good old Anvharian style. Waiting for a sign from me. We'd still be playing by different rules if you hadn't had more sense than I, and finally realized that somewhere along the line we must have got our signals mixed. And I thought you were some kind of frosty offworld celibate." She let her hand go out and her fingers rustled through his hair. Something she had been wanting to do for a long time.

"I had to," he said, trying to ignore the light touch of her fingers. "Because I thought so much of you, I couldn't have done anything to insult you. Such as forcing my attentions on you. Until I began to worry where the insult would lie, since I knew nothing about your planet's mores."

"Well, you know now," she said very softly. "The men aggress. Now that I understand, I think I like your way better. But I'm still not sure of all the rules. Do I explain that yes, Brion, I like you so very much? You are more man, in one great big wide-shouldered lump, than I have ever met before. It's not quite the time or the place to discuss marriage, but I would certainly like – "

His arms were around her, holding her to him. Her hands clasped him and their lips sought each other's in the darkness.

"Gently ..." she whispered. "I bruise easily...."

# XIII

"He wouldn't come in, sir. Just hammered on the door and said, '*I'm here, tell Brandd.*'"

"Good enough," Brion said, fitting his gun in the holster and sliding the extra clips into his pocket. "I'm going out now, and I should return before dawn. Get one of the wheeled stretchers down here from the hospital. I'll want it waiting when I get back."

Outside, the street was darker than he remembered. Brion frowned and his hand moved towards his gun. Someone had put all the nearby lights out of commission. There was just enough illumination from the stars to enable him to make out the dark bulk of a sand car.

"Brion Brandd?" a voice spoke harshly from the car. "Get in."

The motor roared as soon as he had closed the door. Without lights the sand car churned a path through the city and out into the desert. Though the speed picked up, the driver still drove in the dark, feeling his way with a light touch on the controls. The ground rose, and when they reached the top of a mesa he killed the engine. Neither the driver nor Brion had spoken a word since they left.

A switch snapped and the instrument lights came on. In their dim glow Brion could just make out the other man's hawklike profile. When he moved, Brion saw that his figure was cruelly shortened. Either accident or a mutated gene had warped his spine, hunching him forward in eternally bent supplication. Warped bodies were rare – his was the first Brion had ever seen. He wondered what series of events had kept him from medical attention all his life. This might explain the bitterness and pain in the man's voice.

"Did the mighty brains on Nyjord bother to tell you that they have chopped another day off the deadline?" the man asked. "That this world is about to come to an end?"

"Yes, I know," Brion said. "That's why I'm asking your group for help. Our time is running out too fast."

The man didn't answer; he merely grunted and gave his full

attention to the radar pings and glowing screen. The electronic senses reached out as he made a check on all the search frequencies to see if they were being followed.

"Where are we going?" Brion asked.

"Out into the desert." The driver made a vague wave of his hand. "Headquarters of the army. Since the whole thing will be blown up in another day, I guess I can tell you it's the only camp we have. All the cars, men and weapons are based there. And Hys. He's the man in charge. Tomorrow it will be all gone – along with this cursed planet. What's your business with us?"

"Shouldn't I be telling Hys that?"

"Suit yourself." Satisfied with the instrument search, the driver kicked the car to life again and churned on across the desert. "But we're a volunteer army and we have no secrets from each other. Just from the fools at home who are going to kill this world." There was a bitterness in his words that he made no attempt to conceal. "They fought among themselves and put off a firm decision so long that now they are forced to commit murder."

"From what I had heard, I thought that it was the other way around. They call your Nyjord army terrorists."

"We are. Because we are an army and we're at war. The idealists at home only understood that when it was too late. If they had backed us in the beginning we would have blown open every black castle on Dis, searched until we found those bombs. But that would have meant wanton destruction and death. They wouldn't consider that. Now they are going to kill everyone, destroy everything." He flicked on the panel lights just long enough to take a com pass bearing, and Brion saw the tortured unhappiness in his twisted body.

"It's not over yet," Brion said. "There is more than a day left, and I think I'm onto something that might stop the war – without any bombs being dropped."

"You're in charge of the Cultural Relationships Free Bread and Blankets Foundation, aren't you? What good can your bunch do when the shooting starts?"

"None. But maybe we can put off the shooting. If you are trying to insult me – don't bother. My irritation quotient is very high."

The driver merely grunted at this, slowing down as they ran through a field of broken rock. "What is it you want?" he asked.

"We want to make a detailed examination of one of the magter. Alive or dead, it doesn't make any difference. You wouldn't happen to have one around?"

"No. We've fought with them often enough, but always on their home grounds. They keep all their casualties, and a good number of ours. What good will it do you anyway? A dead one won't tell you where the bombs or the jump-space projector is."

"I don't see why I should explain that to you – unless you are in charge. You are Hys, aren't you?"

The driver gave an angry sound, and then was silent while he drove. Finally he asked, "What makes you think that?"

"Call it a hunch. You don't act very much like a sand-car driver, for one thing. Of course your army may be all generals and no privates – but I doubt it. I also know that time has almost run out for all of us. This is a long ride and it would be a complete waste of time if you just sat out in the desert and waited for me. By driving me yourself you could make your mind up before we arrived. Could have a decision ready as to whether you are going to help me or not. Are you?"

"Yes – I'm Hys. But you still haven't answered my question. What do you want the body for?"

"We're going to cut it open and take a good long look. I don't think the magter are human. They are something living among men and disguised as men – but still not human."

"Secret aliens?" Hys exploded the words in a mixture of surprise and disgust.

"Perhaps. The examination will tell us that."

"You're either stupid or incompetent," Hys said bitterly. "The heat of Dis has cooked your brains in your head. I'll be no part of this kind of absurd plan."

"You must," Brion said, surprised at his own calmness. He could sense the other man's interest hidden behind his insulting manner. "I don't even have to give you my reasons. In another day this world ends and you have no way to stop it. I just might have an idea that could work, and you can't afford to take any chances – not if you are really sincere. Either you are a murderer, killing Disans for pleasure, or you honestly want to stop the war. Which is it?"

"You'll have your body all right," Hys grated, hurling the car viciously around a spire of rock. "Not that it will accomplish anything – but I can find no fault with killing another magter. We can fit your operation into our plans without any trouble. This is the last night and I have sent every one of my teams out on raids. We're breaking into as many magter towers as possible before dawn. There is a slim chance that we might uncover something. It's really just shooting in the dark, but it's all we can do now. My own team is waiting and you can ride along with us. The others left earlier. We're going to hit a small tower on this side of the city. We raided it once before and captured a lot of small arms they had stored there. There is a good chance that they may have been stupid enough to store something there again. Sometimes the magter seem to suffer from a complete lack of imagination."

"You have no idea just how right you are," Brion told him.

The sand car slowed down now, as they approached a slab-sided mesa that rose vertically from the desert. They crunched across broken rocks, leaving no tracks. A light blinked on the dashboard, and Hys stopped instantly and killed the engine. They climbed out, stretching and shivering in the cold desert night.

It was dark walking in the shadow of the cliff and they had to feel their way along a path through the tumbled boulders. A sudden blaze of light made Brion wince and shield his eyes. Near him, on the ground, was the humming shape of a cancellation projector, sending out a fan-shaped curtain of vibration that absorbed all the light rays falling upon it. This incredible blackness made a lightproof wall for the recessed hollow at the foot of the cliff. In this shelter, under the overhang of rock, were three open sand cars. They were large and armor-plated, warlike in their scarred grey paint. Men sprawled, talked, and polished their weapons. Everything stopped when Hys and Brion appeared.

"Load up," Hys called out. "We're going to attack now, same plan I outlined earlier. Get Telt over here." In talking to his own men some of the harshness was gone from his voice. The tall soldiers of Nyjord moved in ready obeyance of their commander. They loomed over his bent figure, most of them twice as tall as he, but there was no hesitation in jumping when he commanded. They were the body of the Nyjord striking force – he was the brains.

A square-cut, compact man rolled up to Hys and saluted with a leisurely flick of his hand. He was weighted and slung about with packs and electronic instruments. His pockets bulged with small tools and spare parts.

"This is Telt," Hys said to Brion. "He'll take care of you. Telt's my personal technical squad. He goes along on all my operations with his meters to test the interiors of the Disan forts. So far he's found no trace of a jump-space generator, or excess radioactivity that might indicate a bomb. Since he's useless and you're useless, you both take care of each other. Use the car we came in."

Telt's wide face split in a froglike grin; his voice was hoarse and throaty. "Wait. Just wait! Someday those needles gonna flicker and all our troubles be over. What you want me to do with the stranger?"

"Supply him with a corpse – one of the magter," Hys said. "Take it wherever he wants and then report back here." Hys scowled at Telt. "Someday your needles will flicker! Poor fool – this is the last day." He turned away and waved the men into their sand cars.

"He likes me," Telt said, attaching a final piece of equipment. "You can tell because he calls me names like that. He's a great man, Hys is, but they never found out until it was too late. Hand me that meter, will you?"

Brion followed the technician out to the car and helped him load his equipment aboard. When the larger cars appeared out of the darkness, Telt swung around after them. They snaked forward in a single line through the rocks, until they came to the desert of rolling sand dunes. Then they spread out in line abreast and rushed towards their goal.

Telt hummed to himself hoarsely as he drove. He broke off suddenly and looked at Brion. "What you want the dead Dis for?"

"A theory," Brion answered sluggishly. He had been half napping in the chair, taking the opportunity for some rest before the attack. "I'm still looking for a way to avert the end."

"You and Hys," Telt said with satisfaction. "Couple of idealists. Trying to stop a war you didn't start. They never would listen to Hys. He told them in the beginning exactly what would happen, and he was right. They always thought his ideas were crooked, like him. Growing up alone in the hill camp, with his back too twisted and too old to be fixed when he finally did come out. Ideas twisted the same way. Made himself an authority on war. Hah! War on Nyjord – that's like being an ice-cube specialist in hell. But he knew all about it, though they never would let him use what he knew. Put granddaddy Krafft in charge instead."

"But Hys is in charge of an army now?"

"All volunteers, too few of them and too little money. Too little and too damned late to do any good. I'll tell you we did our best, but it could never be good enough. And for this we get called butchers." There was a catch in Telt's voice now, an undercurrent of emotion he couldn't suppress. "At home they think we like to kill. Think we're insane. They can't understand we're doing the only thing that has to be done – "

He broke off as he quickly locked on the brakes and killed the engine. The line of sand cars had come to a stop. Ahead, just visible over the dunes, was the summit of a dark tower.

"We walk from here," Telt said, standing and stretching. "We can take our time, because the other boys go in first, soften things up. Then you and I head for the sub-cellar for a radiation check and find you a handsome corpse."

Walking at first, then crawling when the dunes no longer shielded them, they crept up on the Disan keep. Dark figures moved ahead of them, stopping only when they reached the crumbling black walls. They didn't use the ascending ramp, but made their way up the sheer outside face of the ramparts.

"Line-throwers," Telt whispered. "Anchor themselves when the missile hits, have some kind of quick-setting goo. Then we go up the filament with a line-climbing motor. Hys invented them."

"Is that the way you and I are going in?" Brion asked.

"No, we get out of the climbing. I told you we hit this rock once before. I know the layout inside." He was moving while he talked, carefully pacing the distance around the base of the tower. "Should be right about here."

High-pitched keening sliced the air and the top of the magter building burst into flame. Automatic weapons hammered above them. Something fell silently through the night and hit heavily on the ground near them.

"Attack's started," Telt shouted. "We have to get through now, while all the creepies are fighting it out on top." He pulled a plate-shaped object from one of his bags and slapped it hard against the wall. It hung there. He twisted the back of it, pulled something and waved Brion to the ground. "Shaped charge. Should blow straight in, but you never can tell."

The ground jumped under them and the ringing thud was a giant fist punching through the wall. A cloud of dust and smoke rolled clear and they could see the dark opening in the rock, a tunnel driven into the wall by the directional force of the explosion. Telt shone a light through the hole at the crumbled chamber inside.

"Nothing to worry about from anybody who was leaning against this wall. But let's get in and out of this black beehive before the ones upstairs come down to investigate."

Shattered rock was thick on the floor, and they skidded and tumbled over it. Telt pointed the way with his light, down a sharply angled ramp. "Underground chambers in the rock. They always store their stuff down there – "

A smoking, black sphere arced out of the tunnel's mouth, hitting at their feet. Telt just gaped, but even as it hit the floor Brion was jumping forward. He caught it with the side of his foot, kicking it back into the dark opening of the tunnel. Telt hit the ground next to him as the orange flame of an explosion burst below. Bits of shrapnel rattled from the ceiling and wall behind them.

"Grenades!" Telt gasped. "They've only used them once before – can't have many. Gotta warn Hys." He plugged a throat mike into the transmitter on his tack and spoke quickly into it. There was a stirring below and Brion poured a rain of fire into the tunnel.

"They're catching it bad on top, too! We gotta pull out. Go first and I'll cover you."

"I came for my Disan – I'm not leaving until I get one."

"You're crazy! You're dead if you stay!"

Telt was scrambling back towards the crumbled entrance as he talked. His back was turned when Brion fired. The magter had appeared silently as the shadow of death. They charged without a sound, running with expressionless faces into the bullets. Two died at once, curling and folding; the third one fell at Brion's feet. Shot, pierced, dying, but not yet dead. Leaving a crimson track, it hunched closer, lifting its knife to Brion. He didn't move. How many times must you murder a man? Or was it a man? His mind and body rebelled against the killing, and he was almost ready to accept death himself, rather than kill again.

Telt's bullets tore through the body and it dropped with grim finality.

"There's your corpse – now get it out of here!" Telt screeched.

Between them they worked the sodden weight of the dead magter through the hole, their exposed backs crawling with the expectation of instant death. No further attack came as they ran from the tower, other than a grenade that exploded too far behind them to do any harm.

One of the armored sand cars circled the keep, headlights blazing, keeping up a steady fire from its heavy weapons. The attackers climbed into it as they beat a retreat. Telt and Brion dragged the Disan behind them, struggling through the loose sand towards the circling car. Telt glanced over his shoulder and broke into a shambling run.

"They're following us!" he gasped. "The first time they ever chased us after a raid!"

"They must know we have the body," Brion said.

"Leave it behind ..." Telt choked. "Too heavy to carry ... anyway!"

"I'd rather leave you," Brion said sharply. "Let me have it." He pulled the corpse away from the unresisting Telt and heaved it across his own shoulders. "Now use your gun to cover us!"

Telt threw a rain of slugs back towards the dark figures following them. The driver of the sand car must have seen the flare of their fire, because the truck turned and started towards them. It braked in a choking cloud of dust and ready hands reached to pull them up. Brion pushed the body in ahead of himself and scrambled after it. The truck engine throbbed and they churned away into the blackness, away from the gutted tower.

"You know, that was more like kind of a joke, when I said I'd leave the corpse behind," Telt told Brion. "You didn't believe me, did you?"

"Yes," Brion said, holding the dead weight of the magter against the truck's side. "I thought you meant it."

"Ahhh," Telt protested, "you're as bad as Hys. You take things too seriously."

Brion suddenly realized that he was wet with blood, his clothing sodden. His stomach rose at the thought and he clutched the edge of the sand car. Killing like this was too personal. Talking abstractedly about a body was one thing, but murdering a man, then lifting his dead flesh and feeling his blood warm upon you is an entirely different matter. But the magter weren't human, he knew that. The thought was only mildly comforting.

After they had reached the other waiting sand cars, the raiding party split up. “Each one goes in a different direction,” Telt said, “so they can’t track us to the base.” He clipped a piece of paper next to the compass and kicked the motor into life. “We’ll make a big U in the desert and end up in Hovedstad. I got the course here. Then I’ll dump you and your friends and beat it back to our camp. You’re not still burned at me for what I said, are you? Are you?”

Brion didn’t answer. He was staring fixedly out of the side window.

“What’s doing?” Telt asked. Brion pointed out at the rushing darkness.

“Over there,” he said, pointing to the growing light on the horizon.

“Dawn,” Telt said. “Lotta rain on your planet? Didn’t you ever see the sun come up before?”

“Not on the last day of a world.”

“Lock it up,” Telt grumbled. “You give me the crawls. I know they’re going to be blasted. But at least I know I did everything I could to stop it. How do you think they are going to be feeling at home – on Nyjord – from tomorrow on?”

“Maybe we can still stop it,” Brion said, shrugging off the feeling of gloom. Telt’s only answer was a wordless sound of disgust.

By the time they had cut a large loop in the desert the sun was well up in the sky, the daily heat begun. Their course took them through a chain of low, flinty hills that cut their speed almost to zero. They ground ahead in low gear while Telt sweated and cursed, struggling with the controls. Then they were on firm sand and picking up speed towards the city.

As soon as Brion saw Hovedstad clearly he felt a clutch of fear. From somewhere in the city a black plume of smoke was rising. It could have been one of the deserted buildings aflame, a minor blaze. Yet the closer they came, the greater his tension grew. Brion didn’t dare put it into words himself; it was Telt who vocalized the thought.

“A fire or something. Coming from your area, somewhere close to your building.”

Within the city they saw the first signs of destruction. Broken rubble on the streets. The smell of greasy smoke in their nostrils.

More and more people appeared, going in the same direction they were. The normally deserted streets of Hovedstad were now almost crowded. Disans, obvious by their bare shoulders, mixed with the few offworlders who still remained.

Brion made sure the tarpaulin was well wrapped around the body before they pushed the sand car slowly through the growing crowd.

"I don't like all this publicity," Telt complained, looking at the people. "It's the last day, or I'd be turning back. They know our cars; we've raided them often enough." Turning a corner, he braked suddenly, mouth agape.

Ahead was destruction. Black, broken rubble had been churned into desolation. It was still smoking, pink tongues of flame licking over the ruins. A fragment of wall fell with a rumbling crash.

"It's your building – the Foundation building!" Telt shouted. "They've been here ahead of us – must have used the radio to call a raid. They did a job, explosive of some kind."

Hope was dead. Dis was dead. In the ruin ahead, mixed and broken with other rubble, were the bodies of all the people who had trusted him. Lea ... beautiful and cruelly dead Lea. Doctor Stine, his patients, Faussel, all of them. He had kept them on this planet, and now they were dead. Every one of them. Dead.

Murderer!

# XIV

**L**ife was ended. Brion's mind contained nothing but despair and the pain of irretrievable loss. If his brain had been completely the master of his body he would have died there, for at that moment there was no will to live. Unaware of this, his heart continued to beat and the regular motion of his lungs drew in the dreadful sweetness of the smoke-tainted air. With automatic directness his body lived on.

"What you gonna do?" Telt asked, even his natural exuberation stilled by this. Brion only shook his head as the words penetrated. What could he do? What could possibly be done?

"Follow me," a voice said in guttural Disan through the opening of a rear window. The speaker was lost in the crowd before they could turn. Aware now, Brion saw a native move away from the edge of the crowd and turn to look in their direction. It was Ulv.

"Turn the car – that way!" He punched Telt's arm and pointed. "Do it slowly and don't draw any attention to us." For a moment there was hope, which he kept himself from considering. The building was gone, and the people in it all dead. That fact had to be faced.

"What's going on?" Telt asked. "Who was that talked in the window?"

"A native – that one up ahead. He saved my life in the desert, and I think he is on our side. Even though he's a native Disan, he can understand facts that the magter can't. He knows what will happen to this planet." Brion was talking to fill his brain with words so he wouldn't begin to have hope. There was no hope possible.

Ulv moved slowly and naturally through the streets, never looking back. They followed, as far behind as they dared, yet still keeping him in sight. Fewer people were about here among the deserted offworld storehouses. Ulv vanished into one of these; LIGHT METALS TRUST LTD., the sign read above the door. Telt slowed the car.

"Don't stop here," Brion said. "Drive around the corner, and pull up."

Brion climbed out of the car with an ease he did not feel. No one was in sight now, in either direction. Walking slowly back to the corner, he checked the street they had just left. Hot, silent and empty.

A sudden blackness appeared where the door of the warehouse had been, and the sudden flickering motion of a hand. Brion signaled Telt to start, and jumped into the already moving sand car.

"Into that open door – quickly, before anyone sees us!" The car rumbled down a ramp into the dark interior and the door slid shut behind them.

"Ulv! What is it? Where are you?" Brion called, blinking in the murky interior. A grey form appeared beside him.

"I am here."

"Did you – " There was no way to finish the sentence.

"I heard of the raid. The magter called together all of us they could to help them carry explosive. I went along. I could not stop them, and there was no time to warn anyone in the building."

"Then they are all dead?"

"Yes," Ulv nodded. "All except one. I knew I could perhaps save one; I was not sure who. So I took the woman you were with in the desert – she is here now. She was hurt, but not badly, when I brought her out."

Guilty relief flooded through Brion. He shouldn't exult, not with the death of everyone in the Foundation still fresh in his mind. But at that instant he was happy.

"Let me see her," he said to Ulv. He was seized by the sudden fear that there might be a mistake. Perhaps Ulv had saved a different woman.

Ulv led the way across the empty loading bay. Brion followed closely, fighting down the temptation to tell him to hurry. When he saw that Ulv was heading towards an office in the far wall, he could control himself no longer and ran on ahead.

It was Lea, lying unconscious on a couch. Sweat beaded her face and she moaned and stirred without opening her eyes.

"I gave her *sover*, then wrapped her in cloth so no one would know," Ulv said.

Telt was close behind them, looking in through the open

door.

"*Sover* is a drug they take from one of their plants," he said. "We got a lot of experience with it. A little makes a good knock-out drug, but it's deadly poison in large doses. I got the antidote in the car; wait and I'll get it." He went out.

Brion sat next to Lea and wiped her face clean of dirt and perspiration. The dark shadows under her eyes were almost black now and her elfin face seemed even thinner. But she was alive – that was the important thing.

Some of the tension drained away from Brion and he could think again. There was still the job to do. After this last experience Lea should be in a hospital bed. But this was impossible. He would have to drag her to her feet and put her back to work. The answer might still be found. Each second ticked away another fraction of the planet's life.

"Good as new in a minute," Telt said, banging down the heavy med box. He watched intently as Ulv left the room. "Hys should know about this renegade. Might be useful as a spy, or for information – though of course it's too late now to do anything, so the hell with it." He pulled a pistol-shaped hypodermic gun from the box and dialed a number on the side. "Now, if you'll roll her sleeve up I'll bring her back to life." He pressed the bell-shaped sterilizing muzzle against her skin and pulled the trigger. The hypo gun hummed briefly, ending its cycle with a loud click.

"Does it work fast?" Brion asked.

"Couple of minutes. Just let her be and she'll come to by herself."

Ulv was in the doorway. "Killer!" he hissed. His blowgun was in his hand, half raised to his mouth.

"He's been in the car – he's seen it!" Telt shouted and grabbed for his gun.

Brion sprang between them, raising his hands. "Stop it! No more killing!" he shouted in Disan. Then he shook his fist at Telt. "Fire that gun and I'll stuff it down your throat. I'll handle this." He turned to face Ulv, who hadn't brought the blowgun any closer to his lips. This was a good sign – the Disan was still uncertain.

"You have seen the body in the car, Ulv. So you must have seen that it is that of a magter. I killed him myself, because I would rather kill one, or ten, or even a hundred men than have everyone on this planet destroyed. I killed him in a fair fight and now I am going to examine his body. There is something very strange and different about the magter, you know that yourself. If I can find out what it is, perhaps we can make them stop this war, and not bomb Nyjord."

Ulv was still angry, but he lowered the blowgun a little. "I wish there were no offworlders," he said. "I wish that none of you had ever come. Nothing was wrong until you started coming. The magter were the strongest, and they killed; but they also helped. Now they want to fight a war with your weapons, and for this you are going to kill my world. And you want me to help you!"

"Not me – yourself!" Brion said wearily. "There's no going back, that's the one thing we can't do. Maybe Dis would have been better off without offplanet contact. Maybe not. In any case, you have to forget about that. You have contact now with the rest of the galaxy, for better or for worse. You've got a problem to solve, and I'm here to help you solve it."

Seconds ticked by as Ulv, unmoving, fought with questions that were novel to his life. Could killing stop death? Could he help his people by helping strangers to fight and kill them? His world had changed and he didn't like it. He must make a giant effort to change with it.

Abruptly, he pushed the blowgun into a thong at his waist, turned and strode out.

"Too much for my nerves," Telt said, settling his gun back in the holster. "You don't know how happy I'm gonna be when this whole damn thing is over. Even if the planet goes bang, I don't care. I'm finished." He walked out to the sand car, keeping a careful eye on the Disan crouched against the wall.

Brion turned back to Lea, whose eyes were open, staring at the ceiling. He went to her.

"Running," she said, and her voice had a toneless emptiness that screamed louder than any emotion. "They ran by the open door of my room and I could see them when they killed Dr. Stine. Just butchered him like an animal, chopping him down. Then one came into the room and that's all I remember." She turned her head slowly and looked at Brion. "What happened? Why am I here?"

"They're ... dead," he told her. "All of them. After the raid the Disans blew up the building. You're the only one that survived. That was Ulv who came into your room, the Disan we met in the desert. He brought you away and hid you here in the city."

"When do we leave?" she asked in the same empty tones, turning her face to the wall. "When do we get off this planet?"

"Today is the last day. The deadline is midnight. Krafft will have a ship pick us up when we are ready. But we still have our job to do. I've got that body. You're going to have to examine it. We must find out about the magter ...."

"Nothing can be done now except leave." Her voice was a dull monotone. "There is only so much that a person can do, and I've done it. Please have the ship come; I want to leave now."

Brion bit his lip in helpless frustration. Nothing seemed to penetrate the apathy into which she had sunk. Too much shock, too much terror, in too short a time. He took her chin in his hand and turned her head to face him. She didn't resist, but her eyes were shining with tears; tears trickled down her cheeks.

"Take me home, Brion, please take me home."

He could only brush her sodden hair back from her face, and force himself to smile at her. The moments of time were running out, faster and faster, and he no longer knew what to do. The examination had to be made – yet he couldn't force her. He looked for the med box and saw that Telt had taken it back to the sand car. There might be something in it that could help – a tranquilizer perhaps.

Telt had some of his instruments open on the chart table and was examining a tape with a pocket magnifier when Brion entered. He jumped nervously and put the tape behind his back, then relaxed when he saw who it was.

"I thought you were the creepie out there, coming for a look," he whispered. "Maybe you trust him – but I can't afford to. Can't even use the radio. I'm getting out of here now. I have to tell Hys!"

"Tell him what?" Brion asked sharply. "What is all the mystery about?"

Telt handed him the magnifier and tape. "Look at that – recording tape from my scintillation counter. Red verticals are five-minute intervals, the wiggly black horizontal line is the radioactivity level. All this where the line goes up and down, that's when we were driving out to the attack. Varying hot level of the rock and ground."

"What's the big peak in the middle?"

"That coincides exactly with our visit to the house of horrors!

When we went through the hole in the bottom of the tower!" He couldn't keep the excitement out of his voice.

"Does it mean that ...."

"I don't know. I'm not sure. I have to compare it with the other tapes back at base. It could be the stone of the tower – some of these heavy rocks have got a high natural count. There maybe could be a box of instruments there with fluorescent dials. Or it might be one of those tactical atom bombs they threw at us already. Some arms runner sold them a few."

"Or it could be the cobalt bombs?"

"It could be," Telt said, packing his instruments swiftly. "A badly shielded bomb, or an old one with a crack in the skin, could give a trace like that. Just a little radon leaking out would do it."

"Why don't you call Hys on the radio and let him know?"

"I don't want Granddaddy Krafft's listening posts to hear about it. This is our job – if I'm right. And I have to check my old tapes to make sure. But it's gonna be worth a raid, I can feel that in my bones. Let's unload your corpse." He helped Brion with the clumsy, wrapped bundle, then slipped into the driver's seat.

"Hold it," Brion said. "Do you have anything in the med box I can use for Lea? She seems to have cracked. Not hysterical, but withdrawn. Won't listen to reason, won't do anything but lie there and ask to go home."

"Got the potion here," Telt said, cracking the med box. "Slaughter-syndrome is what our medic calls it. Hit a lot of our boys. Grow up all your life hating the idea of violence, and it goes rough when you have to start killing people. Guys break up, break down, go to pieces lots of different ways. The medic mixed up this stuff. Don't know how it works, probably tranquilizers and some of the cortex drugs. But it peels off recent memories. Maybe for the last ten, twelve hours. You can't get upset about what you don't remember." He pulled out a sealed package. "Directions on the box. Good luck."

"Luck," Brion said, and shook the technician's calloused hand. "Let me know if the traces are strong enough to be bombs." He checked the street to make sure it was clear, then pressed the door button. The sand car churned out into the brilliant sunshine and was gone, the throb of its motor dying in the distance. Brion closed the door and went back to Lea. Ulv was still crouched against the wall.

There was a one-shot disposable hypodermic in the box. Lea made no protest when he broke the seal and pressed the needle against her arm. She sighed and her eyes closed again.

When he saw she was resting easily, he dragged in the tarpaulin-wrapped body of the magter. A workbench ran along one wall and he struggled the corpse up onto it. He unwrapped the tarpaulin and the sightless eyes stared accusingly up into his.

Using his knife, Brion cut away the loose, blood-soaked clothing. Strapped under the clothes, around the man's waist, was the familiar collection of Disan artifacts. This could have significance either way. Human or humanoid, the creature would still have to live on Dis. Brion threw it aside, along with the clothing. Nude, pierced, bloody, the corpse lay before him.

In every external physical detail the man was human.

Brion's theory was becoming more preposterous with each discovery. If the magter weren't alien, how could he explain their complete lack of emotions? A mutation of some kind? He didn't see how it was possible. There *had* to be something alien about the dead man before him. The future of a world rested on this flimsy hope. If Telt's lead to the bombs proved to be false, there would be no hope left at all.

Lea was still unconscious when he looked at her again. There was no way of telling how long the coma would last. He would probably have to waken her out of it, but he didn't want to do it too early. It took an effort to control his impatience, even though he knew the drug needed time in which to work. He finally decided on at least a minimum of an hour before he should try to disturb her. That would be noon – twelve hours before destruction.

One thing he should do was to get in touch with Professor-Commander Krafft. Maybe it was being defeatist, but he had to make sure that they had a way off this planet if the mission failed. Krafft had installed a relay radio that would forward calls from his personal set. If this relay had been in the Foundation building, contact was broken. This had to be found out before it was too late. Brion thumbed on his radio and sent the call. The reply came back instantly.

"This is fleet communications. Will you please keep this circuit open? Commander Krafft is waiting for this call and it is being put directly through to him now." Krafft's voice broke in while the operator was still talking.

"Who is making this call – is it anyone from the Foundation?" The old man's voice was shaky with emotion.

"Brandd here. I have Lea Morees with me ...."

"No more? Are there no other survivors from the disaster that destroyed your building?"

"That's it, other than us it's a ... complete loss. With the building and all the instruments gone, I have no way to contact our ship in orbit. Can you arrange to get us out of here if necessary?"

"Give me your location. A ship is coming now – "

"I don't need a ship now," Brion interrupted. "Don't send it until I call. If there is a way to stop your destruction I'll find it. So I'm staying – to the last minute if necessary."

Krafft was silent. There was only the crackle of an open mike and the sound of breathing. "That is your decision," he said finally. "I'll have a ship standing by. But won't you let us take Miss Morees out now?"

"No. I need her here. We are still working, looking for – "

"What answer can you find that could possibly avert destruction now?" His tone was between hope and despair. Brion couldn't help him.

"If I succeed – you'll know. Otherwise, that will be the end of it. End of Transmission." He switched the radio off.

Lea was sleeping easily when he looked at her, and there was still a good part of the hour left before he could wake her. How could he put it to use? She would need tools, instruments to examine the corpse, and there were certainly none here. Perhaps he could find some in the ruins of the Foundation building. With this thought he had the sudden desire to see the wreckage up close. There might be other survivors. He had to find out. If he could talk to the men he had seen working there....

Ulv was still crouched against the wall in the outer room. He looked up angrily when Brion came over, but said nothing.

"Will you help me again?" Brion asked. "Stay and watch the girl while I go out. I'll be back at noon." Ulv didn't answer. "I am still looking for the way to save Dis," Brion added.

"Go – I'll watch the girl!" Ulv spat words in impotent fury. "I do not know what to do. You may be right. Go. She will be safe with me."

Brion slipped out into the deserted street and, half running, half walking, made his way towards the rubble that had been the Cultural Relationships Foundation. He used a different course from the one they had come by, striking first towards the outer edge of the city. Once there, he could swing and approach from the other side, so there would be no indication where he had come from. The magter might be watching and he didn't want to lead them to Lea and the stolen body.

Turning a corner, he saw a sand car stopped in the street ahead. There was something familiar about the lines of it. It could be the one he and Telt had used, but he wasn't sure. He looked around, but the dusty, packed-dirt street was white and empty, shimmering in silence under the sun. Staying close to the wall and watching carefully, Brion slipped towards the car. When he came close behind it he was positive it was the one he had been in the night before. What was it doing here?

Silence and heat filled the street. Windows and doors were empty, and there was no motion in their shadows. Putting his foot on a bogey wheel, he reached up and grabbed the searing metal rim of the open window. He pulled himself up and stared at Telt's smiling face.

Smiling in death. The lips pulled back to reveal the grinning teeth, the eyes bursting from the head, the features swollen and contorted from the deadly poison. A tiny, tufted dart of wood stuck in the brown flesh on the side of his neck.

# XV

**B**rion hurled himself backward and sprawled flat in the dust and filth of the road. No poison dart sought him out; the empty silence still reigned. Telt's murderers had come and gone. Moving quickly, using the bulk of the car as a shield, he opened the door and slipped inside.

They had done a thorough job of destruction. All of the controls had been battered into uselessness, the floor was a junk heap of crushed equipment, intertwined with loops of recording tape bulging like mechanical intestines. A gutted machine, destroyed like its driver.

It was easy enough to reconstruct what had happened. The car had been seen when they entered the city – probably by some of the magter who had destroyed the Foundation building. They had not seen where it had gone, or Brion would surely be dead by now. But they must have spotted it when Telt tried to leave the city – and stopped it in the most effective way possible, a dart through the open window into the unsuspecting driver's neck.

Telt dead! The brutal impact of the man's death had driven all thought of its consequences from Brion's mind. Now he began to realize. Telt had never sent word of his discovery of the radioactive trace to the Nyjord army. He had been afraid to use the radio, and had wanted to tell Hys in person, and to show him the tape. Only now the tape was torn and mixed with all the others, the brain that could have analyzed it dead.

Brion looked at the dangling entrails of the radio and spun for the door. Running swiftly and erratically, he fled from the sand car. His own survival and the possible survival of Dis depended on his not being seen near it. He must contact Hys and pass on the information. Until he did that, he was the only offworlder on Dis who knew which magter tower might contain the world-destroying bombs.

Once out of sight of the sand car he went more slowly, wiping the sweat from his streaming face. He hadn't been seen leaving the car, and he wasn't being followed. The streets here weren't familiar, but he checked his direction by the sun and walked at a steady fast pace towards the destroyed building. More of the native Disans were in the streets now. They all noticed him, some even stopped and scowled fiercely at him. With his emphatic awareness he felt their anger and hatred. A knot of men radiated death, and he put his hand on his gun as he passed them. Two of them had their blowguns ready, but didn't use them. By the time he had turned the next corner he was soaked with nervous perspiration.

Ahead was the rubble of the destroyed building. Grounded next to it was the tapered form of a spacer's pinnace. Two men had come from the open lock and were standing at the edge of the burnt area.

Brion's boots grated loudly on the broken wreckage. The men turned quickly towards him, guns raised. Both of them carried ion rifles. They relaxed when they saw his offworld clothes.

"Bloody damned savages!" one of them growled. He was a heavy-planet man, a squashed-down column of muscle and gristle, whose head barely reached Brion's chest. A pushed-back cap had the crossed slide-rule symbol of ship's computer man.

"Can't blame them, I guess," the second man said. He wore purser's insignia. His features were different, but with the same compacted body the two men were as physically alike as twins. Probably from the same home planet. "They're gonna get their whole world blown out from under them at midnight. Looks as if the poor slob in the streets finally realized what is happening. Hope we're in jump-space by then. I saw Estrada's World get it, and I don't want to see that again, not twice in one lifetime!"

The computer man was looking closely at Brion, head tilted sideways to see his face. "You need transportation offworld?" he asked. "We're the last ship at the port, and we're going to boil out of here as soon as the rest of our cargo is aboard. We'll give you a lift if you need it."

Only by a tremendous effort at control did Brion conceal the destroying sorrow that overwhelmed him when he looked at that shattered wasteland, the graveyard of so many. "No," he said. "That won't be necessary. I'm in touch with the blockading fleet and they'll pick me up before midnight."

"You from Nyjord?" the purser growled.

"No," Brion said, still only half aware of the men. "But there is trouble with my own ship." He realized that they were looking intently at him, that he owed them some kind of explanation. "I thought I could find a way to stop the war. Now ... I'm not so sure." He hadn't intended to be so frank with the spacemen, but the words had been uppermost in his thoughts and had simply slipped out.

The computer man started to say something, but his shipmate speared him in the side with his elbow. "We blast soon – and I don't like the way these Disans are looking at us. The captain said to find out what caused the fire, then get the hell back. So let's go."

"Don't miss your ship," the computer man said to Brion, and he started for the pinnace. Then he hesitated and turned. "Sure there's nothing we can do for you?"

Sorrow would accomplish nothing. Brion fought to sweep the dregs of emotion from his mind and to think clearly. "You can help me," he said. "I could use a scalpel or any other surgical instrument you might have." Lea would need those. Then he remembered Telt's undelivered message. "Do you have a portable radio transceiver? I can pay you for it."

The computer man vanished inside the rocket and reappeared a minute later with a small package. "There's a scalpel and a magnetized tweezers in here – all I could find in the med kit. Hope they'll do." He reached inside and swung out the metal case of a self-contained transceiver. "Take this, it's got plenty of range, even on the longer frequencies."

He raised his hand at Brion's offer to pay. "My donation," he said. "If you can save this planet I'll give you the whole pinnace as well. We'll tell the captain we lost the radio in some trouble with the natives. Isn't that right, Moneybags?" He prodded the purser in the chest with a finger that would have punched a hole through a weaker man.

"I read you loud and clear," the purser said. "I'll make out an invoice so stating, back in the ship." They were both in the pinnace then, and Brion had to move fast to get clear of the takeoff blast.

A sense of obligation – the spacemen had felt it too. The realization of this raised Brion's spirits a bit as he searched through the rubble for anything useful. He recognized part of a wall still standing as a corner of the laboratory. Poking through the ruins, he unearthed broken instruments and a single, battered case that had barely missed destruction. Inside was the binocular microscope, the right tube bent, its lenses cracked and obscured. The left eyepiece still seemed to be functioning. Brion carefully put it back in the case.

He looked at his watch. It was almost noon. These few pieces of equipment would have to do for the dissection. Watched suspiciously by the onlooking Disans, he started back to the warehouse. It was a long, circuitous walk, since he didn't dare give any clues to his destination. Only when he was positive he had not been observed or followed did he slip through the building's entrance, locking the door behind him.

Lea's frightened eyes met his when he went into the office. "A friendly smile here among the cannibals," she called. Her strained expression gave the lie to the cheeriness of her words. "What has happened? Since I woke up, the great stone face over there" – she pointed to Ulv – "has been telling me exactly nothing."

"What's the last thing you can remember?" Brion asked carefully. He didn't want to tell her too much, lest this bring on the shock again. Ulv had shown great presence of mind in not talking to her.

"If you must know," Lea said, "I remember quite a lot, Brion Brandd. I shan't go into details, since this sort of thing is best kept from the natives. For the record then, I can recall going to sleep after you left. And nothing since then. It's weird. I went to sleep in that lumpy hospital bed and woke up on this couch, feeling simply terrible. With *him* just sitting there and scowling at me. Won't you please tell me what is going on?"

A partial truth was best, saving all of the details that he could for later. "The magter attacked the Foundation building," he said. "They are getting angry at all offworlders now. You were still knocked out by a sleeping drug, so Ulv helped bring you here. It's afternoon now – "

"Of the last day?" She sounded horrified. "While I'm playing Sleeping Beauty the world is coming to an end! Was anyone hurt in the attack? Or killed?"

"There were a number of casualties – and plenty of trouble," Brion said. He had to get her off the subject. Walking over to the corpse, he threw back the cover from its face. "But this is more important right now. It's one of the magter. I have a scalpel and some other things here – will you perform an autopsy?"

Lea huddled back on the couch, her arms around herself, looking chilled in spite of the heat of the day. "What happened to the people at the building?" she asked in a thin voice. The injection had removed her memories of the tragedy, but echoes of the strain and shock still reverberated in her mind and body. "I feel so ... exhausted. Please tell me what happened. I have the feeling you're hiding something."

Brion sat next to her and took her hands in his, not surprised to find them cold. Looking into her eyes, he tried to give her some of his strength. "It wasn't very nice," he said. "You were shaken up by it, I imagine that's why you feel the way you do now. But – Lea, you'll have to take my word for this. Don't ask any more questions. There's nothing we can do now about it. But we can still find out about the magter. Will you examine the corpse?"

She started to ask something, then changed her mind. When she dropped her eyes Brion felt the thin shiver that went through her body. "There's something terribly wrong," she said. "I know that. I guess I'll have to take your word that it's best not to ask questions. Help me up, will you, darling? My legs are absolutely liquid."

Leaning on him, with his arm around her supporting most of her weight, she went slowly across to the corpse. She looked down and shuddered. "Not what you would call a natural death," she said. Ulv watched intently as she took the scalpel out of its holder. "You don't have to look at this," she told him in halting Disan. "Not if you don't want to."

"I want to," he told her, not taking his eyes from the body. "I have never seen a magter dead before, or without covering, like an ordinary person." He continued to stare fixedly.

"Find me some drinking water, will you, Brion?" Lea said. "And spread the tarp under the body. These things are quite messy."

After drinking the water she seemed stronger, and could stand without holding onto the table with both hands. Placing the tip of the scalpel just below the magter's breast bone, she made the long post-mortem incision down to the pubic symphysis. The great, body-length wound gaped open like a red mouth. Across the table Ulv shuddered but didn't avert his eyes.

One by one she removed the internal organs. Once she looked up at Brion, then quickly returned to work. The silence stretched on and on until Brion had to break it.

"Tell me, can't you? Have you found out anything?"

His words snapped the thin strand of her strength, and she staggered back to the couch and collapsed onto it. Her bloodstained hands hung over the side, making a strangely terrible contrast to the whiteness of her skin.

"I'm sorry, Brion," she said. "But there's nothing, nothing at all. There are minor differences, organic changes I've never seen before – his liver is tremendous, for one thing. But changes like this are certainly consistent within the pattern of homo sapiens as adapted to a different planet. He's a man. Changed, adapted, modified – but still just as human as you or I."

"How can you be sure?" Brion broke in. "You haven't examined him completely, have you?" She shook her head. "Then go on. The other organs. His brain. A microscopic examination. Here!" he said, pushing the microscope case towards her with both hands.

She dropped her head onto her forearms and sobbed. "Leave me alone, can't you! I'm tired and sick and fed up with this awful planet. Let them die. I don't care! Your theory is false, useless. Admit that! And let me wash the filth from my hands...." Sobbing drowned out her words.

Brion stood over her and drew a shuddering breath. Was he wrong? He didn't dare think about that. He had to go on. Looking down at the thinness of her bent back, with the tiny projections of her spine showing through the thin cloth, he felt an immense pity – a pity he couldn't surrender to. This thin, helpless, frightened woman was his only resource. She had to work. He had to *make* her work.

Ihjel had done it – used projective empathy to impress his emotions upon Brion. Now Brion must do it with Lea. He had had some sessions in the art, but not nearly enough to make him proficient. Nevertheless he had to try.

Strength was what Lea needed. Aloud he said simply, "You can do it. You have the will and the strength to finish." And silently his mind cried out the order to obey, to share his power now that hers was drained and finished.

Only when she lifted her face and he saw the dried tears did he realize that he had succeeded. "You will go on?" he asked quietly.

Lea merely nodded and rose to her feet. She shuffled like a sleepwalker jerked along by invisible strings. Her strength wasn't her own, and the situation reminded him unhappily of that last event of the Twenties when he had experienced the same kind of draining activity. She wiped her hands roughly on her clothes and opened the microscope case.

"The slides are all broken," she said.

"This will do," Brion told her, crashing his heel through the glass partition. Shards tinkled and crashed to the floor. He took some of the bigger pieces and broke them to rough squares that would fit under the clips on the stage. Lea accepted them without a word. Putting a drop of the magter's blood on the slide, she bent over the eyepiece.

Her hands shook when she tried to adjust the focusing. Using low power, she examined the specimen, squinting through the angled tube. Once she turned the sub-stage mirror a bit to catch the light streaming in the window. Brion stood behind her, fists clenched, forcibly controlling his anxiety. "What do you see?" he finally blurted out.

"Phagocytes, platelets ... leucocytes ... everything seems normal." Her voice was dull, exhausted, her eyes blinking with fatigue as she stared into the tube.

Anger at defeat burned through Brion. Even faced with failure, he refused to accept it. He reached over her shoulder and savagely twisted the turret of microscope until the longest lens was in position. "If you can't see anything – try the high power! It's there – I know it's there! I'll get you a tissue specimen." He turned back to the disemboweled cadaver.

His back was turned and he did not see that sudden stiffening of her shoulders, or the sudden eagerness that seized her fingers as they adjusted the focus. But he did feel the wave of emotion that welled from her, impinging directly on his empathetic sense. "What is it?" he called to her, as if she had spoken aloud.

"Something ... something here," she said, "in this leucocyte. It's not normal structure, but it's familiar. I've seen something like it before, but I just can't remember." She turned away from the microscope and unthinkingly pressed her gory knuckles to her forehead. "I know I've seen it before."

Brion squinted into the deserted microscope and made out a dim shape in the center of the field. It stood out sharply when he focused – the white, jellyfish shape of a single-celled leucocyte. To his untrained eye there was nothing unusual about it. He couldn't know what was strange, when he had no idea of what was normal.

"Do you see those spherical green shapes grouped together?" Lea asked. Before Brion could answer she gasped, "I remember now!" Her fatigue was forgotten in her excitement. "*Icerya purchasi*, that was the name, something like that. It's a coccid, a little scale insect. It had those same shapes collected together within its individual cells."

"What do they mean? What is the connection with Dis?"

"I don't know," she said; "it's just that they look so similar. And I never saw anything like this in a human cell before. In the coccids, the green particles grow into a kind of yeast that lives within the insect. Not a parasite, but a real symbiote ...."

Her eyes opened wide as she caught the significance of her own words. A symbiote – and Dis was the world where symbiosis and parasitism had become more advanced and complex than on any other planet. Lea's thoughts spun around this fact and chewed at the fringes of the logic. Brion could sense her concentration and absorption. He did nothing to break the mood. Her hands were clenched, her eyes staring unseeingly at the wall as her mind raced.

Brion and Ulv were quiet, watching her, waiting for her conclusions. The pieces were falling into shape at last.

Lea opened her clenched hands and smoothed them on her sodden skirt. She blinked and turned to Brion. "Is there a tool box here?" she asked.

Her words were so unexpected that Brion could not answer for a moment. Before he could say anything she spoke again.

"Not hand tools; that would take too long. Could you find anything like a power saw? That would be ideal." She turned back to the microscope, and he didn't try to question her. Ulv was still looking at the body of the magter and had understood nothing of what they had said.

Brion went out into the loading bay. There was nothing he could use on the ground floor, so he took the stairs to the floor above. A corridor here passed by a number of rooms. All of the doors were locked, including one with the hopeful sign TOOL ROOM on it. He battered at the metal door with his shoulder without budging it. As he stepped back to look for another way in, he glanced at his watch.

Two o'clock! In ten hours the bombs would fall on Dis.

The need for haste tore at him. Yet there could be no noise – someone in the street might hear it. He quickly stripped off his shirt and wrapped it in a loose roll around the barrel of his gun, extending it in a loose tube in front of the barrel. Holding the rolled cloth in his left hand, he jammed the gun up tight against the door, the muzzle against the lock. The single shot was only a dull thud, inaudible outside of the building. Pieces of broken mechanism jarred and rattled inside the lock and the door swung open.

When he came back Lea was standing by the body. He held the small power saw with a rotary blade. "Will this do?" he asked. "Runs on its own battery; almost fully charged too."

"Perfect," she answered. "You're both going to have to help me." She switched into the Disan language. "Ulv, would you find some place where you can watch the street without being seen? Signal me when it is empty. I'm afraid this saw is going to make a lot of noise."

Ulv nodded and went out into the bay, where he climbed a heap of empty crates so he could peer through the small windows set high in the wall. He looked carefully in both directions, then waved to her to go ahead.

"Stand to one side and hold the cadaver's chin, Brion," she said. "Hold it firmly so the head doesn't shake around when I cut. This is going to be a little gruesome. I'm sorry. But it'll be the fastest way to cut the bone." The saw bit into the skull.

Once Ulv waved them into silence, and shrank back himself into the shadows next to the window. They waited impatiently until he gave them the sign to continue again. Brion held steady while the saw cut a circle completely around the skull.

"Finished," Lea said and the saw dropped from her limp fingers to the floor. She massaged life back into her hands before she finished the job. Carefully and delicately she removed the cap of bone from the magter's head, exposing his brain to the shaft of light from the window.

"You were right all the time, Brion," she said. "There is your alien."

# XVI

Ulv joined them as they looked down at the exposed brain of the magter. The thing was so clearly evident that even Ulv noticed it.

"I have seen dead animals and my people dead with their heads open, but I have never seen anything like that before," he said.

"What is it?" Brion asked.

"The invader, the alien you were looking for," Lea told him.

The magter's brain was only two-thirds of what would have been its normal size. Instead of filling the skull completely, it shared the space with a green, amorphous shape. This was ridged somewhat like a brain, but the green shape had still darker nodules and extensions. Lea took her scalpel and gently prodded the dark moist mass.

"It reminds me very much of something that I've seen before on Earth," she said. "The green-fly – *Drepanosiphum platanoides* – and an unusual organ it has, called the pseudova. Now that I have seen this growth in the magter's skull, I can think of a positive parallel. The fly *Drepanosiphum* also had a large green organ, only it fills half of the body cavity instead of the head. Its identity puzzled biologists for years, and they had a number of complex theories to explain it. Finally someone managed to dissect and examine it. The pseudova turned out to be a living plant, a yeast-like growth that helps with the green-fly's digestion. It produces enzymes that enable the fly to digest the great amounts of sugar it gets from plant juice."

"That's not unusual," Brion said, puzzled. "Termites and human beings are a couple of other creatures whose digestion is helped by internal flora. What's the difference in the green-fly?"

"Reproduction, mainly. All the other gut-living plants have to enter the host and establish themselves as outsiders, permitted to remain as long as they are useful. The green-fly and its yeast plant have a permanent symbiotic relationship that is essential to the existence of both. The plant spores appear in many places throughout the fly's body – but they are *always* in the germ cells.

Every egg cell has some, and every egg that grows to maturity is infected with the plant spores. The continuation of the symbiosis is unbroken and guaranteed."

"Do you think those green spheres in the magter's blood cells could be the same kind of thing?" Brion asked.

"I'm sure of it," Lea said. "It must be the same process. There are probably green spheres throughout the magters' bodies, spores or offspring of those things in their brains. Enough will find their way to the germ cells to make sure that every young magter is infected at birth. While the child is growing, so is the symbiote. Probably a lot faster, since it seems to be a simpler organism. I imagine it is well established in the brain pan within the first six months of the infant's life."

"But why?" Brion asked. "What does it do?"

"I'm only guessing now, but there is plenty of evidence that gives us an idea of its function. I'm willing to bet that the symbiote itself is not a simple organism, it's probably an amalgam of plant and animal like most of the other creatures on Dis. The thing is just too complex to have developed since mankind has been on this planet. The magter must have caught the symbiotic infection eating some Disan animal. The symbiote lived and flourished in its new environment, well protected by a bony skull in a long-lived host. In exchange for food, oxygen and comfort, the brain-symbiote must generate hormones and enzymes that enable the magter to survive. Some of these might aid digestion, enabling the magter to eat any plant or animal life they can lay their hands on. The symbiote might produce sugars, scavenge the blood of toxins – there are so many things it could do. Things it must have done, since the magter are obviously the dominant life form on this planet. They paid a high price for the symbiote, but it didn't matter to race survival until now. Did you notice that the magter's brain is no smaller than normal?"

"It must be – or how else could that brain-symbiote fit in inside the skull with it?" Brion said.

"If the magter's total brain were smaller in volume than normal it could fit into the remaining space in the cranial hollow. But the brain is full-sized – it is just that part of it is missing, absorbed by the symbiote."

"The frontal lobes," Brion said with sudden realization. "This hellish growth has performed a prefrontal lobotomy!"

"It's done even more than that," Lea said, separating the convolutions of the gray matter with her scalpel to uncover a green filament beneath. "These tendrils penetrate further back into the brain, but always remain in the cerebrum. The cerebellum appears to be untouched. Apparently just the higher functions of mankind have been interfered with, selectively. Destruction of the frontal lobes made the magter creatures without emotions or ability for really abstract thought. Apparently, they survived better without these. There must have been some horrible failures before the right balance was struck. The final product is a man-plant-animal symbiote that is admirably adapted for survival on this disaster world. No emotions to cause complications or desires that might interfere with pure survival. Complete ruthlessness – mankind has always been strong on this anyway, so it didn't take much of a push."

"The other Disans, like Ulv here, managed to survive without turning into such a creature. So why was it necessary for the magter to go so far?"

"Nothing is necessary in evolution, you know that," Lea said. "Many variations are possible, and all the better ones continue. You might say that Ulv's people survive, but the magter survive better. If offworld contact hadn't been re-established, I imagine that the magter would slowly have become the dominant race. Only they won't have the chance now. It looks as though they have succeeded in destroying both races with their suicidal urge."

"That's the part that doesn't make sense," Brion said. "The magter have survived and climbed right to the top of the evolutionary heap here. Yet they are suicidal. How does it happen they haven't been wiped out before this?"

"Individually, they have been aggressive to the point of suicide. They will attack anything and everything with the same savage lack of emotion. Luckily there are no bigger animals on this planet. So where they have died as individuals, their utter ruthlessness has guaranteed their survival as a group. Now they are faced with a problem that is too big for their half-destroyed minds to handle. Their personal policy has become their planetary policy – and that's never a very smart thing. They are like men with knives who have killed all the men who were only armed with stones. Now they are facing men with guns, and they are going to keep charging and fighting until they are all dead.

"It's a perfect case of the utter impartiality of the forces of evolution. Men infected by this Disan life form were the dominant creatures on this planet. The creature in the magters' brains was a true symbiote then, giving something and receiving something, making a union of symbiotes where all were stronger together than any could be separately. Now this is changed. The magter brain cannot understand the concept of racial death, in a situation where it must understand to be able to survive. Therefore the brain-creature is no longer a symbiote but a parasite."

"And as a parasite it must be destroyed!" Brion broke in. "We're not fighting shadows anymore," he exulted. "We've found the enemy – and it's not the magter at all. Just a sort of glorified tapeworm that is too stupid to know when it is killing itself off. Does it have a brain – can it think?"

"I doubt it very much," Lea said. "A brain would be of absolutely no use to it. So even if it originally possessed reasoning powers they would be gone by now. Symbiotes or parasites that live internally like this always degenerate to an absolute minimum of functions."

"Tell me about it. What is this thing?" Ulv broke in, prodding the soft form of the brain-symbiote. He had heard all their excited talk but had not understood a word.

"Explain it to him, will you, Lea, as best you can," Brion said, looking at her, and he realized how exhausted she was. "And sit down while you do it; you're long overdue for a rest. I'm going to try – " He broke off when he looked at his watch.

It was after four in the afternoon – less than eight hours to go. What was he to do? Enthusiasm faded as he realized that only half of the problem was solved. The bombs would drop on schedule unless the Nyjorders could understand the significance of this discovery. Even if they understood, would it make any difference to them? The threat of the hidden cobalt bombs would not be changed.

With this thought came the guilty realization that he had forgotten completely about Telt's death. Even before he contacted the Nyjord fleet he must tell Hys and his rebel army what had happened to Telt and his sand car. Also about the radioactive traces. They couldn't be checked against the records now to see how important they might be, but Hys might make another raid on the strength of the suspicion. This call wouldn't take long, then he would be free to tackle Professor-Commander Krafft.

Carefully setting the transmitter on the frequency of the rebel army, he sent out a call to Hys. There was no answer. When he switched to receive all he heard was static.

There was always a chance the set was broken. He quickly twisted the transmitter to the frequency of his personal radio, then whistled in the microphone. The received signal was so loud that it hurt his ears. He tried to call Hys again, and was relieved to get a response this time.

"Brion Brandd here. Can you read me? I want to talk to Hys at once."

It came as a shock that it was Professor-Commander Krafft who answered.

"I'm sorry, Brion, but it's impossible to talk to Hys. We are monitoring his frequency and your call was relayed to me. Hys and his rebels lifted ship about half an hour ago, and are already on the way back to Nyjord. Are you ready to leave now? It will soon become dangerous to make any landings. Even now I will have to ask for volunteers to get you out of there."

Hys and the rebel army gone! Brion assimilated the thought. He had been thrown off balance when he realized he was talking to Krafft.

"If they're gone – well, then there's nothing I can do about it," he said. "I was going to call you, so I can talk to you now. Listen and try to understand. You must cancel the bombing. I've found out about the magter, found what causes their mental aberration. If we can correct that, we can stop them from attacking Nyjord."

"Can they be corrected by midnight tonight?" Krafft broke in. He was abrupt and sounded almost angry. Even saints get tired.

"No, of course not." Brion frowned at the microphone, realizing the talk was going all wrong, but not knowing how to remedy it. "But it won't take too long. I have evidence here that will convince you that what I say is the truth."

"I believe you without seeing it, Brion." The trace of anger was gone from Krafft's voice now, and it was heavy with fatigue and defeat. "I'll admit you are probably right. A little while ago I admitted to Hys too that he was probably right in his original estimation of the correct way to tackle the problem of Dis. We have made a lot of mistakes, and in making them we have run out of time. I'm afraid that is the only fact that is relevant now. The bombs fall at twelve, and even then they may drop too late. A ship is already on its way from Nyjord with my replacement. I exceeded my authority by running a day past the maximum the technicians gave me. I realize now I was gambling the life of my own world in the vain hope I could save Dis. They can't be saved. They're dead. I won't hear any more about it."

"You must listen – "

"I must destroy the planet below me, that is what I must do. That fact will not be changed by anything you say. All the offworlders – other than your party – are gone. I'm sending a ship down now to pick you up. As soon as that ship lifts I am going to drop the first bombs. Now – tell me where you are so they can come for you."

"Don't threaten me, Krafft!" Brion shook his fist at the radio in an excess of anger. "You're a killer and a world destroyer – don't try to make yourself out as anything else. I have the knowledge to avert this slaughter and you won't listen to me. And I know where the cobalt bombs are – in the magter tower that Hys raided last night. Get those bombs and there is no need to drop any of your own!"

"I'm sorry, Brion. I appreciate what you're trying to do, but at the same time I know the futility of it. I'm not going to accuse you of lying, but do you realize how thin your evidence sounds from this end? First, a dramatic discovery of the cause of the magters' intransigency. Then, when that had no results, you suddenly remember that you know where the bombs are. The best-kept magter secret."

"I don't know for sure, but there is a very good chance it is so," Brion said, trying to repair his defenses. "Telt made readings, he had other records of radioactivity in this same magter keep – proof that something is there. But Telt is dead now, the records destroyed. Don't you see – " He broke off, realizing how vague and unprovable his case was. This was defeat.

The radio was silent, with just the hum of the carrier wave as Krafft waited for him to continue. When Brion did speak his voice was empty of all hope.

"Send your ship down," he said tiredly. "We're in a building that belonged to the Light Metals Trust, Ltd., a big warehouse of some kind. I don't know the address here, but I'm sure you have someone there who can find it. We'll be waiting for you. You win, Krafft."

He turned off the radio.

# XVII

"**D**o you mean what you said, about giving up?" Lea asked. Brion realized that she had stopped talking to Ulv some time ago, and had been listening to his conversation with Krafft. He shrugged, trying to put his feeling into words.

"We've tried – and almost succeeded. But if they won't listen, what can we do? What can one man possibly do against a fleet loaded with H-bombs?"

As if in answer to the question, Ulv's voice drowned him out, the harsh Disan words slashing the silence of the room.

"Kill you, the enemy!" he said. "Kill you *umedvirk*!"

He shouted the last word and his hand flashed to his belt. In a single swift motion he lifted his blowgun and placed it to his lips. A tiny dart quivered in the already dead flesh of the creature in the magter's skull. The action had all the symbolism of a broken lance, the declaration of war.

"Ulv understands it a lot better than you might think," Lea said. "He knows things about symbiosis and mutualism that would get him a job as a lecturer in any university on Earth. He knows just what the brain-symbiote is and what it does. They even have a word for it, one that never appeared in our Disan language lessons. A life form that you can live with or cooperate with is called *medvirk*. One that works to destroy you is *umedvirk*. He also understands that life forms can change, and be *medvirk* or *umedvirk* at different times. He has just decided that the brain symbiote is *umedvirk* and he is out to kill it. So will the rest of the Disans as soon as he can show them the evidence and explain."

"You're sure of this?" Brion asked, interested in spite of himself.

"Positive. The Disans have an absolute attitude towards survival; you should realize that. Not the same as the magter, but not much different in the results. They will kill the brain-symbiotes, even if it means killing every magter who harbors one."

"If that is the case we can't leave now," Brion said. With these words it suddenly became clear what he had to do. "The ship is coming down now from the fleet. Get in it and take the body of the magter. I won't go."

"Where will you be?" she asked, shocked.

"Fighting the magter. My presence on the planet means that Krafft won't keep his threat to drop the bombs any earlier than the midnight deadline. That would be deliberately murdering me. I doubt if my presence past midnight will stop him, but it should keep the bombs away at least until then."

"What will you accomplish besides committing suicide?" Lea pleaded. "You just told me how a single man can't stop the bombs. What will happen to you at midnight?"

"I'll be dead – but in spite of that I can't run away. Not now. I must do everything possible right up until the last instant. Ulv and I will go to the magter tower, try to find out if the bombs are there. He will fight on our side now. He may even know more about the bombs, things that he didn't want to tell me before. We can get help from his people. Some of them must know where the bombs are, being native to this planet."

Lea started to say something, but he rushed on, drowning out her words.

"You have just as big a job. Show the magter to Krafft, explain the significance of the brain-parasite to him. Try to get him to talk to Hys about the last raid. Try to get him to hold off the attack. I'll keep the radio with me and as soon as I know anything I'll call in. This is all last resort, finger in the dike kind of stuff, but it is all we can do. Because if we do nothing, it means the end of Dis."

Lea tried to argue with him, but he wouldn't listen to her. He only kissed her, and with a lightness he did not feel tried to convince her that everything would be all right. In their hearts they both knew it wouldn't be but they left it that way because it was the least painful solution.

A sudden rumbling shook the building and the windows darkened as a ship settled in the street outside. The Nyjord crew came in with guns pointed, alert for anything.

After a little convincing they took the cadaver, as well as Lea, when they lifted ship. Brion watched the spacer become a pinpoint in the sky and vanish. He tried to shake off the feeling that this was the last time he would see any of them.

"Let's get out of here fast," he told Ulv, picking up the radio, "before anyone comes around to see why the ship landed."

"What will you do?" Ulv asked as they went down the street towards the desert. "What can we do in the few hours we have left?" He pointed at the sun, nearing the horizon. Brion shifted the weight of the radio to his other hand before replying.

"Get to the magter tower we raided last night, that's the best chance. The bombs might be there .... Unless you know where the bombs are?"

Ulv shook his head. "I do not know, but some of my people may. We will capture a magter, then kill him, so they can all see the *umedvirk*. Then they will tell us everything they know."

"The tower first then, for bombs or a sample magter. What's the fastest way we can get there?"

Ulv frowned in thought. "If you can drive one of the cars the offworlders use, I know where there are some locked in buildings in this city. None of my people know how they are made to move."

"I can work them – let's go."

Chance was with them this time. The first sand car they found still had the keys in the lock. It was battery-powered, but contained a full charge. Much quieter than the heavy atomic cars, it sped smoothly out of the city and across the sand. Ahead of them the sun sank in a red wave of color. It was six o'clock. By the time they reached the tower it was seven, and Brion's nerves felt as if they were writhing under his skin.

Even though it looked like suicide, attacking the tower brought blessed relief. It was movement and action, and for moments at a time he forgot the bombs hanging over his head.

The attack was nerve-rackingly anticlimactic. They used the main entrance, Ulv ranging soundlessly ahead. There was no one in sight. Once inside, they crept down towards the lower rooms where the radiation had been detected. Only gradually did they realize that the magter tower was completely empty.

"Everyone gone," Ulv grunted, sniffing the air in every room that they passed. "Many magter were here earlier, but they are gone now."

"Do they often desert their towers?" Brion asked.

"Never. I have never heard of it happening before. I can think of no reason why they should do a thing like this."

"Well, I can," Brion told him. "They would leave their home if they took something with them of greater value. The bombs. If the bombs were hidden here, they might move them after the attack." Sudden fear hit him. "Or they might move them because it is time to take them – to the launcher! Let's get out of here, the quickest way we can."

"I smell air from outside," Ulv said, "coming from down there. This cannot be, because the magter have no entrances this low in their towers."

"We blasted one in earlier – that could be it. Can you find it?"

Moonlight shone ahead as they turned an angle of the corridor, and stars were visible through the gaping opening in the wall.

"It looks bigger than it was," Brion said, "as if the magter had enlarged it." He looked through and saw the tracks on the sand outside. "As if they had enlarged it to bring something bulky up from below – and carried it away in whatever made those tracks!"

Using the opening themselves, they ran back to the sand car. Brion ground it fiercely around and turned the headlights on the tracks. There were the marks of a sand car's treads, half obscured by thin, unmarked wheel tracks. He turned off the lights and forced himself to move slowly and to do an accurate job. A quick glimpse at his watch showed him there were four hours left to go. The moonlight was bright enough to illuminate the tracks. Driving with one hand, he turned on the radio transmitter, already set for Krafft's wave length.

When the operator acknowledged his signal Brion reported what they had discovered and his conclusions. "Get that message to Commander Krafft now. I can't wait to talk to him – I'm following the tracks." He killed the transmission and stamped on the accelerator. The sand car churned and bounced down the track.

"They are going to the mountains," Ulv said some time later, as the tracks still pointed straight ahead. "There are caves there and many magter have been seen near them; that is what I have heard."

The guess was correct. Before nine o'clock the ground humped into a range of foothills, and the darker masses of mountains could be seen behind them, rising up to obscure the stars.

"Stop the car here," Ulv said, "The caves begin not too far ahead. There may be magter watching or listening, so we must go quietly."

Brion followed the deep-cut grooves, carrying the radio. Ulv came and went on both sides, silently as a shadow, scouting for hidden watchers. As far as he could discover there were none.

By nine-thirty Brion realized they had deserted the sand car too soon. The tracks wound on and on, and seemed to have no end. They passed some caves which Ulv pointed out to him, but the tracks never stopped. Time was running out and the nightmare stumbling through the darkness continued.

"More caves ahead," Ulv said, "Go quietly."

They came cautiously to the crest of a hill, as they had done so many times already, and looked into the shallow valley beyond. Sand covered the valley floor, and the light of the setting moon shone over the tracks at a flat angle, marking them off sharply as lines of shadow. They ran straight across the sandy valley and disappeared into the dark mouth of a cave on the far side.

Sinking back behind the hilltop, Brion covered the pilot light with his hand and turned on the transmitter. Ulv stayed above him, staring at the opening of the cave.

"This is an important message," Brion whispered into the mike. "Please record." He repeated this for thirty seconds, glancing at his watch to make sure of the time, since the seconds of waiting stretched to minutes in his brain. Then, as clearly as possible without raising his voice above a whisper, he told of the discovery of the tracks and the cave.

"... The bombs may or may not be in here, but we are going in to find out. I'll leave my personal transmitter here with the broadcast power turned on, so you can home on its signal. That will give you a directional beacon to find the cave. I'm taking the other radio in – it has more power. If we can't get back to the entrance I'll try a signal from inside. I doubt if you will hear it because of the rock, but I'll try. End of transmission. Don't try to answer me because I have the receiver turned off. There are no earphones on this set and the speaker would be too loud here."

He switched off, held his thumb on the button for an instant, then flicked it back on.

"Goodbye, Lea," he said, and killed the power for good.

They circled and reached the rocky wall of the cliff. Creeping silently in the shadows, they slipped up on the dark entrance of the cave. Nothing moved ahead and there was no sound from the entrance of the cave. Brion glanced at his watch and was instantly sorry.

Ten-thirty.

The last shelter concealing them was five meters from the cave. They started to rise, to rush the final distance, when Ulv suddenly waved Brion down. He pointed to his nose, then to the cave. He could smell the magter there.

A dark figure separated itself from the greater darkness of the cave mouth. Ulv acted instantly. He stood up and his hand went to his mouth; air hissed faintly through the tube in his hand. Without a sound the magter folded and fell to the ground. Before the body hit, Ulv crouched low and rushed in. There was the sudden scuffling of feet on the floor, then silence.

Brion walked in, gun ready and alert, not knowing what he would find. His toe pushed against a body on the ground and from the darkness Ulv whispered, "There were only two. We can go on now."

Finding their way through the cave was a maddening torture. They had no light, nor would they dare use one if they had. There were no wheel marks to follow on the stone floor. Without Ulv's sensitive nose they would have been completely lost. The cave branched and rejoined and they soon lost all sense of direction.

Walking was almost impossible. They had to grope with their hands before them like blind men. Stumbling and falling against the rock, their fingers were soon throbbing and raw from brushing against the rough walls. Ulv followed the scent of the magter that hung in the air where they had passed. When it grew thin he knew they had left the frequently used tunnels and entered deserted ones. They could only retrace their steps and start again in a different direction.

More maddening than the walking was the way time was running out. Inexorably the glowing hands crept around the face of Brion's watch until they stood at fifteen minutes before twelve.

"There is a light ahead," Ulv whispered, and Brion almost gasped with relief. They moved slowly and silently until they stood, concealed by the darkness, looking out into a domed chamber brightly lit by glowing tubes.

"What is it?" Ulv asked, blinking in the painful wash of illumination after the long darkness.

Brion had to fight to control his voice, to stop from shouting. "The cage with the metal webbing is a jump-space generator.

The pointed, silver shapes next to it are bombs of some kind, probably the cobalt bombs. We've found it!"

His first impulse was to instantly send the radio call that would stop the waiting fleet of H-bombers. But an unconvincing message would be worse than no message at all. He had to describe exactly what he saw here so the Nyjorders would know he wasn't lying. What he told them had to fit exactly with the information they already had about the launcher and the bombs.

The launcher had been jury-rigged from a ship's jump-space generator; that was obvious. The generator and its controls were neatly cased and mounted. Cables ran from them to a roughly constructed cage of woven metal straps, hammered and bent into shape by hand. Three technicians were working on the equipment. Brion wondered what sort of blood-thirsty war-lovers the magter had found to handle the bombing for them. Then he saw the chains around their necks and the bloody wounds on their backs.

He still found it difficult to have any pity for them. They had obviously been willing to accept money to destroy another planet – or they wouldn't have been working here. They had probably rebelled only when they had discovered how suicidal the attack would be.

Thirteen minutes to midnight.

Cradling the radio against his chest, Brion rose to his feet. He had a better view of the bombs now. There were twelve of them, alike as eggs from the same deadly clutch. Pointed like the bow of a spacer, each one swept smoothly back for its two meters of length, to a sharply chopped-off end. They were obviously incomplete, the war heads of rockets. One had its base turned towards him, and he saw six projecting studs that could be used to attach it to the missing rocket. A circular inspection port was open in the flat base of the bomb.

This was enough. With this description, the Nyjorders would know he couldn't be lying about finding the bombs. Once they realized this, they couldn't destroy Dis without first trying to neutralize them.

Brion carefully counted fifty paces before he stopped. He was far enough from the cavern so he couldn't be heard, and an angle of the cave cut off all light from behind him. With carefully controlled movements he turned on the power, switched the set to transmit, and checked the broadcast frequency. All correct. Then slowly and clearly, he described what he had seen in the cavern behind him. He kept his voice emotionless, recounting facts, leaving out anything that might be considered an opinion.

It was six minutes before midnight when he finished. He thumbed the switch to receive and waited.

There was only silence.

Slowly, the empty quality of the silence penetrated his numbed mind. There were no crackling atmospherics nor hiss of static, even when he turned the power full on. The mass of rock and earth of the mountain above was acting as a perfect grounding screen, absorbing his signal even at maximum output.

They hadn't heard him. The Nyjord fleet didn't know that the cobalt bombs had been discovered before their launching. The attack would go ahead as planned. Even now, the bomb-bay doors were opening; armed H-bombs hung above the planet, held in place only by their shackles. In a few minutes the signal would be given and the shackles would spring open, the bombs drop clear....

"Killers!" Brion shouted into the microphone. "You wouldn't listen to reason, you wouldn't listen to Hys, or me, or to any voice that suggested an alternative to complete destruction. You are going to destroy Dis, and *it's not necessary!* There were a lot of ways you could have stopped it. You didn't do any of them, and now it's too late. You'll destroy Dis, and in turn this will destroy Nyjord. Ihjel said that, and now I believe him. You're just another damned failure in a galaxy full of failures!"

He raised the radio above his head and sent it crashing into the rock floor. Then he was running back to Ulv, trying to run away from the realization that he too had tried and failed. The people on the surface of Dis had less than two minutes left to live.

"They didn't get my message," Brion said to Ulv. "The radio won't work this far underground."

"Then the bombs will fall?" Ulv asked, looking searchingly at Brion's face in the dim reflected light from the cavern.

"Unless something happens that we know nothing about, the bombs will fall."

They said nothing after that – they simply waited. The three technicians in the cavern were also aware of the time. They were calling to each other and trying to talk to the magter. The emotionless, parasite-ridden brains of the magter saw no reason to stop work, and they attempted to beat the men back to their tasks. In spite of the blows, they didn't go; they only gaped in horror as the clock hands moved remorselessly towards twelve. Even the magter dimly felt some of the significance of the occasion. They stopped too and waited.

The hour hand touched twelve on Brion's watch, then the minute hand. The second hand closed the gap and for a tenth of a second the three hands were one. Then the second hand moved on.

Brion's immediate sensation of relief was washed away by the chilling realization that he was deep underground. Sound and seismic waves were slow, and the flare of atomic explosions couldn't be seen here. If the bombs had been dropped at twelve they wouldn't know it at once.

A distant rumble filled the air. A moment later the ground heaved under them and the lights in the cavern flickered. Fine dust drifted down from the roof above.

Ulv turned to him, but Brion looked away. He could not face the accusation in the Disan's eyes.

# XVIII

**O**ne of the technicians was running and screaming. The magter knocked him down and beat him into silence. Seeing this, the other two men returned to work with shaking hands. Even if all life on the surface of the planet was dead, this would have no effect on the magter. They would go ahead as planned, without emotion or imagination enough to alter their set course.

As the technicians worked, their attitude changed from shocked numbness to anger. Right and wrong were forgotten. They had been killed – the invisible death of radiation must already be penetrating into the caves – but they also had the chance for vengeance. Swiftly they brought their work to completion, with a speed and precision they had concealed before.

"What are those offworlders doing?" Ulv asked.

Brion stirred from his lethargy of defeat and looked across the cavern floor. The men had a wheeled hand truck and were rolling one of the atomic warheads onto it. They pushed it over to the latticework of the jump-field.

"They are going to bomb Nyjord now, just as Nyjord bombed Dis. That machine will hurl the bombs in a special way to the other planet."

"Will you stop them?" Ulv asked. He had his deadly blowgun in his hand and his face was an expressionless mask.

Brion almost smiled at the irony of the situation. In spite of everything he had done to prevent it, Nyjord had dropped the bombs. And this act alone may have destroyed their own planet. Brion had it within his power now to stop the launching in the cavern. Should he? Should he save the lives of his killers? Or should he practice the ancient blood-oath that had echoed and destroyed down through the ages: *An eye for an eye, a tooth for a tooth.* It would be so simple. He literally had to do nothing. The score would be even, and his and the Disans' death avenged.

Did Ulv have his blowgun ready to kill Brion with, if he should try to stop the launchings? Or had he misread the Disan entirely?

"Will *you* stop them, Ulv?" he asked.

How large was mankind's sense of obligation? The caveman first had this feeling for his mate, then for his family. It grew until men fought and died for the abstract ideas of cities and nations, then for whole planets. Would the time ever come when men might realize that the obligation should be to the largest and most encompassing reality of all – mankind? And beyond that to life of all kinds.

Brion saw this idea, not in words but as a reality. When he posed the question to himself in this way he found that it stated clearly its inherent answer. He pulled his gun out, and as he did he wondered what Ulv's answer might be.

"Nyjord is *medvirk*," Ulv said, raising his blowgun and sending a dart across the cavern. It struck one of the technicians, who gasped and fell to the floor.

Brion's shots crashed into the control board, shorting and destroying it, removing the menace to Nyjord for all time.

*Medvirk*, Ulv had said. A life form that cooperates and aids other life forms. It may kill in self-defense, but it is essentially not a killer or destroyer. Ulv had a lifetime of knowledge about the interdependency of life. He grasped the essence of the idea and ignored all the verbal complications and confusions. He had killed the magter, who were his own people, because they were *umedvirk* – against life. And he had saved his enemies because they were *medvirk*.

With this realization came the painful knowledge that the planet and the people that had produced this understanding were dead.

In the cavern the magter saw the destruction of their plans, and the cave mouth from which the bullets had come. Silently they rushed to kill their enemy – a concerted wave of emotionless fury.

Brion and Ulv fought back. Even the knowledge that he was doomed no matter what happened could not resign Brion to death at the hands of the magter. To Ulv, the decision was much easier. He was simply killing *umedvirk*. A believer in life, he destroyed the anti-life.

They retreated into the darkness, still firing. The magter had lights and ion rifles, and were right behind them. Knowing the caverns better than the men they chased, the pursuers circled. Brion saw lights ahead and dragged Ulv to a stop.

"They know their way through these caves, and we don't," he

said. "If we try to run they'll just shoot us down. Let's find a spot we can defend and settle into it."

"Back here" – Ulv gave a tug in the right direction – "there is a cave with only one entrance, and that is very narrow."

"Let's go!"

Running as silently as they could in the darkness, they reached the dead-end cavern without being seen. What noise they made was lost in other footsteps that sounded and echoed through the connecting caves. Once inside, they found cover behind a ridge and waited. The end was certain.

~ ~ ~

The magter ran swiftly into their cave, flashing his light into all the places of concealment. The beam passed over the two hidden men, and at the same instant Brion fired. The shot boomed loudly as the magter fell – a shot that would surely have been heard by the others.

Before anyone else came into the cave, Brion ran over and grabbed the still functioning light. Propping it on the rocks so it shone on the entrance, he hurried back to shelter beside Ulv. They waited for the attack.

It was not long in coming. Two magter rushed in, and died. More were outside, Brion knew, and he wondered how long it would be before they remembered the grenades and rolled one into their shelter.

An indistinct murmur sounded outside, and sharp explosions. In their hiding place, Brion and Ulv crouched low and wondered why the attack didn't come. Then one of the magter came in the entrance, but Brion hesitated before shooting.

The man had *backed* in, firing behind him as he came.

Ulv had no compunctions about killing, only his darts couldn't penetrate the magter's thick clothing. As the magter turned, Ulv's breath pulsed once and death stung the back of the other man's hand. He collapsed into a crumpled heap.

"Don't shoot," a voice called from outside the cave, and a man stepped through the swirling dust and smoke to stand in the beam from the light.

Brion clutched wildly at Ulv's arm, dragging the blowgun from the Disan's mouth.

The man in the light wore a protective helmet, thick boots and a pouch-hung uniform.

He was a Nyjorder.

The realization was almost impossible to accept. Brion had heard the bombs fall. Yet the Nyjord soldier was here. The two facts couldn't be accepted together.

"Would you keep a hold on his arm, sir, just in case," the soldier said, glancing warily at Ulv's blowpipe. "I know what those darts can do." He pulled a microphone from one of his pockets and spoke into it.

More soldiers crowded into the cave, and Professor-Commander Krafft came in behind them. He looked strangely out of keeping in the dusty combat uniform. The gun was even more incongruous in his blue-veined hand. After giving the pistol to the nearest soldier with an air of relief, he stumbled quickly over to Brion and took his hand.

"It is a profound and sincere pleasure to meet you in person," he said. "And your friend Ulv as well."

"Would you kindly explain what is going on?" Brion said thickly. He was obsessed by the strange feeling that none of this could possibly be happening.

"We will always remember you as the man who saved us from ourselves," Krafft said, once again the professor instead of the commander.

"What Brion wants are facts, Grandpa, not speeches," Hys said. The bent form of the leader of the rebel Nyjord army pushed through the crowd of taller men until he stood next to Krafft. "Simply stated, Brion, your plan succeeded. Krafft relayed your message to me – and as soon as I heard it I turned back and met him on his ship. I'm sorry that Telt's dead – but he found what we were looking for. I couldn't ignore his report of radioactive traces. Your girlfriend arrived with the hacked-up corpse at the same time I did, and we all took a long look at the green leech in its skull. Her explanation of what it is made significant sense. We were already carrying out landings when we had your call about something having been stored in the magter tower. After that it was just a matter of following tracks – and the transmitter you planted."

"But the explosions at midnight?" Brion broke in. "I heard them!"

"You were supposed to," Hys laughed. "Not only you, but the magter in this cave. We figured they would be armed and the cave strongly defended. So at midnight we dropped a few large chemical explosive bombs at the entrance. Enough to kill the guards without bringing the roof down. We also hoped that the magter deeper in would leave their posts or retreat from the imagined radiation. And they did. It worked like a charm. We came in quietly and took them by surprise. Made a clean sweep – killed the ones we couldn't capture."

"One of the renegade jump-space technicians was still alive," Krafft said. "He told us about your stopping the bombs aimed at Nyjord, the two of you."

None of the Nyjorders there could add anything to his words, not even the cynical Hys. But Brion could empathize their feelings, the warmth of their intense relief and happiness. It was a sensation he would never forget.

"There is no more war," Brion translated for Ulv, knowing that the Disan had understood nothing of the explanation. As he said it, he realized that there was one glaring error in the story.

"You couldn't have done it," Brion said. "You landed on this planet *before* you had my message about the tower. That means you still expected the magter to be sending their bombs to Nyjord – and you made the landings in spite of this knowledge."

"Of course," Professor Krafft said, astonished at Brion's lack of understanding. "What else could we do? The magter are sick!"

Hys laughed aloud at Brion's baffled expression. "You have to understand Nyjord psychology," he said. "When it was a matter of war and killing, my planet could never agree on an intelligent course. War is so alien to our philosophy that it couldn't even be considered correctly. That's the trouble with being a vegetable eater in a galaxy of carnivores. You're easy prey for the first one that lands on your back. Any other planet would have jumped on the magter with both feet and shaken the bombs out of them. We fumbled it so long it almost got both worlds killed. Your mind-parasite drew us back from the brink."

"I don't understand," Brion said.

"A simple matter of definition. Before you came we had no way to deal with the magter here on Dis. They really were alien to us. Nothing they did made sense – and nothing we did seemed to have the slightest effect on them. But you discovered that they were *sick*, and that's something we know how to handle. We're united again; my rebel army was instantly absorbed into the rest of the Nyjord forces by mutual agreement. Doctors and nurses are on the way here now. Plans were put under way to evacuate what part of the population we could until the bombs were found. The planet is united again, and working hard."

"Because the magter are sick, infected by a destructive life form?" Brion asked.

"Exactly so," Professor Krafft said. "We are civilized, after all. You can't expect us to fight a war and you surely can't expect us to ignore the plight of sick neighbors?"

"No ... you surely can't," Brion said, sitting down heavily. He looked at Ulv, to whom the speech had been incomprehensible. Beyond him, Hys wore his most cynical expression as he considered the frailties of his people.

"Hys," Brion called out, "you translate all that into Disan and explain to Ulv. I wouldn't dare."

# XIX

**D**is was a floating golden ball, looking like a schoolroom globe in space. No clouds obscured its surface, and from this distance it seemed warm and attractive set against the cold darkness. Brion almost wished he were back there now, as he sat shivering inside the heavy coat. He wondered how long it would be before his confused body-temperature controls decided to turn off the summer adjustment. He hoped it wouldn't be as sudden or as drastic as turning it on had been.

Delicate as a dream, Lea's reflection swam in space next to the planet. She had come up quietly behind him in the spaceship's corridor, only her gentle breath and mirrored face telling him she was there. He turned quickly and took her hands in his.

"You're looking infinitely better," he said.

"Well, I should," she said, pushing back her hair in an unconscious gesture with her hand. "I've been doing nothing but lying in the ship's hospital, while you were having such a fine time this last week. Rushing around down there shooting all the magter."

"Just gassing them," he told her. "The Nyjorders can't bring themselves to kill any more, even if it does raise their own casualty rate. In fact, they are having difficulty restraining the Disans led by Ulv, who are happily killing any magter they see as being pure *umedvirk*."

"What will they do when they have all those frothing magter madmen?"

"They don't know yet," he said. "They won't really know until they see what an adult magter is like with his brain-parasite dead and gone. They're having better luck with the children. If they catch them early enough, the parasite can be destroyed before it has done too much damage."

Lea shuddered delicately and let herself lean against him. "I'm not that sturdy yet; let's sit down while we talk." There was a couch opposite the viewport where they could sit and still see Dis.

"I hate to think of a magter deprived of his symbiote," she said. "If his system can stand the shock, I imagine there will be nothing left except a brainless hulk. This is one series of experiments I don't care to witness. I rest secure in the knowledge that the Nyjorders will find the most humane solution."

"I'm sure they will," Brion said.

"Now what about us?" she said disconcertingly, leaning back in his arms. "I must say you have the highest body temperature of any one I have ever touched. It's positively exciting."

This jarred Brion even more. He didn't have her ability to put past horrors out of the mind by substituting present pleasures. "Well, just what about us?" he said with masterful inappropriateness.

She smiled as she leaned against him. "You weren't as vague as that, the night in the hospital room. I seem to remember a few other things you said. And did. You can't claim you're completely indifferent to me, Brion Brandd. So I'm only asking you what any outspoken Anvharian girl would. Where do we go from here? Get married?"

There was a definite pleasure in holding her slight body in his arms and feeling her hair against his cheek. They both sensed it, and this awareness made his words sound that much more ugly.

"Lea – darling! You know how important you are to me – but you certainly realize that we could never get married."

Her body stiffened and she tore herself away from him.

"Why, you great, fat, egotistical slab of meat! What do you mean by that? I like you, Lea, we have plenty of fun and games together, but surely you realize that you aren't the kind of girl one takes home to mother!"

"Lea, hold on," he said. "You know better than to say a thing like that. What I said has nothing to do with how I feel towards you. But marriage means children, and you are biologist enough to know about Earth's genes – "

"Intolerant yokel!" she cried, slapping his face. He didn't move or attempt to stop her. "I expected better from you, with all your pretensions of understanding. But all you can think of are the horror stories about the worn-out genes of Earth. You're the same as every other big, strapping bigot from the frontier planets. I know how you look down on our small size, our allergies and hemophilia and all the other weaknesses that have been bred back and preserved by the race. You hate – "

"But that's not what I meant at all," he interrupted, shocked, his voice drowning hers out. "Yours are the strong genes, the viable strains – *mine* are the deadly ones. A child of mine would kill itself and you in a natural birth, if it managed to live to term. You're forgetting that you are the original homo sapiens. I'm a recent mutation."

Lea was frozen by his words. They revealed a truth she had known, but would never permit herself to consider.

"Earth is home, the planet where mankind developed," he said. "The last few thousand years you may have been breeding weaknesses back into the genetic pool. But that's nothing compared to the hundred millions of years that it took to develop man. How many newborn babies live to be a year of age on Earth?"

"Why ... almost all of them. A fraction of one per cent die each year – I can't recall exactly how many."

"Earth is home," he said again gently. "When men leave home they can adapt to different planets, but a price must be paid. A terrible price is in dead infants. The successful mutations live, the failures die. Natural selection is a brutally simple affair. When you look at me, you see a success. I have a sister – a success too. Yet my mother had six other children who died when they were still babies. And several others that never came to term. You know about these things, don't you, Lea?"

"I know, I know ..." she said sobbing into her hands. He held her now and she didn't pull away. "I know it all as a biologist – but I am so awfully tired of being a biologist, and top of my class and a mental match for any man. When I think about you, I do it as a woman, and can't admit any of this. I need someone, Brion, and I needed you so much because I loved you." She paused and wiped her eyes. "You're going home, aren't you? Back to Anvhar. When?"

"I can't wait too long," he said, unhappily. "Aside from my personal wants, I find myself remembering that I'm a part of Anvhar. When you think of the number of people who suffered and died – or adapted – so that I could be sitting here now ... well, it's a little frightening. I suppose it doesn't make sense logically that I should feel indebted to them. But I do. Anything I do now, or in the next few years, won't be as important as getting back to Anvhar."

"And I won't be going back with you." It was a flat statement the way she said it, not a question.

"No, you won't be," he said. "There is nothing on Anvhar for you."

Lea was looking out of the port at Dis and her eyes were dry now. "Way back in my deeply buried unconscious I think I knew it would end this way," she said. "If you think your little lecture on the Origins of Man was a novelty, it wasn't. It just reminded me of a number of things my glands had convinced me to forget. In a way, I envy you your weightlifter wife-to-be, and your happy kiddies. But not very much. Very early in life I resigned myself to the fact that there was no one on Earth I would care to marry. I always had these teen-age dreams of a hero from space who would carry me off, and I guess I slipped you into the pattern without realizing it. I'm old enough now to face the fact that I like my work more than a banal marriage, and I'll probably end up a frigid and virtuous old maid, with more degrees and titles than you have shot-putting records."

As they looked through the port Dis began slowly to contract. Their ship drew away from it, heading towards Nyjord. They sat apart, without touching now. Leaving Dis meant leaving behind something they had shared. They had been strangers together there, on a strange world. For a brief time their lifelines had touched. That time was over now.

"Don't we look happy!" Hys said, shambling towards them.

"Fall dead and make me even happier then," Lea snapped bitterly.

Hys ignored the acid tone of her words and sat down on the couch next to them. Since leaving command of his rebel Nyjord army he seemed much mellower. "Going to keep on working for the Cultural Relationships Foundation, Brion?" he asked. "You're the kind of man we need."

Brion's eyes widened as the meaning of the last words penetrated. "Are you in the C.R.F.?"

"Field agent for Nyjord," he said. "I hope you don't think those helpless office types like Faussel or Mervv really represented us there? They just took notes and acted as a front and cover for the organization. Nyjord is a fine planet, but a gentle guiding hand behind the scenes is needed, to help them find their place in the galaxy before they are pulverized."

"What's your dirty game, Hys?" Lea asked, scowling. "I've

had enough hints to suspect for a long time that there was more to the C.R.F. than the sweetness-and-light part I have seen. Are you people egomaniacs, power hungry or what?"

"That's the first charge that would be leveled at us if our activities were publicly known," Hys told her. "That's why we do most of our work under cover. The best fact I can give you to counter the charge is *money*. Just where do you think we get the funds for an operation this size?" He smiled at their blank looks. "You'll see the records later so there won't be any doubt. The truth is that all our funds are donated by planets we have helped. Even a tiny percentage of a planetary income is large – add enough of them together and you have enough money to help other planets. And voluntary gratitude is a perfect test, if you stop to think about it. You can't talk people into liking what you have done. They have to be convinced. There have always been people on C.R.F. worlds who knew about our work, and agreed with it enough to see that we are kept in funds."

"Why are you telling me all this super-secret stuff," Lea asked.

"Isn't that obvious? We want you to keep on working for us. You can name whatever salary you like – as I've said, there is no shortage of ready cash."

Hys glanced quickly at them both and delivered the clinching argument. "I hope Brion will go on working with us too. He is the kind of field agent we desperately need, and it is almost impossible to find."

"Just show me where to sign," Lea said, and there was life in her voice once again.

"I wouldn't exactly call it blackmail," Brion smiled, "but I suppose if you people can juggle planetary psychologies, you must find that individuals can be pushed around like chessmen. Though you should realize that very little pushing is required this time."

"Will you sign on?" Hys asked.

"I must go back to Anvhar," Brion said, "but there really is no pressing hurry."

"Earth," said Lea, "is overpopulated enough as it is."

THE END

# ABOUT THE AUTHORS

**Murray Leinster** (June 16, 1896 – June 8, 1975) was a nom de plume of science fiction writer **Fitzgerald Jenkins**. He wrote and published more than 1,500 short stories and articles, 14 movie scripts, and hundreds of radio scripts and television plays.

**Harry Max Harrison** (March 12, 1925 – August 15, 2012) was the pseudonym of science fiction writer **Henry Maxwell Dempsey**. Harrison was best known for his character The Stainless Steel Rat and his novel *Make Room, Make Room*, which was the basis for the movie *Soylent Green*.

ABSOLUTELY AMAZING eBOOKS

AbsolutelyAmazingeBooks.com
or AA-eBooks.com

www.ingramcontent.com/pod-product-compliance
Lightning Source LLC
LaVergne TN
LVHW010055110826
845155LV00028B/356

* 9 7 8 1 9 4 9 5 0 4 1 2 5 *